VERYTHING

Beautiful

IS NOT

RUINED

Scholastic Children's Books
An imprint of Scholastic Ltd
Euston House, 24 Eversholt Street
London, NW1 1DB, UK
Registered office: Westfield Road, Southam, Warwickshire, CV47 0R
SCHOLASTIC and associated logos are trademarks and/or registered trade
Scholastic Inc.

First published in the US by Viking Books, an imprint of Penguin Random
First published in the UK by Scholastic Ltd, 2017

ISBN 978 1407 17972 8

A CIP catalogue record for this book is available from the British Library.

Printed and bound by CPI Group (UK) Ltd, Croydon, CR0 4YY
Papers used by Scholastic Children's Books are made from wood grown in
sustainable forests.

1 3 5 7 9 10 8 6 4 2

www.scholastic.co.uk

EVERYTHING Beautiful IS NOT RUINED

DANIELLE
YOUNGE-ULLMAN

SCHOLASTIC

This book is dedicated to my wonderfully generous, kind, hilarious, smart, one-of-a-kind mom, Cindy Ullman . . . who is nothing like Margot-Sophia but who may have sent me on a wilderness trip once upon a time.

Chapter One

🍂 🍁 🍃

"VACATION"

(Peak Wilderness, Day One)

Dear Mom,

Thanks. Really.

I can't wait for this tiny excuse for an airplane to take off into the sky, and then deliver me into the dismal middle of nowhere. Into the stunning, unspoiled lap of Mother Nature, I mean.

I'm not scared, in case you're wondering. It would be much scarier to be looking after small children, or backpacking in Asia unsupervised, like some of my friends. This? It's just trees and lakes. The great outdoors. Nothing to worry about.

Though I gather there will be backpacks. Excursions from base out into the wild. Exotic bugs and plants. Singing, bunk beds, roasting marshmallows, weaving friendship bracelets out of twigs from the forest, awards to those who swim in the coldest water, learning to fish, and so on.

I know you think I'm going to hate it and wimp out and maybe quit. And if that happens, you'll consider me to have reneged on our deal. But you underestimate me, and my determination. You see, I have a new, positive attitude, and I'm not going to continue all huddled, wounded, and tragic like I have been the past few months. I'm done with that. I'm going to have a fantastic time. I'm going to make new friends, connect with my inner Nature Girl, become transcendent and tough and ready for the apocalypse/adulthood/other unforeseen crappy stuff, and I will have fun.

And then you'll see that I am capable enough, and strong enough to make decisions about my own future.

My future.

After everything we've been through, I shouldn't have to prove that to you. I shouldn't have to prove anything. But I said I would, and so I will, setting it all down here in this journal you gave me in your one and only effort to encourage me to "process things." One hundred journals. That's a lot of processing, Mom. I'll tell you this: I'm not turning into a touchy-feely journaling person.

These are just letters.

And it's just camp.

How bad can it be?

Wow. It's been quite a day so far.

Quite an interesting start to this "vacation" of mine.

Remembering that this is supposed to be fun, let's see if I can give you the highlights. . . .

First there was the plane ride. Right away I got such a visceral sense of my mortality. That's probably the very reason they use such a small airplane: so you can really feel the air you're flying through, each harrowing pocket of turbulence, causing you to convert to every religion you can think of and make all kinds of promises to the various gods therein about how much of a better person you will be if only you can live through the experience.

Mission accomplished.

Then, when you finally feel the earth under your feet, despite everything being, let's just say, different from what you expected, you are so freaking grateful, you want to just roll around on it and cry. From happiness, of course. Always happiness.

And maybe it's also for bonding purposes. Because, even though I hadn't worked myself up to the making-friends thing yet, I ended up talking to the very hairy, very smelly (not that the two are necessarily connected, but in this case, maybe) person beside me when it got too bumpy to write, just to distract myself.

Based on first and admittedly shallow impressions, I will confess that I didn't like him. But it's important to move past preconceptions about people and approach them with an open heart in order to see the true person inside.

Right?

The true person inside this Very Hairy Dude revealed himself quickly when I inadvertently grabbed his arm on our shared armrest during one of the more upchuck-inducing air pockets.

I said, "Oh, I'm so sorry!" and removed my hand.

And he said, with such a friendly smile, followed by a downward glance at his lap, "Any part of me you wanna grab, I'm okay with it. Grab away, babe."

I so love being called "babe" and am only a little traumatized by the mental imagery his leering prompted. The point is to be making friends, even if they are disgusting, stinky, hairy perverts . . . on the surface.

Next, we landed.

Enough said.

Actually, I could say more.

We landed in a field, and it took three attempts.

Three, Mom.

The first two times, our little single-engine Cessna approached and got heart-stoppingly low, and then jerked up at the last minute, barely clearing the trees, and in fact snapping a few of the higher branches on our way. I'd have thought that would be frowned upon as our first act when entering nature, but maybe being terrified at the start is supposed to be part of the fun . . . ? It certainly got my attention.

On the third attempt, the pilot actually said, "Field's a little shorter than regulation, but we'll get 'er done. Hang on tight!" over the headsets (reassuring, *non*?), and then we bumped and jerked and shuddered our way forward, almost—I'm not kidding—slamming into the trees at the far end.

Oh, did I mention there wasn't a runway?

Or an airport?

Nope. Just a very bumpy, not quite long enough field.

Finally, the plane was still, and the pilot crowed, "Cheated death again!" and laughed like a maniac. I, pale, wobbly, and shaken to the core, stumbled out of the plane and down the steps onto the ground.

My connection to the earth at that point was intense. Profoundly so. By the time I looked up again, our luggage and a pile of gear had been dumped, and the pilot was back in his little sky buggy. And before any of us had a chance to even think about it—and proving it's only landing and flying he sucks at—he took off in a single attempt and was gone into the blue. . . .

Leaving us in the middle of God knows where, aka Northern Ontario.

I staggered up, stunned and amazed to have been left so abruptly. Stunned, also, at the unfamiliar hugeness of the sky, and the sheer volume of non-city around me, at being here at all, truly, because like so many things, it still didn't feel quite real.

Anyway . . .

What a thrill.

Love,

Ingrid

I perch on my duffel bag and, though I am a bit out of practice with being social, try to make friendly eye contact with my fellow campers (except Hairy Dude, whose eyes I'm avoiding). But everyone is either in their own world or possibly still in shock from the plane ride and landing, and no one returns my interest. This is both weird and discouraging enough to send me into a quick retreat.

And then the mosquitoes descend.

I'm not talking about a reasonable amount of mosquitoes;

I'm talking a veritable plague of mosquitoes, biblical proportions of mosquitoes.

Fortunately, after months of refusing to think about this trip and trying my best to pretend it wasn't happening, a few days ago I finally snapped out of it. I pulled the packing list from the desk drawer I'd stuffed it into back in February, and pored over it obsessively, making sure I had everything on it and more, while simultaneously trying to remember everything my mom's boss's daughter, Ella, had told us about her "life-changing" experience at Peak Wilderness. (Ella's rhapsodic depiction of her adventures, told over dinner at the office holiday party two years ago, complete with words like "intense" and "mystical," was undoubtedly what inspired my mother to force this same experience on me. Also, Peak Wilderness inspired Ella to go to law school.)

All of this to say, I knew there would be mosquitoes, and I am prepared.

I dive into my duffel bag, get my perfume bottle of botanical fragrance that doubles as repellant, and apply it, as directed, to my pulse points.

Around me, my fellow campers are doing the same, but I notice immediately that I'm the only one with the all-natural, nontoxic repellent—everyone else is using something with DEET or one of the other super-stinky kinds. Like none of them got the memo about this trip being all about nature and preserving the environment and so on.

One of the leaders—the man and woman who briefly identified themselves at the airport—will probably set them straight later on.

Two minutes later, I'm still being bitten, even through my clothes, which means pulse points were insufficient. Fine. I take my pretty repellent back out and give my entire body a misting.

Sadly, I soon realize these are super mosquitoes, immune to my fabulous-smelling "natural botanicals." They are determined and hungry, and I am food.

So, I start to kill them one at a time.

I'm on my ninth when I lock eyes with this boy who's suddenly in front of me. At the sight of his face, everything inside me seems to coil up, and for a second I forget to breathe.

He reminds me of Isaac—not that he looks like him, but there's something about his jawline, and the deep-set eyes, that is so Isaac. Of course, after that first crazy coiled-up moment, I see he's actually nothing like Isaac. He's taller and wearing clothes Isaac would never wear—ripped jeans and a T-shirt tight to bursting with his very developed delts, pecs . . . and all those other muscles I studied in health class but forgot the names of. And his head is shaved and he doesn't have even a hint of sweetness about him either. It's really just the eyes—so dark against dramatically pale skin. And even the eyes would only look like Isaac's eyes if someone took Isaac and put him through the military, or in a very tough gang, and then spit him back out into the wilderness.

I'm just being a freak. Because maybe I'm still a little obsessed with Isaac. Still feeling pained and confused every time I think about Isaac.

Dear Isaac . . .

I could write some letters to him, too, in my fancy journal. God knows I've had enough imaginary conversations with him over the last year and a half, while the distance grew between us, thickening like a callus, like an all-day fog, until we were both so well versed in our new roles as people who didn't matter to each other that it was impossible to break through. Still, it doesn't feel properly finished. Dead but not buried. Or buried but not dead.

So what would be the harm of writing him a letter? It's not like I'm planning to send any of them—I just feel lame writing "Dear Diary" or whatever.

No. This is one of those things I need to not think about.

I have quite a few.

My hand drifts to my shin where, three weeks ago, there were stitches. It shouldn't hurt anymore. It doesn't hurt anymore . . . except sometimes, when I start thinking about things I shouldn't, and then it throbs or aches, and occasionally sends hot, stabbing pain up my leg. I know, of course, that this doesn't make any sense, but it's true; when the pain comes, it's real.

I am feeling it right now.

I catch my breath, and another mosquito tries for my nose. I clap my hands together, and this guy says in a very non-Isaac voice, "I doubt that's gonna help."

"Well, maybe not at the moment," I reply, clapping again and mentally tallying the dead mosquito count at eleven.

He cocks a questioning eyebrow and I hesitate. Every action, or lack of action, takes a decision. And a decision takes energy. And every bit of energy taken in making decisions about stupid things takes energy from the important things. That's something I've become aware of, the past few months. I do not have unlimited energy. Sometimes I have none. I have a narrow field of things that I want to let in, and many things that I don't want to let in, and so every bit of my focus needs to stay on the things I want. Only those things. Otherwise, it gets uncomfortable. Painful. Still, I decide to answer the question because this dude looks intense, and therefore it might take more energy not to.

"Every female mosquito lays approximately five hundred eggs," I say, "and if half of the ones that hatch are female, then they each lay five hundred eggs. Then half of that new batch is also female and they lay another five hundred eggs, and that adds up to . . . well . . . a crazy amount of mosquitoes by the time all the reproducing is done, later in the summer. From one female mosquito. And so each mosquito you kill now means, like, potentially millions of mosquitoes that won't be born later on."

See? Nature Girl. That's me. "You can thank me later," I add, "when you don't have the Zika virus."

Not-Isaac studies me for a few long seconds like he's either going to laugh or roll his eyes, and then just slouches away instead.

Unfortunately the bastards are still all over me, and I realize I'm going to have to embrace toxic repellants. I will roll around in them, bathe in them, if only it will keep these damned bugs away.

Of course, I don't have any, and I'm not about to go begging my fellow campers for favors on the very first day—especially when they're so universally shy/weird/unfriendly/pervy. I'm sure there'll be a store or something at the camp where I can buy anything extra I might need. I'll just have to survive—smelling like a house of ill-repute, I might add—until then.

So, although it's steaming hot and we have no shade and it's not going to look cool, I tuck my pants into my socks then go back into my bag, where I briefly consider donning the freak-show mosquito-net hat Mom bought for me. However, I bet my best friend, Juno, that I wouldn't wear it. She wouldn't know, but still. Instead, I pull on a hoodie and tie the hood so tightly that only my nose and eyes are exposed to the mosquitoes.

"Why you covering up, hot stuff?" This from Hairy Dude, of course. "You're ruining my day."

"Likewise," I mutter into my hood as I yank the strings tighter.

Dead mosquito count: thirty-five.

I'm all for nature and everything, but this is ridiculous.

Dear Mom,

Still here in the field.

Apparently we're waiting for a guy in a van, but it's been over an hour, and I have to pee.

I get up and make my way to the two leaders. There's Bonnie, who is all earth-mother-in-camping-gear with long hen-naed hair and wide-set brown eyes. And then there's Pat: sinewy, not much hair, dark skin, and deep-thinking brown eyes. He's wearing a T-shirt worn soft by a zillion washings, hard-core camping pants, and a vest with myriad zippered and buttoned pockets, which he keeps patting. He'll be the guy with the thread, the can opener, the secret stash of protein bars.

"Uh, hi, I'm Ingrid," I say to them.

"Hello, Ingrid," they say in unison, and then Pat says to Bonnie, "I got this." And she walks away.

"I have to . . ." I pause, mortified. You always told me that ladies do not discuss bodily functions, Mom, and so I don't.

"Yes?"

"Uh . . . will we be near any . . . facilities anytime soon?"

"Facilities?" Pat says.

I clear my throat. "A bathroom?"

He frowns.

"Or . . . an outhouse?" I wince saying this. I've been hoping there will be real bathrooms but preparing myself for the worst. I can only imagine how bad the mosquitoes will be in an outhouse. Not to mention the smell.

"No, no, we don't have outhouses here," Pat says.

"Oh. Ha-ha. Phew!" I say, smiling for the first time. "Silly me."

"Yeah, you can just . . ." Pat waves an arm toward the line of trees.

Now it's my turn to frown. "I can just . . . what?"

"Go over there," he says. "You need some TP?"

He starts rummaging in one of the bigger vest pockets and pulls out a small spool of toilet paper.

"Oh, sure, okay," I say, and take some, thinking, Okay, the bathrooms are not well stocked, but at least they're not outhouses. I point in the direction he gestured. "So they're just through there?"

"Sorry . . . what are you talking about?" Pat says. "What are just through there?"

"The bathrooms."

He looks at me as if I'm a lunatic. Hello, he's the one waving vaguely at a mile-long line of trees like I should be able to just find the bathroom in there.

"What bathrooms?" he says.

"The bathrooms. You said the bathrooms were . . ."

My voice dies.

Oh no.

No, no, no.

I clear my throat. "You mean . . ."

"I mean take your TP and find a spot in the woods," he says. "Just dig a hole for the toilet paper afterward. We like to leave nature as we've found it."

"Dig a . . .? I'm sorry . . . what?"

"Never mind," he says. "Bonnie'll go over those details tomorrow. If you don't want to go in the woods, you can just walk off a ways and go in the field where the grass is taller."

"Where the grass is taller . . ." I repeat in confused disbelief as I back away from him. "I'll . . . That's okay. I'll . . . just . . . wait."

So, Mom, I'm waiting. And thinking. And what I'm thinking is that the camp, assuming we ever get there, is going to be a little more rustic than it looked in the brochure.

It's possible, for example, that I may not be able to use my rechargeable flashlight. Fortunately I packed quite a few things that will help make me comfortable no matter what the situation, so I remain optimistic.

Love always,
Ingrid

By the time the dead mosquito count is past one hundred and I'm starting to deal with massive black flies too—these beasts bite through clothing—I capitulate and put on the mosquito-net hat. Everyone else has one on too, except the leaders, Hairy Dude, a girl whose chain-smoking of weird-smelling cigarettes makes it impossible, and another girl who's wearing a ton of makeup and taking photos of herself from above (the better to show her cleavage, I assume) with a phone I know she's not going to be allowed to keep.

Finally I hear something in the distance—a vehicle. It gets louder and then it arrives, driving out from a gap between the trees and coming to a stop right in front of us.

Rescue. Thank God.

The eleven of us—nine campers and two leaders—are going to be pretty squished in there, but I'm so relieved, I could kiss the driver, sight unseen.

A massive, strapping ginger of a man unfurls from the front seat, stalks over, and stands, legs apart, hands on hips, glaring at us like we've woken him from hibernation or stolen his last cup of coffee.

"I'm Duncan," he says, "and I'm in charge of making sure you're properly accounted for, packed, and ready to go." He pulls out a piece of paper, unfolds it, and starts barking out names.

"Seth!"

A cute, flippy-haired guy who's had his standard-issue hiking pants altered to fit like skinny jeans, says, "Y-yes . . . ?"

Duncan nods at Seth, then moves on. "Jin!"

The chain-smoker, a very urban-looking Asian girl with

streaks of blue and purple and blonde in her short black hair, gives him an unenthusiastic wave.

"Melissa!"

A tall, athletic-looking, wide-eyed blonde tentatively raises her hand.

"Bob!"

"Actually, my name is Peace," Hairy Dude says.

A pause. Then, "Registration says your name is Bob."

"I've been rechristened. Peace. It's an important part of my personal journey. I only answer to Peace."

Duncan grunts, then moves on.

Peace? Give me a break.

"Ingrid!"

"Yes, that's me."

"No rechristening for you?"

"Um, no." I smile, ready to share the joke, but Duncan just stares at me until I look away.

"Tavik!"

Not-Isaac with bursting pecs looks up. "Yo."

Next are two boys who've been punching each other in the arm and chortling like six-year-olds. They answer to Harvey and Henry, and appear to be brothers. Possibly twins? And finally there's Ally, the makeup girl, who's stopped with the selfies and is dabbing her face and chest with a bandanna.

"That's the last of you then," Duncan says, then strides over to me. "You—Ingrid."

"Yes?"

"You're not packed."

"Yes I am." I straighten my spine and point to my duffel bag.

"In the backpacks," he says, pointing to a pile of packs I hadn't noticed.

"Oh," I stammer, "no one told us to—"

"No one told us to!" he mimics in a whiny, high-pitched voice. "Are you all sheep?"

Most of us appear to shrink as Duncan looks around, his disapproval sweeping over the group.

"Get yourself a pack, missy," he says, turning his attention back to me.

He's big and growly and in possession of both van and keys, so I'd better do what he says.

I sniff a few of the grungy-looking backpacks, choose the least offensive, then turn to go back to my duffel . . .

And stop in my tracks at the sight of Duncan crouched beside it, going through my things, touching my things, my socks, my T-shirts, my toiletries, my underwear . . . holding them up for people to see and then . . . tossing them onto the ground.

"What are you doing?" I run over and start gathering everything up. He raises my copy of *War and Peace*, looking at it like it's contraband.

"This is not going into your pack."

"But—"

"Each person is responsible for carrying a portion of the food rations," he says.

Maybe it's the fumes—toxic repellants, cigarette smoke, exhaust from the van, plus whatever is wafting up from the backpack—combined with the heat, but I swear I heard him say something about "food rations" and "carrying."

Carrying a portion of the food rations, that was it.

"My job is to make sure you have what you need!" he exclaims as I stand there, gaping. "Only what you need. Five nights from now, when you're in charge of dinner and you've been hiking all day, your fellow campers are going to be pissed when you tell them you brought this book instead."

"Obviously I wasn't going to bring it when we go hiking. But surely at night—"

He guffaws, throws the book down, pulls out something else.

It's my sage-colored microfleece hoodie—one of the ones Mom bought me.

"Don't touch that," I snap.

He snorts, mutters something about my being "a piece of work," but lets me keep it, in favor of continuing to decimate my packing job.

Yes, I studied the packing list. And yes, I did bring three pairs of pants, not two, if you include the ones I'm wearing, and six shirts, not four, and a couple of extra pairs of socks and underwear, plus a bikini in addition to a one-piece. And the journal—the one with the leather cover and ties—and the book because it's on what I hope will be my reading list for the fall. I may as well multitask while I'm out here serving the conditions of my deal with Mom.

Also . . . there are a few things in my bag that weren't on the list, because the list was so sparse, I figured it only covered the basics. Plus, as I thought about the overnight camping trips we'll be taking (Ella's group did three nights in a tent), I started worrying about getting lost, surviving a thunderstorm, and people getting injured. So I added a compass, a reflective rain poncho, candles, emergency flares, a first aid kit, a few packets of instant coffee, and . . . a few other things. None of them unreasonable. All of them there because, never having done anything like this before, I wanted to be prepared.

Regardless, within five minutes I've lost three-quarters of my belongings, including my biodegradable shampoo and conditioner, which were on the list but are apparently supposed to be in travel-size bottles.

The small amount of stuff I'm allowed to keep goes into the stinky backpack, and the rest gets shoved back into the duffel bag. Whether or when I'll get it back is unclear. I press my lips together, swallow hard, and try not to panic.

Duncan goes through everyone else's luggage in a similar manner. Before long I understand his no-nonsense attitude a bit better, as his pile of forbidden stuff expands to include alcohol, baggies of leafy stuff, and even some pills.

As surprised as I am that people tried bringing these substances on the trip, I'm even more surprised that nobody seems to get in trouble for it, beyond having to suffer Duncan's caustic remarks.

When he gets to Jin, however, and tries to confiscate her cigarettes, she puts up a fight, and even produces a letter. "From my doctor," she says, almost snarling. "They're herbal, totally nicotine-free, and I need them."

Duncan scans the letter, then shares a long look with Pat. Pat nods, then Duncan shrugs and lets her keep them.

Finally he helps us divvy up a bunch of gear that includes random-sized metal poles and canvas-covered bundles, plus dense parcels that seem to contain food—making our backpacks full to bursting. Then he instructs us to put our extra luggage in the van, since we'll primarily be using our packs.

By this time I'd like him to drop dead, and regardless of all the illegal substances he found, I think he's taking his job way too seriously.

But he is our ride to the camp.

So.

Fine.

I don't need all that stuff anyway.

War and Peace may have been a tad ambitious, considering my recent state of mind.

And what a relief to be free of ridiculous stuff like clean clothing.

It's only three weeks, right? Two pairs of underwear should be more than enough for a Nature Girl in the making like me. No need for the chorus of hysterics hurtling around inside me.

I heave my bag into the back of the van with a grimace, then go to get my pack.

We're going to be like sardines in that vehicle, and I can't imagine how we'll be in compliance with seat belt laws, but at least there'll be no mosquitoes. And hopefully the trip will be short and not too bouncy, because really, I would be mortified to pee my pants.

But just as I'm attempting to pick up my pack—crap, is it ever heavy!—I hear the van doors slamming shut, and then, as I'm turning around, Duncan jumps into the front seat, closes the door, starts the van . . .

and

drives

off.

As in, away . . .

without me.

Without all of us.

Oh. My. God.

My ears start ringing, presumably from the scream I'm repressing, and I have the sensation of plunging, like from the top of a roller coaster, or a cliff. I'm standing here breathless and unbalanced and unable to think straight or calm myself, and I know it's an overreaction, but I can't help it.

I do not thrive on surprises of this kind, do not like being left . . . and this, after the pilot already left us in this field with no explanation, is twice in one day.

Three if you count my being left at the airport this morning.

Like I don't already have abandonment issues.

Chapter Two

🌿 🍁 🍃

SUN AND MOON

(Ages Six to Ten)

It could have been that I was a child.

It could have been that I was biased because she was my mother.

Or it could have been that Margot-Sophia Lalonde was massive, larger-than-life, riveting, take-your-breath-away vivid, and astonishing.

In spite of all the years and everything since, I still think of her that way.

Up on the stage in performance or rehearsal, or even in one of our living rooms in one of the European cities we lived in so briefly, Margot-Sophia drew breath and opened her mouth, and the sound, the music that came, it shook the air, made all the colors brighter.

My mother's voice pulled something from the depths of me that made me feel everything all at once, things I didn't have names for yet and maybe never would. It was huge, marvelous, magnificent.

It wasn't just me. The vocal coaches and directors and fellow musicians who came in and out of our various temporary homes regarded her with barely disguised awe, and the care required for the nurturing of her—voice, body, soul—was significant. There were special teas, optimum percentages of humidification and temperature, with the requisite humidifiers in every room, house calls from the ENT (ear, nose, and throat) specialist in each city, private teachers of yoga, Pilates, Alexander Technique. She was focused and diligent, and everyone around her was focused and diligent, and practically falling over themselves . . . all to maintain the magnificence.

I took piano and violin and breathed music. I would be a singer too, I thought, or some variety of musician or performer. It was a given. Our life had a sense of purpose, of importance, of largeness.

There are soft memories too—warm, tactile memories—all of these also tied up and infused with music. Mom singing me to sleep on the nights she was home, me waking partway, late in the night when she came into my room after a performance, smoothing my hair and dropping soft kisses on my cheeks and forehead and nose. "Don't wake up," she would whisper. But I wanted to. I always wanted to.

There was my hand in hers everywhere we went: museums, concerts, bookstores, through train stations and hotel lobbies and opera-house lobbies and in greenrooms and dressing rooms, her hand. I can still feel the silkiness of her fingers, the warmth of her palm.

I remember how tall she seemed, how good she smelled,

how loved I was. I remember, when she told me I could be anything I wanted if only I was willing to work hard enough, how I believed her. And how I wanted to be just like her.

But every so often the magnificence faltered. There were days or weeks even, usually between jobs, or after one of our trips back to Canada to check on the house Mom's parents had left her, when Mom was very sad—too sad to do much of anything but lie around, crying and sleeping. It always passed, but it scared me.

Still, life was good.

In Vienna we bought matching coats in elegant red wool.

In Prague we went to the Charles Bridge in the foggy dawn, then had hot cocoa for breakfast.

In Antwerp we gave a mini concert for some of Mom's opera friends, Mom singing and me on piano and violin, and it got written up in the paper.

My education was both odd and interesting. Mom downloaded a hodgepodge of North American and British curriculums for homeschooling, cherry-picking what she thought was important versus not, while still making sure to cover all the basics. She taught some of it to me herself and hired tutors for the subjects she didn't like. Plus there were always the music lessons, history, tennis in certain countries, depending on the season.

In most cities, there would be kids—other opera kids—for me to do my activities with, to take sewing or hat making or dancing or fencing lessons from the costumers, choreographers, or fight directors of whatever opera house Mom was working at. And we would hang out backstage or in the props rooms, or run around the dressing-room area when no one was there, precocious little opera urchins, making nuisances of ourselves until someone shooed us away. Some of the kids I liked better than others, but we were never anyplace for longer than a few months, so while a few of my friendships were intense, they were also short-lived.

There were a couple of girls I exchanged e-mails with for a while, and occasionally I would end up at an opera house with someone I'd met before, but I went into every friendship knowing that sooner or later, I would be saying goodbye.

Still, I had my mom, and so it was okay.

Once, when I was nine, she handed me a Rubik's Cube and told me that was my schoolwork until I figured it out. This seemed awesome, at first.

"Do you know how to do it, Mom?" I asked a few frustrated hours later.

"No, I do not," she said, looking up from her music stand.

"But . . . then . . . why are you making me do it?"

"So you can learn to sort things out on your own," she said. "So you will learn to persevere. So you will be able to do more than one thing."

I didn't get that. To be able to do one thing, if you could do it as well as she did, seemed to me to be more than enough. But when I presented her with the finished Rubik's Cube a few days later, her eyes shone, and that night she let me stay in her dressing room during the show, and the next day we went to a beautiful little café where we had tea Russian-style, from a real samovar, and sat, side by side, drinking it.

A few months later came London. Covent Garden.

Covent Garden was a big deal—in and of itself, but also for Margot-Sophia.

I was used to opera houses, but Covent Garden, with its Corinthian-columned entrance, stunning glass atrium, and seating for over two thousand people, was gorgeous. It was also daunting, being so much bigger, in every way, than any opera house Mom had worked in.

I was entranced, in awe, infatuated.

"This is the place they write the music for," I said to Mom one day near the end of rehearsals, looking up to the three levels of galleries, and farther up, miles up it seemed, to the dome of pale blue with gold filigree.

"Yes." Mom gazed thoughtfully at me, nodding. "The building . . . whoever designed it, aspired to the music, but now the music aspires to it."

I sighed, tucked my hand into the crook of her arm, and she pulled me against her.

"Are you scared? When you go on?"

"Always," she said. "But that is as it should be. And ultimately, I have to believe."

"In yourself."

"Not just myself," she said. "I also have faith in the hours I've spent in preparation, in my skill, and in the magic that comes, when it deigns to come, once you have done all that work."

She didn't need to explain the magic—I had felt it in the very best performances—the thing beyond technical perfection, the thing that made audiences gasp or hold their breath, the thing that shot me straight through and made me feel I might fly or crumble to dust, just from listening.

We believed in hard work, but we also believed in magic.

Just being at Covent Garden was a result of both.

With Covent Garden came a recording, too, the first of many planned, which would ideally bring helpful income for years to come. In addition, the production was going on tour, which would provide more exposure, more stability.

We rented a flat and bought a piano and some furniture: a bohemian mix of antiques and retired set pieces that were donated by various theaters and opera houses for a huge fundraising event. Giddy from her newfound success, and possibly a glass or two of champagne, Mom had gone a little crazy bidding at the silent auction, and won a giant bed, two wardrobes, a non-functional cuckoo clock, and two thrones. It was as settled as we'd ever been or would ever be, I figured. I even made a friend in the building—a girl my age named Emily, whose parents lived across the hall, and whose "normal" life and parents seemed very exotic to me.

By this time I knew there was no father waiting or detained somewhere, planning to come claim us. I was, as Mom put it, "the miraculous result of one very wild, very late, very irresponsible night in the south of Spain," my father long gone, never missed, and never even searched for, because she didn't, in fact, know his name. "But he was handsome," she would say with a smile, "and kind, and knew how to dance the flamenco. I am thankful for him every day, my precious girl, but we are complete without him."

I believed her. And I liked the London flat. We'd still be traveling, Mom said, but we could now afford a home base.

I was in the audience for the opening, dressed in burgundy silk, and breathless, terrified, hanging on her every note.

I had nothing to worry about. Margot-Sophia, statuesque and dramatic with her flowing, dark, un-wigged hair and espresso-colored eyes, was stunning, captivating, perfect, and magical. There were standing ovations, flowers. Reviews were excellent. After years of hard work and slogging through the lesser and medium opera houses of Europe, Margot-Sophia Lalonde had arrived.

It was such a crystal-clear moment, everything coming together. In my memory, though, except for those occasional "sad days," all the years building up to it were beautiful too. My mother was my sun and moon, and all things were infused with soaring music, tiny luxuries, love, and a kind of velvet fabulousness.

Which makes it hard to reconcile where we are now, how we are.

Chapter Three

THE HARD WAY

(Peak Wilderness, Day One, Continued)

Dear Mom,

We have reached the "camp."

I should clarify: we have reached camp after a three-hour hike, much of it uphill.

Also, I held my bladder for seven hours.

And have killed 255 mosquitoes.

See? I have a list of accomplishments already.

Remember how Ella told us how she bonded with the other girls in her cabin? And her story about that too-hot night where the people on the top bunks ended up sleeping on the floor?

Remember the charming log cabins on the brochure you showed me when we first talked about my going on this trip? And the open-air space with picnic tables, and the tiny buildings with wooden moons and stars carved onto their doors?

At the time I thought it looked a little rustic for my first camp experience, but the longer we hiked today, the better that camp became, in my memory. And I figured, maybe that was the point—to exhaust us so much on the first day that we'd be ecstatic just to have a roof over our heads, and a place to call home at the end of the day.

I couldn't wait to get there. I couldn't wait to use the bathroom/outhouse and then have a chance to get indoors and away from the mosquitoes.

But guess what, Mom?

There are no bathrooms.

There are no outhouses.

AND

THERE

IS

NO

CAMP.

No actual, physical camp, that is.

The thing they're calling "camp" is a clearing beside a lake.

The lake is pretty, sure. But there is no camp. There are no cabins. There is no dining hall or cute little store. Not even a canoe rack. For three whole weeks there is nothing but the camp we make every night.

Wow, right?

Now you might be thinking I'm shocked.

Perhaps a little bit confused . . . ?

I mean, I realize I was upset and angry over the past couple of months and not . . . paying attention to some of the finer details of things, but I'm pretty sure this wasn't the plan, Mom.

So did the plan change and you somehow forgot to tell me?

Or did you try to tell me but I wasn't listening?

Did you know I wasn't listening? Did you decide to let me walk into this blind?

I never would have believed it of you before, but now I'm not so sure.

Regardless, you might expect me to be freaking out a little, particularly as I am supposedly "fragile" these days, right?

But no, not me.

I'm just thinking, *How exciting!* as the full picture comes into focus.

How exciting, and what a magnificent opportunity to get in touch with my inner barbarian.

I will be sure to bring her home with me, Mom.

Love,
Ingrid

Once my situation has become clear, I realize I'm going to have to ask a fellow camper for some harsh chemical mosquito repellant after all. Despite my best efforts, my hands and neck and face are covered in bites, and somehow I have them on my legs and stomach, too. I am a ball of sweaty itchiness.

I settle on Ally. She seems really young, and will hopefully be the least likely to mock me.

"No problem. You can have a bottle," she says with a shy smile. "I brought four."

"And Duncan didn't confiscate any of it?"

"After I saw what happened to you, I stashed two of them

in here," Ally says, and pulls her T-shirt down, showing me how she has two smallish bottles of bug spray nestled between her large boobs.

"Wow. That's useful."

"I could serve tea on 'em, as my mama would say," she says, then gives her cleavage a pat, and pulls one of the bottles out. "Honestly, I can tuck about anything in there. I've gone out with my wallet, my phone, and my lipstick all stored in between these girls. And they're very popular on Instagram."

"I'm . . . not surprised," I say, nodding and taking the bottle from her. It's warm and a bit sweaty, but I'm grateful for it. "Thank you."

"Course I'd have been in trouble if the hot Scot had tried to frisk me," she says, her large, round eyes gleaming like maybe she would have liked that.

"Definitely," I say.

"Do I look okay?" she asks me. "Without my phone I have no way to check."

Looking closely at her face, I see her makeup job isn't holding up too well—the mascara smudged, some of the foundation rubbed off, and her lipstick mostly gone. I wonder if she managed to hide and keep some of the makeup, too, and if so, whether she'll actually put on full war paint every day we're out here. All I've got is lip balm with sunscreen in it.

"You look fine," I say, and then, at the slight wilting of her hopeful demeanor, add, "very pretty."

"Thank you." She is smiling tentatively, and simultaneously pulling at her shirt and patting her waist, and kind of sticking her chest out. "I need all the help I can get."

I am supposed to say, *No, you don't* or *Don't we all!* or *No, you're the most naturally gorgeous girl I've ever seen, and I wish my boobs were popular on Instagram!* or some other reassuring/complimentary thing in response to this, but there's something so sad about her for a second that I feel sort of . . . crushed by it. My throat gets tight, and then I feel ridiculous, and all I manage to say is, "Yeah, I know, I mean, no, uh, you *so* don't . . ."

Two minutes ago I was completely fine (albeit itchy and desperate), but now it seems I'm unable to have a normal conversation without feeling weird and overly emotional.

I hold up the bug spray. "I should get some of this on."

She nods.

"Thanks again."

I've just gotten myself properly doused when Bonnie gathers the nine of us together and says, "Now for your first challenge . . ."

Like the day hasn't been one long string of challenges.

"Each of you has tent components in your pack," she continues.

Aha—that's what the metal poles, et cetera, are.

"Get the components out, match them together, put up the tents," she says. "Go."

We look around at one another, then back at Bonnie.

"Ah, Bonnie?" says one of the guys—the cute hipster, Seth.

"Yes, Seth?"

"I've never put up a tent before. Are there instructions?"

"No."

"It's not exactly difficult," sneers Peace-Bob.

"You're not going to help us?" Seth demands, keeping his focus on Bonnie . . . who gives her answer by walking away.

Needless to say, it turns out I'm not the only person here who's never been to camp, much less gone camp*ing*. Cue chaos.

We eventually figure out there are three tents (more information that would have been helpful) via counting the components. Nine irritable, mosquito-bitten people equals the counting ability of a first grader, but we somehow manage it. Then we learn the hard way that each tent is slightly different and that the parts do not mix and match.

Jin sits on the side, smoking and rolling her eyes at everything, which I don't understand. I'm not exactly here by choice, but I figured I was the only one. This is one of those "once in a lifetime" experiences that people supposedly jump at the chance to participate in. Jin, though, is not jumping. In fact, except for the shock and panic I'm trying to keep in check, she looks how I feel—unimpressed.

Sporty blonde Melissa is eager and earnest, organizing poles and parts by size and color like she is the Gwyneth Paltrow of camping, and Ally stands by, looking overwhelmed but trying to help. Henry and Harvey decide it will be funny to start swiping components from them and running around hollering and hooting, obviously hoping one of the girls will run after them. Melissa goes pale and stalks off. Ally runs after them at first, but soon is huffing and gasping, holding her chest, and muttering about needing two bras if she's going to run.

I take the stakes and set them near the corner of each tent while Tavik deals with Harvey and Henry, then he and Peace nearly come to blows because each of them is certain he is the only one who knows what to do, and neither of them is willing to listen to the other.

Meanwhile, farther down near the beach, Pat and Bonnie get their tent up in five minutes, and sit chatting on a rock by the lake, glancing at us every so often, but seemingly unconcerned.

It takes us an hour, and the tents, once up, are tilted, floppy, and haphazard.

"They're like a parody of themselves," I mutter. "Faux tents."

"Speak English, bitch," says Jin from behind me.

I whirl around, flushing with a mix of anger and fear. I've dealt with this type of person before, and there's a fine line between not backing down and making things worse.

"Maybe you can spray some of your perfume on them," she adds with a sneer.

"If you don't help, I don't see how you have the right to criticize the result," I say, with a gaze that's steadier than I feel.

"I can do whatever the hell I want," she says.

"Sure, you go ahead," I say, a sudden bleakness settling on me and making it hard to maintain my bravado. "I really don't care."

She looks away a second before I do, and then we both look back at the tents.

I've been doing some math.

Nine of us. Five guys—Peace, Tavik, Seth, Harvey, Henry—and four girls—Jin, Ally, Melissa, me.

And there are three tents, each sleeping three.

People start heaving their packs toward the tents . . .

Jin gets up, stamps on her cigarette, and marches to the front of the least wobbly tent, grabbing Melissa on the way there.

I join them.

Ally joins us.

On the threshold we stop, look at one another.

"We're not all going to fit," I say, stating the obvious.

"Duh," Jin says.

"This can't be right," Melissa says. "Maybe there's . . . another tent somewhere?"

"I don't think so," Ally says, glancing nervously around.

Pat chooses this moment to wander over and check out our progress.

"Pat, we have a problem," I say.

"Tents are up, I see," he says with a nod.

"That's not the problem," Melissa says, suddenly eager and helpful again, and explains.

"Oh. Well," Pat says, patting his vest pockets, "this trip is coeducational."

"You're saying one of us has to share a tent . . . with them?" Melissa asks, her pitch going up along with her obvious level of alarm. "I don't think—"

"Look," Pat says, "here at Peak Wilderness, we choose not to make assumptions about people's sexuality, or even gender; therefore dividing by male and female is irrelevant. We have a strict no-sex rule, the breaking of which will result in expulsion from the program. The size of the campsites dictates that the tents be close together, and the rule of three people in a tent ensures no two people are left alone in a possibly compromising situation."

Sex . . . ! had not crossed my mind. I was way further back, worrying about basics like privacy and personal space and the fact that boys are known to snore and fart and smell at close quarters. Now I'm nauseous.

Meanwhile, Jin mutters, "Dude, you don't think three can be compromising?"

Oy.

"Beyond that," Pat continues like he didn't hear her, "we expect you to be respectful, use your best judgment, and work it out."

And then he steps away to talk to the boys.

Great.

"Rock-paper-scissors?" Ally suggests.

"No, no," Melissa says, clutching her stomach and looking like she's going to pass out. "No, I can't. Please."

"What about two and two?" I suggest. "Two girls and, say, Seth? And the other two with—"

Melissa is starting to hyperventilate. "I can't. I can't," she gasps.

My insides twist, and again what I feel is how someone else looks—Melissa this time. Only I'm obviously more practiced at hiding it.

"All right." I swallow, and put a hand on Melissa's arm. "We'll figure something out . . . ."

"Figure something out? Someone . . . has to sleep with two strange boys," Ally says, eyes wide, face red, and looking like it's all just dawning on her now. Based on my earlier observations of Ally, I'd have expected her to be excited about this, or at least pretend to be, but she is genuinely freaked out.

Ally's comment is followed by a long, awkward pause in

which we all wait for a solution to magically appear, or in my case, for the entire thing to just go away.

Because that always works.

"It's not fair," Ally says.

"Life isn't fair," I say, surprised, and surprisingly pained, to hear my mother's voice and favorite mantra coming so easily and automatically out of my mouth.

Life isn't fair.

This whole trip could have been set up to prove it to me once and for all. Life isn't fair, and anything is possible. Even your own mother might believe you are too much of a dreamer, too soft for the life you want to pursue, and she might make a deal with you and then change the terms without telling you. Pull the rug out from under you, just because you dared to want something badly enough to defy her, badly enough even to hurt her. Pull it out again, just in case it hasn't happened enough times already. Or maybe just to make sure you're ready for all the not-fair stuff that's coming in life. Like I didn't already know. Like I wasn't already reeling from a truckload of not-fair.

She might have. She wouldn't have. I go back and forth, but the fact is, I don't know anymore, and I'm not going to figure it out in the next five minutes.

I look at Melissa and Ally, both melting down now—Melissa rigid and pale and looking like she might fall over, and Ally red-faced, with tears welling up. Meanwhile, Jin has planted her feet firmly in front of the entrance to the tent. She doesn't seem so much like she cares about the possibility of sleeping with boys. More like she cares about *winning*, and about the fact that she got here first.

And then I think about Mom again and realize one thing for certain: she may have sent me to a different program than Ella's, by mistake or on purpose; she may have deceived me, or she may not have; but she would *never* have knowingly sent me on a trip where I would be sleeping in a tent with boys—full-grown men, practically—if she'd known about that part.

I think about how she would have a freaking cow over this.

And then?

"I'll do it," I say. "No big deal."

And that is how I end up with Tavik and Peace-Bob for tentmates.

Awesome.

Chapter Four

CURTAIN

(Age Ten)

Pop stars and rockers get nodes—calluses on the vocal cords, usually from overuse, usually because they are not paying attention and/or think they can push through. Opera singers do not push through.

Opera singers know that, unless they are superstars, they can be replaced in two seconds flat, and therefore have their throats scoped regularly to make sure they are not developing nodes or polyps, and at the slightest hint of them, everything stops. All singing, all talking, all sound, dunzo. Out come the extra humidifiers, the cups of tea, the voice therapists.

Opera singers work hard, work tirelessly, but when it comes to their voices, they do not push through.

Except . . .

Maybe . . .

When they are in the middle of a career breakthrough run at Covent Garden, and they get a little hoarse, just a little tiny bit hoarse . . .

And, because they can't bear the thought of taking time off in the middle of such an important role, tell themselves it's just a cold, and fail to go to the ENT, and keep going to the theater and singing because not performing might mean losing all the momentum, months and years of building to this, all to be shoved back down to the bottom of the heap. . . .

I was in the audience on the night it happened. At first, it was just a pause where there wasn't supposed to be one. Only someone who'd heard her rehearsing this part thousands of times would have heard it. Still, I squirmed in my seat.

Then there were a couple of funny notes. I whipped out my opera glasses, zoomed in on her, and stared. Up close she still seemed . . . fine . . . but normally she was better than fine. I started to sweat, my heart beating too quickly. She could get booed for this. Opera audiences are passionate, vocal, and unforgiving.

Then, during the second aria, her voice went crazy, zooming from the notes she was supposed to be singing to other notes way up or down the scale. Wrong notes. Screechingly, undeniably wrong notes that rose and fell in what felt like slow motion, each long second worse than the last.

The final time she opened her mouth to sing, nothing came out.

I sat there in the dark, insides shredded. It was just her voice, but it seemed to me like she was literally dying up there.

Everything stopped for a long, excruciating moment as hundreds of people held their breath at the same time. Even the orchestra paused. And then my mom, Margot-Sophia Lalonde, face flushed, eyes bright with terrified, unshed tears, made a dramatic, in-character gesture with her arms, and the conductor sprang back into action. The music started back up, faster than before, and Mom moved to the marks she was supposed to and did all her choreographed actions, and essentially mimed the rest of the piece, finishing on her knees in the spotlight, agony streaming down her face.

And then the curtain, blood red and edged with gold, fell.

Mom's friends converged upon us in London.

Everyone had heard; the drama of Margot-Sophia Lalonde losing her voice partway through a performance had even made the papers. Her cover, which is what they call understudies in opera, had arrived at the theater within the fifteen minutes specified by her contract (that's how fast you can actually be replaced in opera—fifteen minutes) and sung from the wings while Mom walked the rest of the part. I had watched in anguish from the back, unable to stay in my seat, equally unable to turn away.

Now our flat was full, with doctors coming and going, visitors arriving with gifts of specialty teas, honey cakes, scentless bouquets of flowers, bits of amusing gossip. Mom communicated via signals and signs, or with paper and pen, in a pretty silk-covered notebook someone had brought her.

There were trips to the hospital, examinations, consultations, and always Mom told me everything would be fine, but that she needed more rest. She did not get sad and go to bed; she continued to take obsessively good care of herself and stayed positive.

The run of the show ended.

The tour began . . . without us.

Mom remained positive.

But fewer and fewer people came to visit as the weeks turned into months, and those who did come started to seem awkward, apologetic. Pretty soon no one came except the vocal therapists, yoga teacher, and ENT.

I went between hovering over my mother and hiding out at my friend Emily's.

Finally there was surgery. She'd hoped to avoid it, because of cost, because of the recovery time, and because there was no guarantee it would work. But now it was time to try. She didn't say it, didn't act it, but I felt it: this was the last chance.

Recovery was slow, more days and weeks passing and then came the attempts to sing, carefully at first and supervised by the doctor. Her lower register was fine, sounded beautiful. But the upper register . . . didn't sound good.

And it didn't improve with further attempts.

I will never forget the sorrowful face of Mom's handsome ENT when he told us what we already suspected: Mom's singing voice was destroyed. It was over.

"The good news," he said, "is your speaking voice, and the lower part of your register . . . both are fine. And you may use them as much as you like."

"Yes. Thank you." She was so dignified, so strong, her speaking voice still so rich and nuanced, her articulation clear and perfect from all the years of classical training.

He could be wrong, I thought. This was too painful to be real. *We'll keep trying. We'll try again tomorrow.*

But tomorrow came, and Margot-Sophia Lalonde, grim-faced but with perfect composure, began to sell the furniture.

She never cried, so neither did I.

The curtain was falling. Had fallen.

And we were out of magic.

Chapter Five

AT RISK

(Peak Wilderness, Day One, Continued)

Dear Mom,

Here's a quick fact I'm sure you'll enjoy: if you cook on a campfire in the dark or semidark, bugs, lots of bugs, especially mosquitoes, will fly into the food. And when you go to eat, it will be so dark, you cannot see the bugs well enough to pick them out of your bowl.

Apparently this is no problem, because the boiling sterilizes the bugs.

And they are a good source of protein.

While they are fresh bugs, and certainly local, I am not the only person who was disgusted. Ally cried. Seth and I barely ate, both of us determined to pick as many out of our bowls as possible, which meant there wasn't much actual food left. Meanwhile, Melissa surprised me by shrugging it off and eating everything, and Peace ate with relish and talked about how eating bugs is the way of the future because the beef industry isn't sustainable.

(Dead mosquito count: 438, not including the ones we cooked and ate.)

Love,
Ingrid

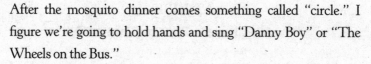

After the mosquito dinner comes something called "circle." I figure we're going to hold hands and sing "Danny Boy" or "The Wheels on the Bus."

We convene on a rocky outcrop above the lake, our faces lit by moonlight and flashlights. Pat gives us a big welcome, and Bonnie echoes it, and then we're instructed to introduce ourselves and talk about why we chose to sign up for the trip and what our goals are.

Chose. Ha. I can't wait for my turn.

Pat and Bonnie begin. Pat's background is in social work. Bonnie is a psychotherapist.

"I see this as an opportunity to marry two of the things I'm passionate about—the great outdoors and today's youth," Pat says, "particularly at-risk youth. My goal is to help empower you as individuals and to foster a sense of connectedness, of responsibility to ourselves and the earth."

On one hand, I'm almost moved.

On the other, I'm trying not to barf.

And on another hand, if I had a third hand, I'm wondering about the word "at-risk."

Bonnie is next with more of the same—nature and leadership, troubled youth and learning to work as a team, blah, blah, blah.

If I wasn't "troubled" before, I am now.

Seth, whom I am fervently wishing were my tentmate, if I have to stay with boys, is first.

He clears his throat. "I'm from a very . . . traditional family. And I'm here to get tougher. Mentally, physically, spiritually. I'm here to get closer to God and to strengthen myself against . . . temptation and sin."

He says "temptation and sin" like he wants to swallow the words.

"What sort of sin?" Bonnie asks, face neutral.

"All of them," Seth says, looking at the ground in front of him, his shoulders slumped. "My dad . . . that is . . . let's just say I'm not acceptable to God. And if I'm not acceptable to God, I'm not going to have a family anymore and I love my family, so . . . I have to change. I have twenty-one days to change. That's my goal."

Right, so he's gay/bi/trans, or something, and he's from one of those ignorant, asshole families that will disown him for it. Now I *really* wish he were my tentmate. And I want to throttle his parents.

Harvey and Henry, who are fraternal twins but still look very much alike, go next. Well, technically it's Harvey first, then Henry, but they basically speak together, and they're here because they thought it would be "totally extreme," and they want to kick each other's asses in a variety of nature-related challenges.

"Plus—" says Harvey.

"Dude," says Henry, "no."

"Who cares, man?" Harvey says to him, then turns back to the circle. "Plus we had a party and, uh, trashed the house."

"*Half* the house."

"Yeah, half the house," Harvey amends. "Totally by accident, though, and the really bad part wasn't even us. Someone drove their car through the living-room window."

"So our parents . . . Well, they almost canceled this trip, they're so pissed, but on the other hand, they don't want to see us for a few weeks."

"Time to get out of Dodge."

"So here we are," Henry finishes.

"Do you have a history with this type of incident, Henry?" Bonnie asks.

"Well, not exactly," Henry says, just as Harvey says, "Oh, totally!"

"I asked Henry," Bonnie says, with a hard look at Harvey.

"Same difference," Harvey says.

"But you are not, in fact, the same person," Bonnie says.

"Okay, sure," Harvey says. "Floor's yours, bro."

Henry, who wears his medium brown hair shorter than Harvey, looks annoyed, but I can't tell whom he's annoyed with— Bonnie, or his brother.

"We get into a bit of trouble sometimes," he says. "But nothing too serious."

"Are you kidding?" Harvey practically shouts. "We are epic! We're legendary!"

"Sure, okay," Henry says, looking distinctly un-legendary. "But it's all in fun."

"Potato guns! Smoke bombs! And there was that time we

took Principal Carter's phone and—"

"Dude, shut up!" Henry says, punching his twin in the shoulder. "Be cool, okay?"

"Right," Harvey says, and subsides. "We're Boy Scouts. That's all we've got to say."

"Hmm," Bonnie says, studying them. "We'll come back to this another time. How about you, Jin?"

Jin throws her cigarette into the fire and sweeps the circle with a glare, meeting each person's eyes with defiance. "I was on the street," she says. "I was making my way all right, then one night a few months ago, I got thrown into jail for . . ."

"Yes . . . ?" Pat says when Jin fails to continue, and suddenly I get the feeling that he knows—whatever she's about to say or not say, he already knows.

"Solicitation," Jin says, glaring steadily at Pat.

He nods, cool as a cucumber.

"Right, well. My parents refused to come for me. I'm a humiliation. But they called my aunt. Probably because she's richer than they are and cares less about the opinions of everyone in our community. Plus they don't want to spend any more money on me. Unstable investment."

Bitterness oozes from her with this statement.

"Anyway, she offered to take me in," Jin continues. "I was . . . tired. And so I accepted. But she's strict and she had conditions—no drugs, which sucks because I'm really only a recreational user—and I have to catch up in school, and she thought I should do this, too. Get as far away from the 'bad in-fluences' as possible. Definitely no chance to call a dealer from out here anyway."

Harvey laughs.

Bonnie and Pat gaze at Jin with dead-serious listening faces, and Harvey stops laughing.

"Anyway, I figured if I can survive on the street, this is child's play," she says with a shrug.

"How long have you been clean?" Pat asks.

"I'm not an addict. I just like to have fun. But as far as being clean, technically . . . except for a few weak moments, I've been clean, including from nicotine," she says with a nod toward her herbal cigarette, "for . . . two months."

A few weak moments within the last two months does not sound particularly clean to me, but what do I know? Her smoking suddenly bothers me a lot less, though.

"All right. Good for you," Pat says.

"And now, Peace?" Bonnie says.

Peace-Bob stretches his legs out, looks around the circle.

"I reject the way we live," he says.

Here we go.

"I reject the commercialism, the waste, the selfishness. I reject Western relationship boundaries, organized religion, war. I reject my former self."

It's not quite in the spirit of things, but I reject his current self.

"My mission in life, starting with this trip, is to be peaceful, to live as one with nature, to be authentic. Someday I hope to find a group of like-minded individuals and band together to live off the land. . . ."

I work very hard not to roll my eyes as he goes on.

Bonnie finally (tactfully) hastens him along, and Melissa

is next. Other than her intense reluctance to share a tent with anyone male, she's been pretty quiet. I'm expecting, due to her looking so fit, to hear she's in training to climb Everest or something.

"I just escaped from a cult," she says.

Wow. Not Everest.

"I disappeared. Until six months ago I hadn't seen the sun for over a year. That's how long I was gone. Anyway. I'm a mess, and it's been hard trying to . . . relate . . . to my family, to my old friends. No one knows what to say to me, and I don't easily . . . trust people. Or myself. So when my mom and dad suggested this, I figured it might help. My goal is just to get stronger, feel better, and maybe figure out . . . how this happened to me."

We are all silent for a few moments, and again I get the sense that neither Bonnie nor Pat is shocked, or even surprised.

"That's it for me," she says, her voice suddenly chipper. "Ally?"

Ally is still weepy about the bugs-for-dinner situation, but pulls herself together enough to tell us she goes to a "special" high school that's going to give her a credit for this. Plus she'd like to lose weight. Plus she'd like to get back custody of her one-year-old girl, who is currently in foster care due to Ally not being able to provide a stable environment. This is partly because Ally's own parents are raging partiers in both senses—they are wild and loud when they're having fun, and wilder and louder when they're fighting, causing most of the neighbors to have the police on speed dial.

Some government grant is covering Ally's fee to be here.

She can't be older than sixteen.

My shin is aching, and I'm starting to feel sick inside and wondering where the genuine nature enthusiasts are (I refuse to count Peace-Bob), because that's who the brochure said this trip was for, and that's the type of people Ella met when she did Peak Wilderness. Nature enthusiasts.

Tavik (my other tentmate) is next, and though he's not exactly rocking that vibe, I'm hoping *he's* a nature guy. Like maybe he's a snowboarding, dirt-biking, ATV-riding, rock-climbing nature guy.

I'm envisioning this when he says, "I just got out of jail."

I haven't said a word thus far, but at this I find myself blurting, "What?"

"Ingrid, you may speak when it's your turn," Bonnie says in a level tone.

"Sorry," I mutter.

"Yes, I was recently incarcerated," Tavik continues, eyes now on mine. "Not that it's anyone's business. My parents are dead. I'm on parole. Some genius of a social worker thought this would be good for my rehabilitation and got me in as a charity case."

"And what are your personal goals for your time here, Tavik?" Bonnie asks, all serene and unfazed.

The impression I keep getting is that neither she nor Pat is fazed by any of it. This fits with the luggage search and Duncan's lack of surprise about finding alcohol and drugs. Maybe the more messed-up campers come with a file, or the leaders have been briefed in advance about all of us. If so, what would they have been told about me? That I'm a wuss of a city girl who needs her ass kicked by the wilderness in order to . . . what? Build character? I certainly have no behavior or incidents on the scale of these people—nothing of significance, anyway. But still, Bonnie and Pat might know I've had a hard time lately.

Tavik looks at Bonnie and laughs at her question. It's not an unkind laugh or even a bitter one. He sounds genuinely amused, and for a second he reminds me of Isaac again.

"What's funny?" Bonnie says. "Surely you have goals. Maybe even dreams . . . ?"

"Oh yeah," he says. "White picket fence, chocolate lab, a pretty little wife who likes it from both sides."

I flinch, and a choking sound comes from someone across the fire—Melissa, I think.

Bonnie just waits.

"All right, sorry," he says finally. "I guess my goal is to stay out of trouble and spend some time looking at the sky. I've been thinking maybe I haven't seen enough sky."

The wind shifts, I look upward, and a clean, clear breath of air goes into my lungs as I look at the shockingly bright stars and try to get "both sides" out of my head.

"Your turn," Tavik says, looking at me.

I give myself a shake.

"I . . . I'm sorry, but what is going on here?" I say.

"We're sharing," Pat says.

"I understand that part," I say, trying to calm myself, trying to sound normal, and failing. "I mean, what kind of trip is this? Because I am certain I had a brochure that showed *cabins*. And smiling teenagers with 'leadership potential.'"

"What, you don't think I have leadership potential?" Tavik says with a bark of laughter.

"I didn't mean . . . I just mean . . ." I break off as heat rushes to my face. "I didn't mean to hurt anyone's feelings. I just . . . expected something totally different from this."

Pat and Bonnie exchange a glance.

"We do have a couple of physical camps, and some of the expeditions are run from them," Pat says carefully. "And some, like this one, are not. For this group there is more of an emphasis on wilderness survival, group dynamics, and yes, leadership."

"Is . . . is there a chance I'm supposed to be at one of the other ones? The camp ones?"

"This is the only Peak Wilderness program running at the moment," Bonnie says, shaking her head.

"Why don't you tell us why you're here, Ingrid?" suggests Pat in his gentle-with-steel-underneath way.

I look around the circle, an aching, burning sensation pulsing inside me as I attempt to digest the fact that Mom has sent me for almost a month of actual camping, in the wilderness, with a bunch of junkies, criminals, and lunatics.

I remember seeing that "camping" might be involved in some of the trips, and I can imagine Mom deciding to book me into one of the more intense programs, and not telling me because she was angry, or because she honestly thought it wouldn't be so different from what we discussed, or to teach me a lesson, because she doesn't think I'm self-reliant enough.

But throwing me in with a group like this? I have a hard time believing she'd have done that on purpose.

Regardless, I made a deal. A promise. I said I would do Peak Wilderness, and I didn't specify which program. And if I complete this, I get to spend my senior year at school in London, England. I get to live the life I want.

Bonnie, Pat, and the rest of the group are staring at me, waiting for an answer. I realize I'm rubbing my lower leg again, and stop, clasping my hands tightly together.

I shouldn't be here.

I am a model citizen and paragon of stability compared to these people.

Okay, there were a couple of months when I could barely eat. And there was the incident with the ax. But only one person knows about that, and he promised he wouldn't tell anyone. And I'm fine now. Mostly healed, and much calmer, and really, it was an accident. The throbbing shin is totally psychosomatic—has to be. Anyway, none of that had even happened yet when Mom signed me up for this trip, and frankly, there's no way she knows about it now, either. Point being? No way I'm talking about any of that stuff, or about my relationship with Mom. Not unless I suddenly want all these unbalanced people thinking they've been invited to dig into my psyche, which is never happening. It's not relevant to why I'm here. Not relevant, period.

Bonnie and Pat probably know something, but whatever they know or don't know, they can't force me to talk about it.

And yet, I get the feeling that the music-school thing isn't going to play well for this crowd, and I have to say something.

"I had a bad year . . . at school," I say finally. This is partially true—I had to complete eleventh grade via homeschooling. "I was having trouble." (True-ish.) "I missed some school. . . ." (True.) "So . . . my mom decided . . . on my behalf . . . that over the summer, a . . . a change of scenery would be good for me."

Decided a change of scenery would be good for me. . . .

That's funny, right?

Chapter Six

ISAAC

Dear Isaac,

Uh, hi.

I thought of you today. And I'm so far from everything and everyone that despite our being nothing but tense pretend-friends for the last long while . . . I thought I'd write.

Did I ever tell you how my mom believes music saved her life? Not just her sanity, her actual life. I think you could call that ironic.

Anyway, that's not what I wanted to write about; I'm just filling space, bullshitting really, which is totally, hilariously, a waste of time in this context. Bullshitting in my own journal. Pathetic.

How about I just dive in?

It's my fault, our being pretend-friends. Mostly mine, anyway. I have no business writing to you. And yet . . . here I am, so far away from where you are, and who knows what's going to happen in our lives from this point forward. You probably noticed I didn't come back to school after New Year's, and we might not be in the same place in the fall, either. I got accepted into this incredible school in England, and I might do my final year there. I plan to, actually. Not that I expect you to even care anymore. You probably don't. And I'll never show you this, anyway.

I realized, just now, that I liked knowing you were close by, after we broke up, if you could call it a breakup when maybe we weren't officially together. Even when I was mad as hell, and hurt, it was nice knowing you were down the hall in another classroom, or right next to me but pretending I didn't exist, or a couple of subway stops away on weekends. I thought I wasn't thinking about you anymore, but I was. Am. I could see you, hear you, smell you if you got close enough. Now I can't.

It's funny how many things we never talked about. That's (at least partly) my fault too. I had so much going on at home, and I didn't tell you any of it. The thing is, I got used to dealing with things on my own, and even if I'd wanted to talk to you, I didn't know how. So you didn't know how fragile I was, how screwed up. You didn't know how much I needed to feel I could trust you, even though I wasn't, in fact, trusting you. Ha. You didn't know how complicated and full of contradiction I was, either, and hey, at least I saved you from that.

So, my mom, when she was little, she says she was "moody," which . . . there's probably a diagnosis for it now, but the point is, she had trouble staying afloat. She didn't feel normal—not at home, not at school, not anywhere.

You and I both have felt that, I know.

Anyway, she had trouble. She couldn't be happy. And her parents—my grandparents, whom I never met—didn't know how to help. My impression is they were of that stoic, Victorian, chin-up generation where they didn't talk about things.

She used to climb out her window at night and lie there on this short bit of roof with a steep incline, and wish that the stars would come to life, and fly away with her. One time she started to fall asleep out there, and almost fell off. For a whole three days after, she felt incredible—amazingly energized and happy—that's what she told me. Near-death experience = happy.

Weird reaction, right?

Then when she was eleven, she started piano lessons. She was late starting, compared to a lot of kids, but she said that in music she finally found something to grab on to. The rest of the time she'd just been drifting.

I have that sometimes—a drifting feeling.

Her parents didn't get it, really, but music was at least a proper activity for a young girl to be engaged in. Like I said, she says it saved her life.

Because, what—otherwise a star would have come to take her away?

You know, Isaac, I spent half my life on guard against that star. For the longest time she was all I had, the center of my universe, and I just had to be vigilant. Later, it felt like I was always trying to get her back—the real her. But it wasn't just her, it was my childhood, the shining-ness of it. That time in my life was like a state of being I could somehow get back to, an anchor, like music was her anchor.

She says it saved her, so it probably did.

What is going to save me?

Ingrid

Chapter Seven

PEACE OUT

(Peak Wilderness, Day One, Continued)

Finally it's bedtime—time to go sleep with the agro-hippie and the ex-con. The good news is there should be no mosquitoes in the tent. The bad news is I don't know how I'll even get to sleep in such a foreign, freaky situation.

I take a deep breath, unzip the door, and scramble in.

Tavik is already there and he's taken the uphill side. I slide over to the other side, which leaves a mere two feet between us for Peace-Bob.

Tavik's got a tiny LED light on, and my jaw drops when I see what else he's holding—a book, wrapped in what looks like a zippable waterproof cover.

"How'd you manage to keep that?"

"Unlike you, I didn't just stand there and let the guy unpack and repack all my shit for me," he says.

"I noticed you lost a few things."

"My stash, you mean?"

I nod. He'd had a sizable bag of weed that Duncan confiscated.

"I meant to lose that."

"What, so you could smuggle in a book?"

"You jealous?" He gazes at me, unblinking.

"Depends on the book."

"It ain't your hardcover Dostoyevsky."

"Tolstoy."

"Same thing."

"Actually, Dostoyevsky's writing was much more symbolic, more infused with ideological discussion, whereas Tolstoy puts you right in the center of—"

"Sure, nerdo. But dead Russian dudes are fucking pretentious reading for a wilderness retreat."

"Not if you like dead Russian dudes."

He grunts, and goes back to reading.

"Anyway," I say, unable to stop myself, "does this seem like a retreat to you? I'm thinking 'retreat' is a word that could only be used ironically for this trip so far. Is this what you were expecting?"

"Pretty much."

"Huh. You never said what you're reading."

"Porn."

I suck in a breath. He smirks.

"If you're nice, I might let you borrow it when I'm done."

I doubt I'm ready for his version of "nice," so I ignore this comment, unroll my sleeping bag, bundle up the sage hoodie to serve as a pillow, and try to figure out how I'm supposed to change into my pajamas.

The most logical thing would be to ask Tavik to leave. But can I manage to open my mouth to ask that? No. Not after the porn comment. Not with the perma-smirk he's wearing even while supposedly reading, as if he knows I'm mortified and un-comfortable and have never spent a night sleeping with a boy, much less two.

Changing outside isn't an option—less private, creepy, and I'll be eaten alive by mosquitoes. So I'm left with being too embarrassed to change with Tavik here, and too embarrassed to ask him to go.

Finally I lie down on top of my sleeping bag, fully clothed, and stare at the canvas above me. I'll just sleep in my clothes. And tomorrow I'll figure out a better system—one that includes getting to the tent first so I can have some damn privacy.

Peace-Bob, though, has no such scruples.

Oh no.

He charges in, unpacks in record time, and then, before I have the foresight to look away, hunches down in the middle of the tent, peels off his pants *and* underwear, hanging his hairy ass—I am not exaggerating—right over my head.

(I believe I mentioned he is odiferous?)

My throat closes on itself, and I roll away from the horror, almost choking, and making a disgusted sound in the process.

"What?" he says.

Tavik (the jerk) is laughing.

"I don't need to see your . . . bare butt, thank you," I say, staring at the side of the tent but seeing his butt over and over again in my mind's eye.

"The body is a natural thing," he says. "There's nothing to be ashamed of. Personally I love to be naked."

"Oh my God."

With that I pull my hood down over my eyes and get to work on trying to un-see what I just saw.

Chapter Eight

🍂 🍁 🌿

DIVA'S BED
(Age Eleven)

Three months after our life in London was over, we had moved into Mom's childhood home, a charming coach house on a tree-lined street of Toronto. Mom's parents had died a few years back and we'd been renting the house out, but now the renters were gone. We'd had our things shipped and un-packed, and gotten me registered in my first "normal" school. And I would be going with my real last name: Burke. Lalonde had only been Mom's stage name—her way of separating her-self from parents who never understood, or approved of, her career choice.

I liked Lalonde better. I was used to it and wanted to keep it, and no matter what, my mom would always be Margot-Sophia Lalonde to me, because that was what she had chosen for her-self. But now she was choosing something else, and since Burke was our legal name, arguing was pointless.

So, fine. New name. New start. I would be in sixth grade in the fall, and I was excited, figuring I'd finally have a chance at having friends—the kind you don't have to say good-bye to after a few weeks.

Meanwhile, Mom had gone from positive to stoic, had soldiered on.

But once she got us settled in Toronto, she went to bed.

I watched and waited and hoped she would get back up after a few days, like the times this had happened when I was younger, but days turned into weeks.

At school I discovered that I knew too much of many things and not enough of others to be trying to make friends just yet, and quickly decided to aim for invisibility instead. Every day I would come home, let myself in, and listen from the foyer, hoping to hear Mom up and about. Hearing nothing, I would then slip off my shoes, coat, and backpack, and tiptoe upstairs and stand outside her bedroom door and listen again, every bit of my being focused on her, on willing her heart to be beating and her lungs to be taking in air, at least.

Sometimes I would still hear nothing, and it was such a loud nothing, like the sound of that curtain falling—soft to nonexistent, and yet so final.

And so I would slip forward carefully, one foot and then the other, the door swishing against the ivory carpet as I gently pushed it open, just enough to step into the room.

In the darkened, stale-aired space was the giant bedstead from the silent auction in London—one of the few pieces that Mom refused to sell, and insisted on shipping to Canada, despite the impracticality and expense. It had a gold-leaf headboard and a canopy hung with diaphanous sky-blue, white, and gold silk, with long tassels. The top part of the canopy was so tall, we'd had to have it affixed to the ceiling.

Once I was close enough and standing very still, I would detect the subtle rise and fall of the sheet, and all the rigid, frightened pieces of me would come back together in relief. I would creep closer and then just stand, breathing with her, each breath dissolving small portions of the dread I carried with me all day long at school, and then on the way home, and worse and worse down the block, and then up the stairs and inside.

I wanted to touch her. Climb up onto the bed and curl into her, around her. But then I might wake her, and I couldn't bear the things she said when she was awake.

"I want to go to sleep and never wake up."

You would have to be an idiot to miss the meaning of that.

Curtain.

Stay with me, I would beg in my mind, sending my will through space to the defeated form on the bed. *Stay.*

I was not an idiot.

As the months of sixth grade passed and my mother failed to die, I also wanted her to *get up and live.*

I didn't want to be mad. I knew what she'd been through. But after the initial worry and subsequent terrifying realization that she wasn't going to just snap out of it, I was like an orphan—alone in a new house in a new city, nothing familiar, no friends or family, and motherless.

I knew why. Of course I knew. But I started to boil inside.

I started to stare down at her in the bed, the words *GET UP* screaming in my mind.

Get up. Get up.

I need you.

How she could drop me into this new life and then just abandon me to fend for myself, I could not fathom.

Get. Up.

She was a crumpled, diminished, washed-out, fireless shell. But the mom I knew, the dedicated, optimistic, magical mom— she was in there somewhere and I wanted her back. I felt terrible and guilty for being so angry, so full of hate sometimes. It was the wrong feeling, I knew.

But I had lost the same things she lost. Plus her. Not the same, exactly, but still. At eleven years old I wasn't supposed to be buying groceries with my mother's credit card, depositing dividend checks from the modest investment portfolio my grandparents had left us, making all my own meals plus someone else's, not that she ate.

I didn't have to be a math genius to see the dividend checks weren't going to be enough for us to live on.

Please get up.

There were days she tried, days I'd come home to find her in the kitchen, having cooked half a meal, or sitting in the living room with a stack of self-help books, trying to read.

"Is there anything in there that can help?" I asked one day, pointing at the book in front of her.

She looked up, met my gaze, and then started to shake. "I can't even read. I can, but . . . nothing goes in." She pointed to her head. "And everything is so . . . slow. Thick."

"Mom, you need to see a doctor."

"I've had quite enough of doctors," she muttered. "I just need to rest."

"What about what I need?"

"Oh, sweetheart . . ." Tears formed in her eyes.

"You can't just stay in bed forever, Mom," I said, my repressed anger bubbling toward the surface. "You can't just lie around feeling sorry for yourself. You have a daughter, in case you haven't noticed."

A wailing sob came out of her at this, and she got up and hobbled, hunched over and crying, and threw her arms around me. I hugged her back and eventually managed to get her upstairs and into her bed, where she cried for five solid hours. I sat outside the door, feeling helpless, remorseful, and still furious.

The next day she got up and made breakfast and was awake and cooking more food than we could possibly eat when I got home from school, and then she stayed awake all night, walking back and forth, up and down, weeping and talking to herself. She'd been drinking Red Bull and taking super doses of vitamins.

It wasn't an improvement. And the next day she crashed back down again, staying in bed for a solid month.

I felt like setting the house on fire, calling in the army, howling at the moon, anything, just to make something happen. But I was also afraid of anything happening, because it wouldn't necessarily be good, as evidenced by the Red Bull/vitamin incident.

Then a letter arrived. It was from one of the few friends—a costume designer from Vienna—who'd made a small effort at keeping in touch.

The envelope contained, in addition to a chatty letter, a newspaper clipping containing a review about a brilliant new soprano—someone we knew, but not well—in a breakout performance. *Screw it,* I thought, and delivered it to Mom on the pretty bamboo tray I'd been using to bring her anything I thought would tempt her to eat.

"Want me to read it to you?"

"I'm fine," she said, scanning it from her reclined position on the pillows.

"Okay . . ."

"A slap in the face," Mom muttered a couple of minutes later, and dropped the clipping onto the floor. And then she sat up a little straighter. I was about to pat her arm, but drew back when I saw fire in her eyes.

Fire was good. Fire was better than despair—it had to be.

Yes. Get up. Get up and fight.

I picked up the clipping.

"Take it away," Mom said.

I went softly out, heart pounding, and dropped the clipping into the bathroom garbage.

Something will happen now, I thought, and I was right.

From Mom's bedroom came a ripping sound, followed by a bellowing roar: "Down!"

I froze.

"Bring it down!"

I unfroze, shot back to Mom's room, and found her out of bed and wild-eyed.

"Bring it all down," she cried, gripping one of the diaphanous bed curtains in both hands and pulling at it until it

ripped from the ceiling. Bits of plaster fell down all around us, and the beautiful curtains lay pooled at her feet. "Bring it down!"

"Mom, stop!" I cried, crossing the room. This, again, was not what I'd been hoping for. "Mom! You'll bring the ceiling down on us! Come, you love this bed; it's your diva bed!"

It was the wrong thing to say, the diva part. I knew that right away. And if there'd been any doubt, the wail that rose up, seemingly through the depths of the earth all the way through Mom's weakened body and up through her damaged vocal cords, made it clear.

Wrong thing.

Another curtain, this one seeming to shriek as it tore along the seams.

"Mom, Mom, stop . . ." I was forced to move, and almost tripped in my haste to get out of the way as Mom launched herself across the bed to attack the curtains on the other side.

"Stop it, stop it, stop it!" I continued to shout, my voice barely penetrating through the wailing and the ripping and tearing and the raining plaster. And then Mom started to pick up other things—a ceramic cat, a music box—and throw them at the wall. The smashing sounds were epic. "No, you're ruining everything, all the beautiful things! Please, please, stop . . ."

"Everything beautiful is already ruined," Mom roared, proving she was listening, at least.

"It isn't!" I snapped, so tired, so frightened, so tired of being frightened, and so very frustrated. "Margot-Sophia!" I hollered, and I flew across the room to the bedroom door, grabbed the handle, and began to slam it—open and slam, open and slam—over and over as hard as I could.

"*Margot-Sophia!*" (*Slam, swoosh, slam.*)

"Get hold of yourself!" (*Swoosh, slam, swoosh.*)

"Get hold of yourself and stop being so baroque!" (*Slam.*)

"You stop this!" I slammed the door hard, three times, my voice a roar that came from my deepest depths. "*Now.*"

Mom stopped, her dark hair still flying around her face for a few seconds after the rest of her paused, holding in one hand a figurine from Germany dressed in frothy-looking porcelain lace.

Her eyes locked on me as I stood, hand on the doorknob, ready to slam it again.

For a long moment I figured the doll was going to come flying at me and thought about how that lace might be sharp at certain velocities.

And then Mom's lips twitched and her body quivered, and I figured we were about to go back to the shaking and crying, maybe for days, maybe worse this time. Maybe I'd made a terrible mistake.

But then she began to laugh.

She laughed. Laughed until she was helpless, until once again I feared for the doll, and therefore stepped forward and took it from her, setting it back on the writing desk.

Mom was still laughing, which meant maybe after all this she was actually losing her mind. But if it was madness, I would take it, because she came to me and took me in her arms and I started laughing too. If it was madness, maybe we would just go mad together.

We laughed until we had tears coursing down our cheeks,

laughed ourselves onto the floor among the mistreated curtains and crumbled plaster, laughed until our stomachs hurt and our throats were dry.

And then she grabbed my hands and said in her beautifully focused, intense way, "Oh my dear, my sweetheart, of course you are right."

"That you were being baroque?"

She snorted. "That too."

"That the ceiling is going to come down?"

At this, she took my face, kissed me on both cheeks, then stared into my eyes and said, "That everything beautiful is not ruined."

Chapter Nine

SHIT HOLE

(Peak Wilderness, Day Two)

Dear Mom,

How refreshing to wake up in nature like this.

In two inches of water, to be specific.

TWO INCHES.

This is just what I needed after a long night of listening to Peace-Bob snort and snore, and re-seeing his hairy bare butt, nether orifice, and family jewels in my mind's eye, and being squished by large male bodies sliding downhill toward me in their slippery sleeping bags.

Lovely, fresh rainwater, to wash the night away.

So invigorating.

All my clothing, the clean and the dirty, is wet. My sleeping bag is soaked. The only things that are not wet are this journal, the hoodie/pillow, and the few things I stashed in the top pockets of my pack last night—none of it wearable.

Fortunately the rain has stopped and the sun is up and I did get to keep one bar of biodegradable soap, so I figure I'll have the chance to wash everything in the lake and hang it out to dry in the sunshine. It'll probably smell amazing.

I'll try my best to keep a positive attitude, because really, it has to get better from here.

Sunshine and rainbows,
Ingrid

Dear Mom!

I had my positive attitude for at least five minutes, until the morning's first "lesson."

How to Dig a Hole to Poop In.

You think I'm kidding?

I wish.

But no, these are the "details" Pat must have been referring to yesterday, back when I was innocent and naïve—i.e., worried about having to use an outhouse and whether the mattress on my bunk would be comfortable.

I am going on a no-fiber diet.

Apparently it's a hiker's rule—you can't just take a crap in the woods and leave it. First you find yourself a good stick, then you dig a nice little crap-size hole, then you, uh, whip your pants down and do your thing (hopefully you'll have good aim), then after, you cover it all up with dirt and leaves.

Oh, and it gets better. Because next, when none of us

asked any follow-up questions about the hole digging (because we were all so revolted and in shock, I assume), Bonnie stepped in to give a demo for the females, about how to lean back onto a tree while peeing.

She stayed fully dressed, but the detail of the demonstration was mortifying. Why this had to be done in front of everyone, and not in a private session with females only, I do not know.

And then came the final delight.

"Now listen up! We're trying to leave nature as we find it," Bonnie said, and then handed each of us a large Ziploc bag. "Anyone know what these are for?"

"Antibacterial wipes?" I suggested, feeling hopeful.

"No. This is for your toilet paper," she said.

Right. This actually made sense to me, especially after the water issue of this morning.

"Your used toilet paper," she clarified.

My mouth opened to respond, but nothing came out.

"All used toilet paper goes into your Ziploc," she confirmed, "and you keep it with you until the end of the trip."

Used

Toilet paper.

Keep with you . . .

I closed my eyes . . .

and somehow managed to keep my scream on the inside.

"Doesn't . . . shouldn't toilet paper biodegrade?" This was Seth, who looked a little pale.

"I believe I just said that we aim to leave nature as we find it," Bonnie said in a tone that made it clear there would be no debate. "And animals don't use toilet paper."

"That's disgusting," Jin muttered, and as I glanced around I could tell almost everyone was thinking the same thing. Maybe I'm not the only underprepared person on this trip. Maybe Peak Wilderness deliberately omits these gross details from their literature, and you didn't know about them either, Mom . . . ? Because my fellow campers were responding with quite a bit of horror and surprise.

All except Peace-Bob, of course, who was nodding his approval and will probably use his nasty Ziploc as a pillow.

And I thought, *Save me.*

And then I thought, *How is this, in any way, helpful preparation for my spending a year away, in a completely civilized city, at a school that has plumbing and everything else? How does it apply?* And then I answered my own question, Mom: *it doesn't.*

I am having these moments, asking myself WTF I am doing here, and thinking about you, and in those moments, thousands of tiny knives stab me from the inside and I can't breathe and I want to take up the ax again. Hack at things with a sharp object.

"Time to pack up," Pat said in a cheery voice, just as if Bonnie hadn't dropped a shit bomb on us. "Duncan will be here soon with the boat."

The group dispersed, but I was shivering in my still-wet clothing and couldn't imagine how I was supposed to participate all day in this state, so I approached Pat and explained about all my things being soaked.

"Oh yes. I noticed last night that your tent wasn't in the best location," he said.

"You . . . noticed last night?" I said, blinking in disbelief.

"It's best to set a tent on high ground," he said.

"Really."

"Yes," he said, nodding. "That way the rain runs downhill from where you are."

"Aha," I said, nodding along with him, wanting to wring his scrawny neck. "I see that now."

"Basics of gravity," he continued, oblivious—or pretending to be oblivious—of my fury. "Plus your rain fly should not be touching the tent proper—it ruins the seal. So I'll bet you had water dripping from above too."

"Wow. Yes, we did."

"Yup. Not surprised you had a problem."

"You're not surprised," I repeated.

"Nope," he said.

I thought my head might explode. Or that I might, despite being a generally peaceful human being, kick him in the shins.

But you brought me up to be polite, Mom. So instead I took two deep breaths, gripped my Ziploc, and asked if I might have some extra time before we left for the day, to hang my things, plus our tent, out to dry.

Pat shook his head. "We've got a two-hour boat ride and then a long hike before we reach camp tonight. I'm sorry, but it'll have to wait."

"I'm sorry too," I said, oh so politely, and went to pack.

So, Mom, that is how you find me: filthy, exhausted, starving, grossed out, and miserable, on the deck of a ferryboat. And before you ask, I did try taking my things out to dry on the boat . . . and promptly lost a pair of shorts overboard. My only pair.

Love anyway,
Ingrid

Soon enough we're standing on a beach in the middle of some supposedly awesome national park—I should call it that: Supposedly Awesome National Park—poring over the maps Bonnie and Pat have given us. When I see where we are, my heart sinks.

I thought dropping us in the middle of a field yesterday, then confiscating half our belongings and taking us on a four-hour march that ended in bugs for dinner and leaky tent-sleeping with strange men was more than enough to give me the sense of being removed from every single thing of familiarity and comfort. But evidently we needed to get even farther from civilization.

Everyone else is oohing and aahing about nature and the incredible views, and all I can think about is that there isn't a building or human-made thing to be seen, anywhere. Not even a cell tower. We've been left in the middle of nowhere, many days' hike from civilization, and I don't find it inspiring at all.

I find it terrifying.

In fact, my breathing is getting short and I am feeling a powerful urge to ditch my backpack and start running. It's almost like reverse claustrophobia, if there is such a thing.

"Can you feel that?" Melissa says, coming up beside me, eyes intense.

"Feel what?" I ask, thinking maybe she's having a similar experience.

"The farther we get out here, the more I feel like the layers are peeling off me," she says, and I realize that her intensity is of the ecstatic variety.

"Really?" I say, trying to swallow back my own sense of panic.

"Yes!" She reaches her arms out in a stretch, then turns to me and asks, "What do you see?"

"Pardon me?"

"When you look at me, what do you see?"

"Um . . ." I have the distinct feeling this is a trick question. "I see a tall blonde girl with pretty blue eyes, fit looking . . ."

"A perfect girl," she says.

"Y-yes . . . ? Well, I mean no one's—"

"A perfect girl from a perfect family. That's what I was," she says, steamrolling over my response with bitter words from what sounds like a speech she's been mentally rehearsing for a very long time. "Perfect and effortlessly meeting everyone's expectations. Pretty, thin, sporty but not too sporty, smart but not so smart as to be off-putting, friendly, and with appropriate friends, appropriate interests. An intelligent career in front of me, oh, unless someone 'discovered' me on the street, as they surely would, and then I would be the next Karlie Kloss. But it wasn't ever effortless."

All I need to do is nod. In fact I get the feeling I am barely required at all, for her to have this conversation. Or maybe I am, because she really needs to talk.

"My family—they like to keep a lid on things. My dad's best and only advice, ever, even after this cult thing, is, 'Get your head screwed on, Melissa!' As if I could literally, you know, go to a chiropractor and have that done."

"That'd be nice," I say.

"Seriously. My therapist thinks I was vulnerable to . . . the cult . . . because I wanted so badly to break from all that. I was going crazy under all that expectation. So I escaped from one sort of control into a worse one. And now I'm back at home with them, and it's . . . the expectation, and how they're freaking out without ever saying they're freaking out . . . and . . . oh . . . sorry . . . I'm talking too much."

"No, it's fine," I say.

"What was I on about in the first place?"

"Layers . . . ?"

"Yes. So, that's a layer—expectation. I'm away from everything, and that feels . . . good. For the moment, anyway. They're like voices in my head I can't turn off, sometimes. And then his voice, too, like everyone is just fighting for control of me. And I'm scared."

"Why?"

She looks at me, eyes haunted. "Because sometimes all I want is for someone to tell me what to do."

I am trying to formulate a response to this when Pat calls us to gather around.

It's time to set out for today's hike. Bonnie and Pat give us the briefest of instructions: one of us is always to be in the lead, one at the back making sure no one trails behind. The lead must spot little piles of rocks called "cairns" in order to find and follow the path.

They take volunteers for each position.

Never having hiked anywhere, I don't volunteer. In fact, I do my best to make myself invisible, because pretty much everyone is better qualified for this than me. Ally, Melissa, and Seth hang back too, and Jin somehow gives the impression that these jobs are for suckers and she wants nothing to do with them.

Henry volunteers for the back end, and, surprise, surprise, Peace-Bob takes the lead and starts looking for the cairn. We all look for it, but past the beach is a dried-up riverbed, all rock, practically made up of boulders, and there are rocks everywhere else, too, so finding a piddling little pile and distinguishing it as human-stacked is near impossible.

We stand around the beach for a few minutes, then follow Peace-Bob up one side, where he thinks he sees something.

He's wrong, so back to our starting place we go.

Each time, Peace-Bob is sure, barks out, takes off with enthusiasm, and we follow.

Pat and Bonnie do not assist, and claim not to know where the path is.

But I can't help recalling how they let us set up our tent in a water trap last night. . . .

Finally Peace-Bob takes off along the side of a wide riverbed where he thinks he *really* sees a path. Our backpacks are excruciatingly heavy, mine even more so because everything in it is soaked. The heaviness makes balancing difficult—every step feeling like I'm either going to pitch forward and fall on my face, or backward to land like an upside-down turtle. In addition, my skin is rubbed raw at the shoulders and at the waist, where there's a clip that's supposed to help distribute the weight of the pack. The chest clip squashing my boobs is the least of my worries, but also uncomfortable.

I look down at the supposed path and put one foot in front of the other.

Soon we are forced out onto the riverbed, because of course the path Peace found is not a path. No one has seen a damned cairn. The rocks are strangely angular and unstable, and most have barely enough surface to put a foot on. Even without the backpacks, it would be slow going and deathly hard to balance. With them, it's treacherous. Someone is going to sprain an ankle, or break their neck, and/or die. Probably me. Hopefully me.

Finally we clamber off the riverbed to another supposed path.

"What the hell was that?" Tavik says, staring at Peace-Bob like he wants to take his head off. "You trying to kill us?"

"What, are you upset about a few rocks?" Peace-Bob retorts, beads of sweat dripping from his facial hair. "Shut up."

I kill mosquitoes number 836 to 846.

"We are exactly two minutes' distance from where we started," Jin says. "And that was hours ago."

"Three hours," Tavik says.

"So," Bonnie says in what I'm beginning to recognize as her therapy voice, "let's assess what's happening here."

I let my pack down, and sigh.

"Ingrid," Pat says. "You look like you want to say something."

"Nope." I shake my head, awash with frustration and exhaustion. "Not me."

"Come on. What's your assessment? How are you feeling?"

"Awesome," I say tonelessly.

Jin snorts.

"No, really, I'm a whole new person. This is fabulous," I say. "I hope every day is just like this."

Tavik laughs.

Pat steps closer, pins me with his gaze. "I would like to hear what you're really thinking and feeling—what's behind the sarcasm."

"Seriously?"

Pat nods.

Everyone is looking at me.

I take a moment, look around, considering. I am accustomed to keeping a lot in, holding my head high, et cetera. This is about dignity, survival, about having walls up for a reason, about the show going on no matter what, even when it becomes the *Nothing to See Here, My Life Is Perfect* show. I have been trained this way from birth, practically, and by now it's like part of a pact—a pact between Mom and me.

But I'm starting to feel like it's a rotten pact.

"Ingrid?" Pat is waiting.

"All right," I say. "First, I think it's not Peace's fault, or not all his fault anyway, that we're in this situation. Second, regarding how I'm feeling? I feel like crap and everything hurts, and I'm pissed off."

Pat smiles like he's won something. "Why is that?"

"Because I don't appreciate you letting us wander around

like idiots all afternoon, risking our necks walking on the damned rocks with zillion-pound backpacks when I'm sure you know exactly where the real path is."

"What makes you think that?"

"Well, if you don't, then you'd better use your emergency cell to get Duncan back here, because in that case neither of you is qualified to keep us safe out here, and we should all get our money back. But I don't buy it. And I especially don't buy it after what you did to us with the tents. Based on that, I don't trust you. I believe this is the same crap, and I think it's wrong, and I also think it's unsafe."

"Hmm," Pat says, and shares a look with Bonnie.

"So, actually, I'm not going to go anywhere until we have this sorted out." I fold my arms over my chest and sit down.

"You're not willing to follow Peace anymore?" Bonnie says.

"I'm perfectly willing to follow him, or anyone else, once we're on the actual path. But until I'm sure we're not wasting our time and energy and going in circles, no."

Seth murmurs something that sounds like agreement and sits down next to me. Tavik sits down too. Melissa just looks at her shoes. Ally bursts into tears. Harvey and Henry are barely listening, and instead are engaged in a silent game of poking each other with sticks. Jin stays on her feet, still glaring at Peace-Bob.

"All right," Bonnie says finally. "I think I can help. Follow me."

As we set off, Pat turns and gives me a wink.

"Thanks for your participation," he says.

Participation, my ass.

Chapter Ten

MARSHMALLOWS

(Peak Wilderness, Day Two, Continued)

Bonnie takes us straight to the trail, and we hike in silence for the rest of the afternoon. The terrain is tough, the path like a small roller coaster, up and down literally every few feet. There is zero flat surface, and it's always more up than down—we're ascending onto a ridge of some kind. My glutes and quads are screaming, quivering, threatening to pack it in with every step. In addition to the hills, it seems like every other step there's another tree root to trip over, or another small rock to roll one's ankle on. And my feet inside my not-so-broken-in hiking boots? I'm afraid to look, but they feel like hell.

I am not the only one in pain. While I keep quiet about mine, Ally is near the end of the line, falling apart to the point that Henry has to stop us multiple times so she can rest. He and Harvey eventually start taking turns carrying her backpack because it's the only way we'll ever get to the end of today's trail.

During the course of this god-awful hike, I try (a) pretending

I'm somewhere else, (b) being stoic, and (c) channeling the dark side of the Force—i.e., being really, really angry, and sending that anger into every step I have to take.

(C) is the most effective, though the energy it gives me begins to fade with the daylight.

It's almost dark again when we finally arrive at the campsite.

This is worse the second time because now I know it means mosquitoes for dinner, and zero chance of my clothing and tent getting a chance to dry out. But I'm starving and so sore all over, and will therefore probably just close my eyes and eat. And I'm tired enough that maybe the wet sleeping bag/pajamas/tent won't bother me.

Ally collapses onto the sand and pulls her boots and socks off, making a pitiful sound. Her feet are covered in blisters, many of them burst and rubbed raw, and she is even bleeding in a few spots. I search in my pack, find some Band-Aids, and bring them to her, but Bonnie is there already, with antiseptic ointment and gauze and some heavy-duty wrapping.

I am relieved to see Bonnie making this effort—the way things are being run, I'd almost expected them to send Ally out into the woods, barefoot, to find magic herbs with which to make her own cure, and leaves to wrap her feet with in lieu of bandages.

Tavik and I get straight to finding a nice, non-sloping, high-ground spot for the tent. And then, with Peace's help, get it put up in a completely cooperative, nondramatic way. Miracle. It's still wet inside and out, especially on the side I slept on, but there's a bit of wind and the tent fabric is thin, so there's some hope it will be partially dry by bedtime.

As soon as the two guys wander off, I scramble into the tent, zip both layers of doors closed behind me, set my pack on the dry side, and then pull out my bathing suit and put it on, watching the door every second.

Suit on, I start to assess the situation with the rest of my clothes. There is the dirty pile of stuff I wore yesterday and today—socks, underwear, bra, cargo pants, T-shirt, hoodie—and the damp pile of clean things—basically all the same items, plus one pair of flannel pajamas and a small towel. (Don't even talk to me about how long flannel is going to take to dry.)

I have one bar of soap.

And it's gotten chilly since the sun went down.

And I have basically nothing that is both dry *and* clean to put on once I come out of the lake, except the hoodie, which isn't long enough to cover my butt.

In the end I lay the damp clean clothing, plus my sleeping bag, on a large rock, hoping this will help, and ball up the dirty clothes, all except my underwear, socks, and bra, in my corner of the tent. I have no illusions that I'll be given any extra time tomorrow morning to get these things dry if I were to wash them, but perhaps if we get to camp with a couple of hours of daylight tomorrow afternoon, I can do it then.

And so I head to the lake, leave my tiny towel on the beach, and walk into the water with my bar of soap plus bra, undies, and socks, because these items are nonnegotiable in terms of cleanliness.

The water is take-your-breath-away cold. And not the kind that becomes refreshing and awesome once you've swum around in it for a few minutes. More like the kind that gives you hypothermia.

Melissa, Jin, and Tavik all test the temperature with hands and feet before backing away.

"You're a nutcase, going in there," Jin says from the shore.

"I c-c-can't disagree," I say, teeth chattering. "B-b-but I can't s-stand the s-s-smell of myself."

Jin rolls her eyes and blows her herbal smoke at me. "You'd suck as a street kid."

"You m-mean that as an insult, right?"

"Totally."

I hop and wade farther in, gasping, until I'm chest-deep, then dunk backward to wet my hair, gasp some more, and proceed to give myself and my stuff a thorough soaping, followed by the best rinse I can manage. The blisters on my ankles and feet sting like hell at first, but the good news is, soon I can't feel them anymore.

I emerge, a triumphant icicle, the heavenly, clean scent of soap all around me, and shiver my way back up the beach.

Peace is in the tent, so I decide to check on the sleeping bag and damp clean clothes instead of going in there and enduring whatever disgusting comments he's guaranteed to make. I'm going to have to wear the damp undies with the damp pajamas, and/or the sweater, and hope they dry from the currently non-existent heat of my body.

At the rock, I am dismayed to see that everything I put there has blown off into the sand.

I want to throw myself on the ground and give up.

Instead I drop the soaking wet (clean) clothing from the lake onto the rock in a bundle, and then shake as much sand out of everything else as possible. But the sand is fine, and doesn't shake all the way out.

I never imagined "I have nothing to wear" as such a literal sentence.

I'm standing there, teeth chattering and shaking my head and trying to tell myself how ridiculous it is that I want to cry. I am making a pitiful attempt to summon back the anger I've been feeling—and using—all day, when Bonnie comes over.

"What's up?" she says.

I tell her through gritted teeth.

She regards me gravely, then thinks for a moment.

"I say you put on the damp pants—skip the underwear— with the sweater for now, then get a stick, or a couple of sticks— long ones—rig them up somehow like a drying rack, and hang everything on there."

I nod.

"You need to hang things to get them dry," she adds.

Gee, I never knew that.

"All right . . ." I say, keeping the snide thought to my- self, since I'm grateful she's at least willing to give me some direction—probably only because it would look bad on her re- cord if I died of exposure, but still.

"Ideally it'll dry overnight. If it doesn't rain," she adds.

"Right," I say, nodding again, shivering . . .

"Actually," she says, glancing over to where Harvey and Melissa are on campfire/dinner-making duty. "Anything you really want to be sure to get dry, you could hold near the fire."

This is, for real, the best idea I've heard all day, since we'll be around the campfire for dinner and then likely for circle, too.

Dear Mom,

With all the ladylike modesty you tried to teach me, I'm sure you'd love to see me now . . . sitting around a campfire with a bunch of strangers, sans underwear and bra, roasting my undies on a stick.

You know, like marshmallows.

But not.

Dead mosquito count: 1,050.

Love,
Ingrid

I'm on dish duty after dinner, which means I leave the stick with undies, bra, and a pair of socks I added, carefully balanced on a log near the fire.

"Um . . ." I look at Jin, who's there having a smoke before circle.

"What?" she says, exhaling in the opposite direction of my stuff, which is considerate-ish, for her.

"Could you . . ." I gesture to my stick. "Make sure no harm befalls my . . ."

"You're hilarious," she says, without smiling.

"Look," I say, feeling my cheeks getting red. "I'm mortified as it is."

"I know," she says. "That's what's so hilarious. That and how you sound like a walking literacy textbook."

"Well, will you? Watch them?"

"Oh, all right."

Back to the lake I go, this time to wash the pots.

After, I stand for a few moments looking out over the water, the moon reflecting off its glass-like surface. It's beautiful, yes. But the beauty doesn't reach me the way it's supposed to because I feel like it's been shoved down my throat. I register the stark gorgeousness of the dying day, and what it fills me with is unease, and an ominous sensation of cracking inside—of cracking open, of a corresponding excruciating pain I have kept at bay by incredible discipline beginning to seep toward the surface.

I don't want to be cracked open.

Cannot be.

Have to stop thinking about this, thinking at all.

Nevertheless, I let myself wonder again why—why my mom would knowingly sign me up for such a hard-core, no-comforts version of Peak Wilderness, *if* that's what she did.

Why would she do it when she herself—a very proper, elegant person, who always bought the best she could afford, even when we couldn't afford much, who never left the house without makeup, who considered it unladylike to even *say* the word "underwear"—would have hated every second of this?

My throat tightens and my eyes start to well up, and I stay turned toward the lake, hoping no one will see.

Damn it. I'm not a crier. I am brave-face-mess-inside, like her. But everything that makes me feel safe and normal has been yanked from under me, and I'm stuck out here feeling naked, beaten-up, and far too vulnerable.

I pull myself together in time for circle and find a semi-comfortable log, close enough to the fire to continue my embarrassing-but-necessary roasting project, to sit on.

"Let's talk about today," Bonnie says, starting things off. "I think we had some fairly big happenings. I'd like to hear from every person."

And so we go around the circle, each getting a turn to offer our insights on the day.

Ally is completely falling apart. Her eye makeup—which she did, in fact, find time to reapply this morning—is smudged and smeared beyond repair, her boobs-out, Instagram-ready posture is gone, and she looks like hell.

"I want to leave," she says to Bonnie and Pat. "Please, can you call Duncan and get him to come get me? I quit."

"You can't quit yet," Jin says. "Are you serious?"

"Look at my feet!" Ally cries. "How am I even going to walk?"

"Your feet will heal and then toughen up," Bonnie says. "We'll keep them well wrapped and in a couple of days, you'll be fine."

"It's not just that," Ally says, her entire body quivering. "I'm fat!"

"And . . . ?" Bonnie says, just as I'm about to say the reflexive *No, you're not!*

"Well . . ." Ally says, confused by Bonnie's nonreaction.

"Is it possible that seeing yourself as fat is causing you to believe you are limited . . . when that's not, in fact, true?" Bonnie says.

"Huh?" Ally says, her bewilderment momentarily stopping her tears.

"The size of your body doesn't determine what it can do, unless you believe it does," Pat says.

"Maybe you'll surprise yourself," Bonnie adds. "Tell me again what your most urgent goal is, for these three weeks."

"I want to get Angel back," Ally says, new tears spilling over. "And completing the program and getting the credit . . . will look good on my file. My caseworker says it might tip the scales because . . . in addition to my parents being . . . how they are, I tend to quit things—jobs, summer school . . ."

"So," Bonnie says, nodding, and focusing on Ally like they are the only people here, "maybe you find a way, when you feel like quitting, to focus on that goal."

"Okay," Ally whispers.

"And stop thinking that quitting is an option."

Pat then teaches us a meditation exercise that involves looking into the flames of the fire to clear our minds.

Meanwhile, I am obsessed and humiliated and hyper about how everyone can see my undies and bra, and thinking if I move them, it will attract more attention. But leaving them means Peace feels he can make disgusting tongue movements and then look pointedly at them every time my gaze comes anywhere near him. I'm so distracted that when we're supposed to be meditating, all I can think about is how I'd like to shove Peace's nasty tongue straight into the fire. Or stab him with a burning stick.

Each person takes a turn, and when they do, Bonnie and/or Pat zeros in on what they're saying, and what they maybe don't realize they're saying. They dig and push for more details before finally imparting some advice, a piece of wisdom, food for thought.

Melissa repeats her observation about feeling freer of expectation, but in a group she is more shy, and I notice now that she doesn't make eye contact with any of the boys, or Pat.

Seth, who has moved to put a comforting arm around Ally, has so many mosquito bites, plus a few black fly bites, that his face and neck are puffy. He reports that they even got him through his pants.

"I can't feel God," he says, his expression bleak. "I thought I would feel Him out here, closer to nature. But I don't. If it's a test, I'm failing."

"Is God, to you, a feeling?" Bonnie asks.

"Sometimes," Seth says. "That's what faith is about— believing even when you don't feel it. So . . . maybe it's a test."

"Or maybe you've bought into a bullshit patriarchal system of oppression," Jin says, "and so there's nothing to feel."

Seth looks stricken.

"Please give each person space to talk," Bonnie says, putting her hand up to stop Jin. "And let's be constructive. We're not here to fight about religion."

It goes on.

Jin admits she'd have taken drugs if anyone had had any, during the stress of trying to find the path, but it comes out like bragging. Pat and Bonnie dig, but Jin somehow manages, even while telling the truth, to keep up an impenetrable wall.

Bonnie makes some comments on how addicts' brains are

wired, and how new neural pathways can be built. Like roads. And how, during these three weeks, Jin may begin to build a new road that leads away from her addictions. How we all might build these roads for ourselves.

I wonder if this new-road building can be done for recurring sorrows. Like you can just build a new road, or a bridge, to take you up and out of them. Because there are people like my mom, who occasionally fall into deep trenches, troughs of sorrow that they can't seem to climb out of, and wouldn't it be nice if you could just build yourself a road out of it?

"Your turn, Ingrid. How was today for you?"

"Awesome," I mumble, arms clutched over my chest to keep people from looking at my braless boobs. "Nice nature."

I have no intention of telling them how the giant sky with trees and water and not a single sign of civilization has totally freaked me out, and how I'm swinging between wanting to hit something and wanting to run away.

"I think we saw a new side of you," Bonnie says.

New compared to what? I want to shout. *You don't even know me!*

"I think we heard your true voice," Bonnie continues, despite lack of encouragement from me.

"My true voice?"

"Half the time you act like you're not really here," she says, "like you're just floating along and engaged elsewhere. You don't want to take responsibility for things, don't volunteer to lead."

"So?" I say, getting into it despite my best intentions. "Not everyone can be the leader, and not everyone wants to be. That's why there's just one leader."

"Try this on for size," Pat says, and then takes on an unintentionally funny, I'm-saying-something-important-now tone. "Each person should be their own leader."

"Uh-huh," I say, not impressed.

"Yes, and my point *being*," Bonnie says, "I see you not speaking your mind most of the time, not giving your opinions, but you do have them. Strong ones, maybe good ones. We all lose, and you lose most of all, when you keep them to yourself."

"I don't like to fight," I say. "It never achieves anything."

"It doesn't have to be a fight," she says. "I'm saying I see you keeping things in, and maybe you do it because you think voicing those things might be detrimental, but today . . . Ingrid, you cut through. What you said earlier wasn't diplomatic, but it was honest, and it was perceptive, and it cut to the heart of the situation and led to a moving forward that we needed."

"I only had to do it because you guys were bullshitting us," I say, arms crossed even tighter, and glaring at her now.

"We are here to help test you," she said, eyes locked on me and not denying it. "We're here to create challenges for you, and supervise you as you rise to meet them."

"Or not."

"Yes, or not." She nods. "We're here to see you try and fail, and try again, too. We're here to bring out the best in you."

"So, you want me to shoot my mouth off all the time? You think that's the best of me?"

"I think you have a powerful instinct to fight for yourself, and to fight for the right thing, in general, but that you quash it."

This statement strikes me like an arrow through a lung: sharp, specific, and painful.

"You met me yesterday," I say, angry and trying to rally from the blow. "So you don't actually know anything. I don't have the energy to fight about every little thing I disagree with because then I would be fighting all the time. And I have bigger fish to fry. More important things to spend my energy on."

"All right, what are they?"

Bam—there's the trap.

Everyone seems to lean forward, like I'm about to reveal the depths of my soul. Ha.

"What do you need that energy for?" she says, focused on me like a laser.

"I am not obliged to share my thoughts and feelings with you," I spit out. "I didn't come on this trip to be forced into some big overhaul of myself. I haven't done anything—" I stop at the sudden, stabbing pain in my leg, and gasp.

"What's wrong?" Bonnie says.

"Nothing!" I clap a hand over my shin, force slower breaths, and stare at the fire like we just learned to. She can know whatever she knows about me, or thinks she knows, but I'm not talking. No chance. But jeez, I'm a freaking wreck. "I'm fine. I just . . . lost focus in school and said I'd do this trip. I promised I would. So I came to do it, and get it done. That's all."

"That's fine," Bonnie says in a therapy voice. "But just so you know, when you're ready, you can trust us with the real you."

"This is the real me."

And my fighting energy is already fully engaged, just in simple survival.

93

I leave my stick by the fire, and head to the tent, only to find that Tavik has beat me there again, which means once again I have the changing problem. I need the fleece hoodie I'm wearing for a pillow, and I'm not sleeping in my pants again, thank you.

I steal a glance at Tavik, sitting there reading his porn and pretending I'm not there, and my stomach rolls over. Fat chance he's going to be all gentlemanly and offer to leave. And if I ask him to, it only makes the whole thing more awkward, and will make me seem naïve, uptight, conspicuously virginal. And this to a guy who's been in prison. Recently. For what, I have no idea and am afraid to ask. Regardless, it's much better if I can be cool, seem like one of the guys.

I turn my back to him, set my damp pajamas between me and the wall of the tent, then change my mind and put the bottoms beside me on the left and the top on my right. Then I turn my flashlight off, hoping Tavik will take the hint and turn his off too. Although, there would be a certain awkwardness about that, if he did. In fact, now I feel like a total dork. Like I've created tension where there shouldn't be any.

He turns a page and keeps reading, not seeming to notice anything at all. Meanwhile, I have overthought myself into a tizzy of embarrassment and am nearly paralyzed.

Where's my true voice now?

"Tavik?" I say, though it comes out like a croak.

"Yeah?"

"Would you . . . uh . . ." I trail off, hoping he'll pick it up from there.

"What? I'm trying to read here."

"Would you mind turning the light off? Or . . . turning around?"

"Huh?"

"So I can *change*?" I say, frustration lending strength to my request.

Tavik starts to laugh, a guttural, startling sound that starts low and deep and increases in tone and intensity until he is positively cackling, his LED light jerking up and down in his hands and creating a light show to accompany my humiliation.

"So happy to amuse you," I say. I am sweating and there are tears in my eyes. I should have just stripped.

"Oh, screw it," I mutter, then pull my arms out of the sleeves, and yank the hoodie over my head, giving him a full view of my bare back. If he didn't notice I wasn't wearing a bra earlier, he knows now, assuming he's watching. And I do assume he's watching—I can feel him watching. Still, it's just my back.

I'm fumbling at my right side, trying to get my pajama top without turning at all, when the front of the tent unzips suddenly, and Peace-Bob is there, flashlight shining right on me and getting a full side view of my naked torso.

All my fake who-cares attitude disappears and I shriek, flinging my arms around my chest.

"Whoa," Peace-Bob says. "Babe . . ."

"Is it possible," I say through clenched teeth, "for a person to get thirty seconds of privacy?"

"Well, that's not fair—Tavik's getting a show."

"Get. Out. Get out!" My shout comes out like a roar, big and deep.

"Sure, sure." He clicks the flashlight off and backs out of the tent.

"Everything all right in there?" The voice is Pat's, and I realize everyone in the camp must have heard me shriek.

"No!"

I've got one hand still clutched over my boobs and the other is feeling around, trying to find my damn pajama shirt, which I know was right there beside me.

"You need me to come in?" Pat says.

"No!" Just what I need, *another* male in here. "Stay out!"

"Okay," Pat says, "but just shout if you need anything—don't be shy."

Tavik, still behind me with his light, cackles.

"Screw you," I hiss.

In a rare moment of mercy, he turns his light off.

"You looking for this?" he says in the darkness, and I feel the flannel of my top being pressed against my shoulder.

"Yes," I say. "Thank you."

For a second I'm genuinely grateful, then I wonder if he was hiding it all along.

"You're welcome," he says. "I can't wait to see what you do about your pants."

Me neither.

But the pants are not such a problem. I simply perform the entire change within my sleeping bag and then stay in it. If I could only breathe while lying in it headfirst, that's where I would spend the rest of the night. Instead I wriggle down as low as I can and call out to Peace-Bob that he can come in.

"About time," he says, flashlight blazing as he stomps in, his smell coming with him.

"Sorry," I say, though it would be hard to say what exactly I'm sorry for.

"Hey," he says, and puts both hands up, palms out, "your issues, not mine. I told you last night, the body is a natural thing. There's nothing to be ashamed of."

"It's nothing to do with shame," I say.

"Like I said, your issue," Peace-Bob says. "Personally—"

"You love to be naked," I say. "We know."

Tavik chuckles.

I turn away, just in time to avoid the stinking, hairy ass over my face.

Which means, I guess, that I've learned something.

Chapter Eleven

METAMORPHOSIS
(Ages Eleven to Twelve)

After the bed-destroying incident, Mom finally went to a doctor who prescribed some medication. Slowly she got better, and got back to paying bills, buying groceries, talking to me about my homework, my day, normal stuff.

I was so relieved. At the same time, I remember thinking my tutors and teachers had missed something when they taught metamorphosis, because it seemed that it could go backward.

My mom started out as a butterfly—a magnificent, opera-singing butterfly-diva. And then she damaged her vocal cords and finally ran out of energy to fight her grief and seemed to go back into the chrysalis, dragging her damaged-butterfly self into bed. I was happy she reemerged at all, but when she did . . . well, it wasn't quite back to caterpillar form, but more like a moth—herself but with all the color gone.

By the time Moth-Mom had fully emerged, I'd been

through one invisible year of school (sixth grade) and was about to turn twelve.

"I got a job," she told me one day. "I'm going to be an admin assistant at an accounting firm."

"Mom, you could teach at one of the universities. Why don't you do that? You'd be an incredible singing teacher."

"No," she said, her face suddenly pale. "Never. Do you think I want to be known as a tragedy every day of my life? Not to mention, it's impossible to demonstrate technique when my upper register sounds like nails on a chalkboard."

"Okay, but you could teach piano, violin. . . . It doesn't have to be singing."

"Ingrid." She held her hand up. "No."

"Why not?"

"It would hurt too much," she said, her eyes beseeching me. "It would be like . . . Every day it would be like trying to get back something that's gone. Desperate and crawling and pathetic. It's gone. We move forward. Shed the past and move forward with our heads held high."

"All right," I said, but obviously not with enough conviction.

"I'm trying, Ingrid," Mom said. "Can't you see that I am trying to take care of you? Of us? I'm doing it the only way that makes sense to me. The only way I can. Do you understand?"

At the new job she dressed in beige ("I cannot dress like a diva to do photocopying, Ingrid") and cut her hair short, and told them to call her Margot, which somehow morphed into "Marg" with a hard g.

This, on top of losing Lalonde, was horrible.

"Mom, you are not a Marg."

"What does it matter?" she said, and sighed.

Teaching fledgling opera singers might have hurt Mom, but her acceptance of "Marg" hurt me. More than hurting me, though, it worried me. Depression, despair, and grief were one thing; this was something else.

It was resignation.

It was the light of her, fading.

Margot-Sophia Lalonde to Marg Burke.

Butterfly to moth.

A year after emerging from the chrysalis, Mom was still Marg.

And Marg was busy answering phones, receiving packages, scheduling meetings, sending memos, and living without music, which meant I was too.

But there was hope.

Because one day in late spring, into the accounting firm walked a man in a linen suit. He had wavy brown hair just long enough to tuck behind his ears, beautiful olive skin, and a velvety speaking voice with just a trace of an accent.

Even as Marg, Mom was elegant, and as much as she was trying to live a whole new existence as a moth, she had never lost her perfect posture, her presence, or her very particular, dramatic beauty. Under the beige suits and low heels and subdued makeup, she was still something more than what she appeared, day to day.

And this man, Andreas, saw it.

He took one look at Mom, reached for her hand, and gazed deep into her eyes. "You don't belong in this place," he said.

"You should come with me."

She thought this was hilarious, and she brushed him off.

But she told me about him, and despite her protests, I Googled him. Andreas came from a corporate background, but now owned and ran a high-end coaching and consulting firm that was based in Toronto, specializing in helping executives and entrepreneurs take their careers to the next level. He had a team of coaches working for him, but was also a sought-after coach himself with a veritable who's who of international clients.

Mom's boss was his accountant.

So, he wasn't a crackpot or a phony. He was successful, and he did something interesting, and he presumably liked helping people.

Andreas kept coming back—apparently his tax situation was complicated that year because he'd gained so many new international clients. Every few days he would visit, and chat with Mom, drawing her out. And each time he came bearing little gifts—gourmet chocolates from Belgium, antique buttons, specialty cheese, a silk scarf, books, and finally, a Fabergé egg–style Russian music box that played music from Puccini's opera *Turandot*.

I happened to be there, that day. I'd come after school to wait for her, and was sitting a few feet away in the entry lounge, doing my homework.

He hadn't noticed me, and Mom made no move to introduce us, or even acknowledge to him that I was there. I was staring goggle-eyed at the beautiful egg, though, and I nearly died when she lifted the lid and the familiar music came pouring out.

It might have backfired. It almost did. Because she gasped and got to her feet behind her modular beige desk when she heard the music, and I thought she might burst into tears.

But then he said, with such sweetness, "I hear music when I look at you. Please, will you let me take you somewhere?"

"Where . . ." She was shaky still, but starting to recover. "Where do you think you're going to take me?"

"Is that a yes?"

I couldn't help myself, I got up and made sure I was in her line of sight, just over his shoulder, and started to jump up and down, waving and nodding and mouthing the word *yes*.

"Yes!" she said, with a little more force than was strictly needed and a sharp look at me, clearly directing me to sit the hell down before I embarrassed her to death.

"Wonderful," he declared, a hand on his heart. He was handsome (for a grown-up), and expressive. Google hadn't given me any info on his background, but I thought he might be Italian, or maybe Spanish.

"The moon, the ocean, the top of the world . . . whatever you wish. Copenhagen, Rome, Prague, Paris . . ."

"Why don't we start with dinner?" she said, laughing, eyes sparkling with something I hadn't seen in a long time, or maybe ever. "I have responsibilities that prohibit space travel, at the moment."

"Dinner, then," he said.

When he left a few minutes later, her phone numbers and e-mail address in his contacts, he blew her a kiss, and then, just as he was turning to go, he met my eyes, grinned, and gave me a very jolly wink.

I was ordered to hide upstairs when he arrived.

"No man gets to meet my daughter on the first date. Or the second, if there is one."

"Have you looked in the mirror? There'll be one."

She shrugged, but she had to know she looked stunning, with her finally growing-out hair half up, half down; a touch of red lipstick and a little mascara; a flowing black-and-red jumpsuit I'd convinced her to wear by threatening to burn all her beige clothing while she was out if she didn't; and pair of strappy sandals.

"You'll be all right here?" she asked.

"I'm actually old enough to babysit, you know. If we knew any babies."

"Stay inside, keep the shades down, don't answer the door or tell anyone over the telephone or Internet that you're alone here," she instructed.

I was tempted to comment that I'd survived for months in the house with her practically comatose, but I figured it was a bad subject to bring up.

When the doorbell rang, I dutifully scampered up the stairs, but then ran into the bathroom to get a hand mirror, and set myself up on the floor, just out of sight, with the mirror tilted toward the front foyer. I'd be able to see how it went without Andreas or my mother catching me. Once the door opened, though, Andreas was looking only at her.

He loved her already. I could see it as clear as anything, even through the tiny mirror. Why he did, or how he could in such a short time was unclear, but I was certain it was so.

They had dinner on a ship in the harbor, that first night.

And then there were more dinners, and plays and movies and sporting events, and he even got her to go to a rock-climbing gym, though she refused to don a harness once there, stating that the look (from below, I assume) was undignified.

To my intense relief, she asked him to call her Margot-Sophia, not Marg. This was a good sign, and not just about their relationship. At least that's what I hoped. By then, Andreas knew to look for me at the top of the stairs when he picked her up. On the fourth date he slid a book from his jacket and set it on the entryway table.

Mom pretended to ignore it, but she was smiling.

Smiling all the time.

It was a good book, too. *The Secret Garden.* I read it in three nights.

Date number five was on a Saturday afternoon, and they were going horseback riding. Andreas stood in the foyer, never having been invited farther into the house.

"I wonder . . ." he said to my mom, after a surreptitious glance at me, up in my hiding spot.

"Yes?"

"Does she turn into a pumpkin when she comes downstairs?"

My eyes widened and I retreated so Mom wouldn't see me if she looked up.

"Pardon me?" she said.

"Or does she have some terrible disease so that she becomes

a troll when confronted with the outdoors? I promise, no matter what it is, she won't frighten me."

I was technically too old for such silliness, but I was giggling—silently at first, and then not so silently, and no longer strictly in hiding.

Mom was looking from Andreas to me, and back.

"Or is it me?" he said, touching her arm. "Because otherwise . . . perhaps she would like to come riding with us?"

"Yes!" I said, leaping up, but then reminding myself to act like a twelve-year-old, not an overeager puppy. "I'd love to. I'm Ingrid, by the way. Thank you for the book. I loved it."

I walked down the stairs at a measured pace, and came to stand in front of him.

"Wonderful to meet you, Ingrid," he said, and proffered his hand, which I shook. "I am Andreas."

"Hello," I said, in my best grown-up voice. "Nice to meet you. Mom? Can I come?"

She hesitated for a moment, and I could tell she was worried this was happening too fast, but finally she gave a sharp nod, and said, "Yes."

After that I was invited most of the time, unless it was a school night. Andreas was fun and funny and generous, though he did sometimes treat me like I was younger than I actually was. Regardless, he clearly understood I was part of the package, and acted as though he *wanted me* as part of the package.

It turned out Andreas was part Greek, part Moroccan, and his dad had been a diplomat, which meant he had spent a lot of time moving around, and been educated at international schools. He was worldly, and had many interests, and I worried for a long time that he would have liked us better in our old life, that the way we lived now might be too small for him, that Mom would eventually become too mothlike.

But she began to read—something she hadn't had much time for when she was a singer. She read newspapers, books, science journals. At first I think it was because she, like me, was afraid she wouldn't have enough to talk about with Andreas, especially since she didn't want to talk about her past. But it became a passion for her—knowledge, history, current events, city politics, debates about the state of the world, the latest novels—she was insatiable for it all, and it was clear she had been in need of something to exercise her excellent mind on.

She also took up tennis, and convinced Andreas to ballroom dance with her—something she already had the basic skills for from the old life. And together, they cooked—fun, amazing meals, a bottle of wine always nearby, laugher and chatter and the occasional verbal sparring match.

She was alive again. Still beige at work, still working the beige job, but alive.

And so I was, too.

Chapter Twelve

PARIAH
(Age Twelve)

Dear Isaac,

You thought I was weird about singing. The fact is, I thought I couldn't.

I had all these lessons as a kid, and then they stopped. Long story. Anyway, they can't accurately assess the quality of your voice when you're really young. For a girl, they don't know until you're eleven or twelve if you've got something worth training. We were way past lessons, and our musical life, when I got to that age.

In fact, our house was a no-music zone. No one ever said it was a rule or anything; it just happened. Once in a while I'd listen to something, but only when Mom was out, which felt very wild and rebellious, not to mention dangerous.

One of those times, when I was twelve, I had some pop music not just on but blasting full volume in the kitchen, and I was singing along. The song was something embarrassing, I'm sure.

I was dancing and going crazy the way you do when you think you're completely alone. You know, pretend microphone, striking poses, acting like a rock star—blackmail material if anyone had got it on video. But I thought I sounded pretty good.

And then, holy shit, the music was gone and my mom was there, her hand on the power button, my lonely voice suddenly hanging awkwardly in the air.

I stopped.

Her face was ghostly white.

I stood there, gaping. Hot and cold and confused and somehow deeply ashamed. For a second she'd looked so pained, and I didn't know if it was the music itself, or if it was because my voice sounded horrific, or if it was, instead, because my voice sounded good. All I knew was that it—the moment itself—was so very bad.

She recovered first, and reached out to pat me on the head.

"Well," she said, clearing her throat, "at least we'll be spared that."

"Spared what?" I said.

"The possibility of your having a career as a vocalist," she said, with a rueful smile.

"Oh," I said, my humiliation doubling. "I don't sound good? I mean, I know I don't sound like you . . . used to . . . but . . ."

I could have sworn . . .

"Trust me, Ingrid," she said. "I don't want to hurt your feelings, but . . . that voice of yours . . . is not going to be your path to fame and fortune."

I died a little then. My mom knew about voices, so if she didn't think it was good, it wasn't.

"But that's just as well, isn't it?" Mom continued brightly. "Because look at where all of that got me? Poverty, instability, gruelingly hard work, and then a broken heart. You deserve better. You're smart, and you have a world of choices open to you. Don't be sad, darling. If you want to sing in the kitchen, or the shower or whatever, you go right ahead."

I couldn't, though. Not after that.

And now I think she lied to me. Or, if it wasn't exactly a lie, it was a deliberate misdirection, a deception. And look at me here on this trip, thinking I was going to camp, speaking of deception, if that's what it was. For my own good, supposedly, both times. But I don't know. . . . If you deceive someone for their own good, how can any real good come of it?

I hate the feeling of being angry. I don't want to be angry with her. It hurts.

A lot of things hurt.

By the way, I've been thinking: I wish I had seen you naked.

And vice versa.

How's that for random and shockingly honest?

Yeah, yeah, it's my true voice. And it's staying here, in this book.

Wistfully yours,
Ingrid

I first met Isaac in a closet, and not the metaphorical kind.

It was seventh grade and we were locked in a utility

closet at lunchtime at our lovely school.

No lights.

With a bunch of eighth graders heckling us from the other side of the door, because, wow, shoving people into closets was fun.

Isaac was a geek of the quintessential variety, complete with horribly fitting clothes, straw-like hair that looked like his parents cut it with an actual bowl over his head, blotchy freckles, glasses, braces, and a fabulous brain combined with a socially suicidal eagerness to show his mental prowess in every conceivable academic subject.

I was new. Or I was considered new, not having been noticed in any way whatsoever the year before, when I'd *actually* been new, and apparently that was reason enough for people looking for someone to pick on.

This closet thing had been happening to me a lot, but I assumed it was a first for Isaac, who was gasping and shivering. I backed myself up against one wall, trying to give us both space.

"Sorry about this," I said.

"Not your fault," Isaac said.

We'd never spoken before. When you already have problems, it doesn't help to align yourself with people who have the same problems. It would be nice to think you can team up and that would alleviate the situation, but based on my observations during my first year and a half of "real" school, this wasn't the case.

"What do we do?" Isaac said.

I shrugged, then realized that of course he couldn't see it. "Usually I just wait until lunch ends. And hope at some point it will all be over."

"But they said they want proof that we—"

"*Hey, Ingrid, are you on your knees?*" came a shout from the other side of the door.

"They can't make us do anything," I said through suddenly gritted teeth.

"No, I just thought . . . maybe we could mess ourselves up? So we look—"

"Mess ourselves up? No. Eww."

"Okay! I didn't mean to be offensive."

"I'm not offended. I didn't mean it like that. I'm just so sick of these Neanderthals."

"Okay, but you sound mad."

"Well, I'm locked in a closet against my will. Again. And I ran out of time to eat my lunch in advance, so I'm hungry. And the people at this school are awful and unoriginal. And this is our local school, so I can't leave until ninth grade, and then apparently they'll all be at the same high school too. And I had a better life than this, once. So actually yes, I am mad. But not at you."

"Oh, okay," Isaac said, clearing his throat and not sounding okay at all himself. "I guess it could be worse. They could be beating us up, instead."

"Wow. That's so comforting."

"Of course they still might."

"Oh my God."

"Sorry. I'll shut up."

"Thank you." I endured the silence for forty-two counted seconds before I gave in and asked, "Have they? Uh, beaten you up?"

Isaac made another gasping/choking sound.

"Never mind; you don't have to tell me."

After that we stood, breathing in the cleaning-product fumes and trying not to listen to the catcalls and abuse from outside the door. It was loud out there, but inside the closet was its own little sound capsule and this meant I could hear Isaac's breath accelerating and a wheeze starting.

"What's wrong?" I asked.

"Other than the obvious?"

"Yeah."

"I am showing manifestations of not liking . . . I don't like . . . small closed spaces."

"You're claustrophobic?"

"Whatever. The point is, if I were going to choose a place to be forced to supposedly, uh, hook up with someone, this would not be it."

"Not to mention we're *twelve*."

"That too."

"So . . . are you going to freak out? Pass out? What?"

"I don't know. I'm . . . trying to stay . . ." he said, his voice coming out half strangled. "But these assholes . . . these Neanderthals, although I think it's actually an insult to the Neanderthals . . ."

"True."

"They're making my life difficult already and now this is . . . just . . . great."

Standing there in the dark I realized a few things.

1. This might be some kind of test, and if I were smart (plus evil and ruthless), I would pass it by finding a

way to throw Isaac under the bus—humiliate him, cut him down, thus giving myself a chance at a better social status and perhaps a reprieve from the closet lunches and the rest of it. After all, Isaac's status was established and fixed, whereas mine wasn't. At least I hoped it wasn't.

2. On a cosmic, karmic, "being a decent person" level, this was a test of a different kind.

3. It was unlikely I could pass both of these tests.

4. That sucked.

Meanwhile, his distress was ramping up.

"Isaac, what can I do?"

He didn't answer.

"How do you get yourself out of this? Okay, you probably need to . . . breathe. I mean, breathe slower. Meditate or something."

"Sometimes"—he gasped—"I do math."

"Of course you do. All right, do some math."

"I can't. I can't get started."

"One plus one is—"

Isaac half gasped, half chuckled. "It has to be harder than that . . . formulas . . . fractions . . ."

"Well, sorry, I'm crap at math," I said, then reached across the small space. "Give me your hands. Or your arms."

"Okay."

I took him by the forearms, squeezed, then slid my hands to his and held them. They were ice-cold.

"I can't lose it in front of those people," he said.

"You're not going to." He *was* going to, at this rate. "Listen, what about music? Doesn't music stimulate the math part of the brain?"

I dug into my memory banks, pulled up my favorite Bach cello suite, and started to hum, taking it slow because at regular tempo the notes were too fast for humming. I kept hold of his arms, stood close, and envisioned pitching my voice so it would go straight to his brain and his nervous system.

"Keep going," he said when it was done.

He sounded a little calmer, so I moved on to the next thing that came to mind—a Verdi aria. At first I was humming, but soon I was singing the words.

It was working. He'd stopped gasping for air and his hands weren't so cold anymore, so I just kept going. I sang a folk song, some Mozart, Puccini, more Bach, mostly from Margot-Sophia's repertoire or my own music lessons. It was all still there inside me and it felt like finding water in the desert. Although I never forgot about the assholes on the other side of the door, the music helped me hook into something that caused me to just not care, that caused me to remember the very big world outside this hellish school. And anyway, it was too loud out there for them to even hear.

"Don't stop," Isaac said when I paused at the end of the lament from *Dido and Aeneas*.

And so I chose another.

And another.

And then one more . . .

Until all around us was just music and everywhere else a tight silence . . . a pause, a seeming break in space and time, like the moment between one breath and another . . .

And then, when I'd run out of everything I knew offhand, and Isaac was calm and breathing slowly, I stopped.

"Better?"

"Holy cow," he said. "You . . . you sing."

"No, I just know some songs."

"If you say so. But it helped. Thank you."

"Don't thank me yet. I didn't think they'd hear me, but . . . it's pretty quiet out there all of a sudden . . ."

"You still helped." He squeezed my hands; I squeezed back. He hummed a couple of bars from the cello suite, and I smiled at him across the darkness.

And then the door flew open, bringing blazing fluorescent light, colder, fresher air, and faces.

"Oh, look, they're holding hands," Elizabeth, queen of the assholes, crowed. She was the big evil, and not the typical two-faced, maybe-dumb, pretty-girl evil—she was viciously smart, preppy, and sporty, with long curly brown hair, fair skin, freckles, and piercing blue eyes. She wasn't pretty, and she wasn't trying to be, but she had an amazing laugh and a magnetic personality. She was trying to rule the world, and she would probably succeed. She was the one who'd noticed me in early September and decided to make me her target.

"They had a romantic date," she sneered now, "and he made her sing."

Yep, they'd heard me. Uh-oh.

"What'd ya do to make her sing, big boy?" said Zac, Elizabeth's nightmare boyfriend, yanking Isaac into the hallway and throwing a fake-friendly arm over his shoulders.

"You must have some hot moves to make a girl sing like

that," Elizabeth added. "And you . . . such a songbird."

"That's just how she begs for it," Zac said, and all around them their minions cackled.

"That's just how she gets her mouth ready," said one of Zac's nasty followers, earning screeches of approval.

My eyes met Isaac's and I could see he was angry, ready to fight. I gave a subtle shake of my head.

Don't.

If we kept our mouths shut and let them have their stupid jokes, maybe it would be over with nothing worse happening.

Maybe.

"She's a songbird and they're lovebirds . . ." continued Zac in the same asinine manner, and because he was Zac, everyone laughed.

But then Isaac broke in with: "Oh come on, that wasn't even funny."

Crap. I closed my eyes for a second, and by the time I opened them, Zac's fist was connecting with Isaac's gut, and Isaac was going down, kicks and punches landing on him all the way.

"Stop!" I shouted, but no one listened.

"Get up, lovebird," Zac said, hauling Isaac up from behind and passing him off to two burly guys who'd come forward as if summoned by mind-speak. "Hold him."

At the same time, someone grabbed me from behind and shoved me forward and up against Isaac.

"Show us, lovebirds," Elizabeth said. "Show us your love."

I only came up to just below Isaac's chin, so I couldn't see his face.

"How about a big, sloppy kiss? Make your loverboy feel better," Zac said. "C'mon."

I'd never kissed anyone, at least not in the romantic sense.

Not that this was—at all—in the romantic sense. It was the opposite of romantic.

I could have refused, or helped myself by saying something nasty to Isaac in that moment, but I was way past being able to do that and still live with myself. So I went up on my tiptoes and gave him a superfast peck, aiming for the lips and landing the kiss half on, half off.

"Tongue, tongue, tongue," they chanted.

I felt my cheeks heating up and tears prickling at the backs of my eyes. I had no idea how to even do what they were asking and was generally grossed out by the concept and certainly never wanted to try it in front of a group of hostile kids whose sole purpose was to humiliate me.

But they'd already been beating Isaac up, and things might get worse.

"C'mon, songbird." It was Elizabeth, standing behind me, talking right into my ear. "He's soooo sexy."

I tried to shove away from her, but that only brought me closer up against Isaac, who was looking panicked again. If he didn't like closed spaces, he probably wasn't dealing well with this chanting, crushing mob, either.

Our eyes met and he said, "Just do it."

Grim-faced, he leaned down and I got onto my toes again.

The crowd was laughing, jeering, and people were still holding our arms, pushing us together from all sides.

We inched closer and I tried to pretend we were alone, back in the closet.

With music.

Then Zac was there, a hand on the back of each of our heads, and in one powerful move he smashed our faces together and held them there.

Our lips may have met in the process, but so did our teeth, noses, and foreheads.

I was still dazed, head ringing, when he let us go, but then I saw blood coming from Isaac's left nostril, and the pain and humiliation landed hard.

That's when I flipped.

It's a bit of a blur, but I remember a surge of fury and the feeling of my elbows flying and my feet stomping and kicking and I think I may have been screaming. I'm not sure I hurt anyone, but I definitely surprised them . . . and hurt myself, because it turns out kicking and punching people actually hurts the person doing it.

I remember tasting blood in my mouth and then thinking that this was it, I was so dead.

And then the bell rang, and there were teachers coming out of the staff room down the hall, and like magic, everyone disappeared.

Except us. Isaac and I, bruised and dazed, stayed at the end of the hallway.

"Are you okay?" I asked him. "Of course not—you're bleeding. I'm taking you to the nurse."

"I need to get to geography."

"Seriously, you're worried about class?" I wrapped an arm

around him and propelled him along the corridor.

"Well . . . yes," he said, huffing along beside me "This stuff happens to me all the time. Not exactly this, I guess. Anyway, it's not going to stop me from going to class."

"It is today," I said, as we arrived in front of the closed office door.

"Wait, Ingrid," Isaac rasped. "You can't tell him. How this happened, I mean."

"Uh, yeah, my death wish only goes so far."

Mr. Moore, the school nurse, cool-looking in red jeans and a coordinating red-and-burnt-orange button-down, took one look at Isaac and ushered him into the outer office.

"You need me, too?" Mr. Moore asked me, looking me over and then meeting my eyes with an assessing gaze.

"I'm fine."

"You want to tell me what happened?"

"He ran into a door," I said.

"Huh. All right." He didn't believe me, but I guess he could tell that was all I was going to say. "Get to class, then."

I gave an encouraging smile to Isaac, waved, then spun away, moving as fast as I could without breaking into a run. I made it to my locker, put everything I could fit into my backpack, shoved my coat on, walked down the hallway, pushed my way out the doors, and let the November wind freeze my tears on the long walk home.

I wasn't going to spend another second in that school, and it would be three years before I saw Isaac again.

I was lucky, when I told Mom in no uncertain terms that I would never go back to that school, to have Andreas around. We were at an impasse. Mom was unwilling to pull me out of school without another school lined up, and half determined that I should go back and gut it out regardless, and I was desperately trying to hold my ground despite having no viable alternative plan of my own.

Andreas, however, was an incorrigible fixer. It wasn't just what he did in his coaching business; it was who he was. Because of this, he had a lot of connections. And it so happened that Andreas knew of a school—a very special school—and Mom agreed that we could at least check it out.

Godark Academy is housed in a former church that was later converted into a building with two theaters, and finally into a school. It is a crumbling gothic folly, drafty and creaky, with an old heating system that produces "boiling," "freezing," and nothing in between, and it holds a corner of the West End with ghostly charm.

It's an alternative public school with a smallish student population all in grades six through twelve. Entrance was via lottery and then interview, but Andreas knew the principal and thought he might get me in via a "humanitarian" plea.

"What, like I'm a refugee?"

"Like you are a very special person to me," he said.

My throat tightened. It was a big thing for him to say.

Upon entering the lobby I gazed up and up, eyes landing on stained-glass windows. I felt the gray stone walls rising up around me, the many-bulbed chandelier floating eerily in the space above. I breathed in and out, feeling the musty, old-book-scented air drop deep into my lungs, soothing me.

It felt like Hogwarts on a budget.

It felt like a downtrodden opera house.

It felt like home.

I stood, my feet on the stone-tiled floor, and wished to sprout roots so I could stay.

I glanced up at Mom, wondering if this was evoking the past for her, too, and if so, whether it would be in a good way, or not.

"I believe the rate of university acceptance upon graduation is quite high," Andreas murmured, seeming to know already what would hold the most weight for Mom. Her attitude toward the arts—all of them—had taken a big hit since we moved to Canada, and in every conversation we'd had about education and career, she had stressed practicality and stability. I was to get fabulous marks and plan for a smart career. Andreas had obviously taken this in.

"Ninety-six percent university acceptance, actually," replied a smooth new voice.

I turned to discover the voice came from a white-haired, swan-like personage of difficult-to-determine gender, whom Andreas introduced as Rhea. (Ray-uh. I soon realized she was a she.) "Rhea is Head of School—the principal, in other words."

I watched Mom as she and Rhea shook hands and studied each other, each seeming to sense some kind of je ne sais quoi in the other.

There was to be a tour and a description of the curriculum and philosophy of the school, and then an interview. I didn't need a tour. I would have taken any school besides the one I was in. But as we went through, popping in and out of various classrooms and so on, I got all good vibes. Students waved at us and smiled at me, and even visually, there was diversity here; a variety of races, plus people didn't all dress the same, or do their hair the same, et cetera.

I was transferred within the week, and matched with a "buddy" on my first day.

"The buddy thing sounds cheesy, but it's cheesy on purpose," said my "buddy," a girl named Juno, with carrot hair and giant green eyes. "Basically Rhea's picked me to be your insta-friend. And she's a good judge of character, so there's an excellent chance we'll get along."

"That's . . . okay; that's good," I said.

"Rhea has an instinct. She can do friendship voodoo, in a good way."

"Great." I liked Juno. I could tell she was smart, and she had a bluntness that I appreciated. I so badly wanted to make a good impression, which meant I had to figure out a way to be friendly, cool, and not desperate.

"I'm responsible for your having a smooth start. My job is to introduce you around, help you get oriented, and make sure nobody messes with you."

"Messes with me?" I must have looked panicked, because Juno started shaking her head.

"No, no, like, someone might give you the wrong directions on purpose or whatever—stupid things, trying to be funny. But they won't. And don't worry; it's not like you have to stay friends with me if you don't want to."

"No, I . . . I want to. I mean, if *you* want to."

"Of course. But I mean, although so far I like you quite a lot, I won't be heartbroken."

"Does everyone get assigned someone like this? Or is it . . ."

Just the freaks who've been pariahs at other schools . . . ? I knew Andreas had told Rhea everything he knew and I hoped she would keep it private and I could have a fresh start.

"Anyone new, and anyone who starts late," Juno said.

"Oh, good. All right. And thank you."

"By the way, you have to be ready, if we're going to be friends, to help me deal with some boy drama," she says.

"Boy drama? Like a boyfriend?"

"No." Juno made a face. "A boy who's a friend—my best friend, growing up, but he's been weird since, I don't know, last year? He'll be acting normal one minute, and like he doesn't even know me the next—you know, pretending he's too cool for me. And I will not tolerate that garbage from a boy I used to play dress-up with. So I'll be like, 'Toff, I've seen you naked a hundred times and you once pooped in my bathwater!' right in front of his friends, which embarrasses him almost to death, which causes him to act like even more of a jerk toward me."

"Wow," I said, not sure whether to laugh. "So what do you need from me? Talk to him when you're talking to him, ignore him when you're not?"

"Sure. And . . ."

"And . . . ?"

"If he ever says anything about me . . ."

"I doubt he's going to talk to me, but of course I would report back to you if he ever did," I said, hoping this was what she wanted.

And it must have been, because Juno smiled, then suddenly reached out and gave me a hug, and I hugged her back and tried not to cry from relief.

Chapter Thirteen

SMOKED

(Peak Wilderness, Days Three to Six)

Dear Mom,

I have massacred many mosquitoes by now.

And yet the bites are so numerous, I'm not sure my skin will ever recover.

Meanwhile, I'm sure you're concerned about what happened to my wet things—my undies and bra in particular. Like, did they dry, are they off the stick and no longer making an inappropriate spectacle of themselves, are they clean, am I wearing them now? Admit it—you are obsessed.

Before bed, Pat gave me a small piece of canvas and together we hung it over some low branches in a less windy spot, back from the beach. Under that I rigged my stick drying rack so that everything could hang overnight (not including the sleeping bag, which I obviously needed) without fear of rain or dew making them all wet again.

Last night was cold, though, and this morning everything is still damp. (Don't even talk to me about sleeping in the wet sleeping bag.)

But let me tell you about campfires, Mom, because I don't believe you've ever encountered one up close.

Yes, they are hot, with warming and drying capabilities.

You know what else campfires are?

Smoky.

And do you remember what else was happening around that campfire last night?

Smoking.

At the time I was in the midst of it, and therefore desensitized.

This morning, though, my sense of smell is working at full capacity.

So.

Consider that while I did my best washing everything, all I had to work with was a small bar of biodegradable soap. Consider the socks and underwear that I hiked in, slept in, sprayed bug spray in and around for two days.

And the other set that sat wet and moldering in my pack in the hot sun most of the day yesterday? Consider that.

And then imagine how these items smell this morning, after being fire-and-stinky-herbal-cigarette-smoked last night.

Imagine putting these items on under cold, damp clothing, and then imagine the smell of them, wafting up from your feet, chest, and nether regions. It is a unique stench, and quite inescapable, like wearing an inferno, and not the Disco kind.

Imagine how this will develop today, as, for example, my feet get sweaty.

Meanwhile, Bonnie, trying not to choke when she comes near me, has suggested that for the purposes of airing the other pair of underwear out—the ones I'm not wearing—I hang them on the outside of my backpack for the day.

So, yes, I have mounted my undies like a flag on the back of my pack.

You know, in case anyone failed to get a good look at them last night.

Smoked love,
Ingrid

I wake feeling dreadful on Day Three. I've barely slept. I was awake shivering and shaking, cycling from furious to scared to confused and back, and trying not to let panic overtake me. It's been here all along, but I've been fighting it off. Now, however, with every muscle in my body aching, with everything stinking and wet, myself included, with my every action under scrutiny—of the emotionally intrusive kind by Bonnie and Pat, of the uncomfortable kind by people like Jin and Tavik, and of the creepy kind by Peace-Bob—I'm losing the fight. I am too tired even to fight, so I am just losing.

And there's no out. We're in the middle of nowhere, days of hiking from civilization, so even if I wanted to renege on my deal with Mom, it's impossible. I'm trapped.

After having my morning pee in the woods and getting dressed, I sit down to write to Mom about the smoked undies, bra, and socks. The angry bite of these letters I'll never send has been oddly grounding. (Maybe they're written in my true voice, in which case my true self is a sarcastic bitch.) Today it doesn't help much, but I do it anyway. And then, as I close the journal and tie the leather straps and look up at the sky, I feel, again, like everything is closing in on me. My heart races. I start to shake again, then tell myself I cannot do this, cannot fall apart, because if I do that out here, with a bunch of strangers who don't give a crap about me, I'm toast.

I just have to survive another . . . eighteen freaking days. No problem. Ha-ha.

Breakfast is ready. I can't imagine how I'll eat, but I know I can't hike all day with no food.

I just have to survive. I'm good at that. Right?

Bonnie comes to sit beside me as I spoon hot cereal into my mouth.

"Ingrid . . . ?" she says. "How are you today?"

"Fucking terrible," I find myself saying. "And you?"

"I'm sorry to hear that," Bonnie says. "Do you want to talk about it?"

"No."

"Are you upset about Peace walking in on you changing last night?" Pat says, barging clumsily into the conversation. Harvey and Henry look up, interested. In fact, everybody except Peace is here, listening.

"If I am, do you think I want to revisit the experience over breakfast, with everyone sitting here, listening?" I say, face flushed and barely managing not to throw my bowl at him.

"I'm . . . sorry," Pat says.

"It's fine," I say. "Forget it."

"So what's wrong?" Bonnie says, a hand reaching up to rub my back.

"Nothing!" I say, trying to shift away from her. God, I hate these people poking into my business all the time. "Nothing, I'm just having a bad morning."

"Why?" she says.

"Why do we need to talk about every little thing?" I say, getting up and moving to another log, away from her.

"We're here together," she says. "And each person's mood affects the entire group."

"Also," Jin pipes up, "if you're going to answer 'how are you?' with 'fucking terrible,' you have to know people are going to ask why. You're practically begging people to ask why. So? What's your problem?"

"Look, I just don't want to be here, that's all."

"You changed your mind?" Bonnie asks.

"No, I *never* wanted to be here."

"You thought you were going to a camp . . . ." Bonnie says, in a voice that sounds like her professional I'm-being-calm-because-I'm-talking-to-a-crazy-person mode.

"No, I didn't want to do it at all. Even when I thought it was camp. I made a deal that I would do it, but I never wanted to."

"Why did you, then?" Jin says.

"Because my mother wanted me to."

"Seriously?" Jin sneers. "You do everything she says?"

"No," I say, glaring at her, wishing she would stay out of it.

"Is she trying to control you?" Melissa asks quietly. "Because that's very controlling behavior."

"No! No one is controlling me, or trying to control me."

"You're obviously upset, though," Bonnie observes again.

"Look," I say, standing up and backing away from the fire. "I'll hike, and cook and clean up when it's my turn, but all the rest, all this talking, all these questions . . . I'm not up for it. I'm not doing it. So stop asking me."

Dear Mom,

I still haven't told them about Ayerton, or my flip-out on the night of the spring dance: the ax, the garage. It's not why you sent me. It's none of their business. What would be the point in telling them I'm such a loser, I accidentally chopped myself in the leg? While not-accidentally hacking at the roof of our garage? And how the hell could I explain to them that this action—the roof, not the leg—made perfect sense to me at the time, and still does?

And meanwhile, all I am trying to do is use everything you taught me. Shed the past. Move forward. Chin up, head high. And what you did earlier in your life—follow your own path and work your butt off going after what you want. But that's practically impossible when you, via this damned trip, have stripped away everything that makes me feel comfortable or safe, every possibility of a coping mechanism. Why? Whatever the degree of trickery that was involved, you sent me here, and you knew it was going to be rough even if it had been a proper camp with cabins and some level of civilization. Is Melissa right: Is it to control me? Well, sure, but it's more than that. Are you trying to break me? I promise you, I do not need breaking. And the gall of you thinking you know what I need at this point is . . . well, it's extraordinary.

Love (which often sucks),
Ingrid

Once again, I hike in the middle of the group, thinking, with each step, that I just have to get through the day. Ally starts out in front of me, the gauze her feet are wrapped in sticking out the tops of her boots.

We begin in silence, and soon it's the sound of her huffing and puffing that I'm hearing louder than anything else. I ask her if she's okay, and she only nods and keeps going. Before long she's limping and slowing down, and I can see her shoulders shaking.

"Ally? Do you need a break?"

Ally pauses, looks back at me, and I stop. Behind me, Jin stops.

"I n-need a break every two minutes," Ally says, tears streaking down her face, which she has, I notice, made up again today. I have to admire the optimism.

"We can't exactly stop every two minutes," Jin says from over my shoulder.

"I know," Ally says, sniffling.

I turn and glare at Jin, then say to Ally, "Why don't you have some water?"

She nods, pulls out her water bottle, takes a drink.

"I'm never going to survive this," she says, looking at me with wide, drippy eyes. "Everything hurts."

Seth, who has been walking ahead of Ally, has come back to see what's wrong, and up ahead I can see that everyone has stopped.

"Ally?" Seth says, getting an immediate sense of the situation. "What's her name again? Angel?"

Ally nods, sniffling.

"Come on," he says, reaching out to take her hand. "Every step, just . . . do what they suggested last night. Think about Angel. Every single step gets you closer to her."

I nod along with Ally, and she murmurs, "Angel," and starts walking.

"You can do it," I say, though I'm not really sure she can. I'm not even sure I can.

"That's right," Seth says. "Let's go."

Seth keeps hold of her hand even though it's obviously awkward to do while walking single file, and we all start moving forward again.

"About time," Jin mutters from behind me.

"You're just chock-full of kindness and empathy, aren't you?" I respond, shaking my head.

"Endless supply," she says, totally deadpan, and I almost laugh.

For the next couple of hours, I find myself thinking,

"Angel," with almost every step, too, almost like a mantra. Sometimes it even helps.

Five days in, Ally has shifted from weepy, limping, and slow to not crying at all and hiking, albeit grimly, at a steady pace. She starts doing stretching and push-ups with Seth before dinner. I'm a little worried she's developing a crush on Seth, which can't end well, but she's much better, and at the end of the fifth day, even volunteers to lead the next day's hike.

That night, I'm on firewood duty. When I arrive at the fire pit with my last armful of wood, something is off between Melissa and Peace, who are in charge of dinner.

"What is your problem?" Peace is saying. "I can't have an opinion?"

Melissa's face is rigid, and she doesn't respond.

"I'm just being nice," Peace says, as Melissa assembles ingredients on a flat rock. "I'm trying to help. Fine. Make dinner yourself. I'm out."

He stalks off into the woods, leaving Melissa there, breathing fast and looking like she's going to pass out from . . . I'm not sure what the emotion is.

"Are you okay?" I ask her.

She doesn't answer, just turns like some kind of automaton and continues with the dinner prep. Since Peace has left her on her own, I help, and attempt to engage her in conversation, but she seems to have shut down completely. She goes through the entire evening, including circle, without saying a word.

Ally does a decent job leading us on Day Six, but we're still taking hours longer than the map estimates to get to camp every night.

She is having an easier time, but Melissa is not.

Harvey and Henry get into a fistfight on the trail, so they're obviously not either.

And I am not.

I have fantasies about hot showers.

I have nightmares, waking in a cold sweat once or twice a night.

And day and night, I feel like I'm trapped in purgatory, panic rising and falling, and the fury that's been keeping me afloat coming and going. I try to distract myself by thinking about other people's problems—there's certainly enough of that around me—but more and more the fury gives way to other things: blankness, bleakness, a sense of shattering betrayal.

Chapter Fourteen

PHANTOM LIMB

(Ages Thirteen to Fourteen)

"This, this, this . . ." Mom was tossing things into an ever-growing recycling pile. "Out it goes."

I'd been at Godark just over a year, and after much discussion, Andreas had agreed to sell his waterfront condo and move in with us. The three of us had looked at a few houses, thinking to move, but seeing other places only caused us to realize how unique and cozy the coach house was, and we decided it was more than large enough for the three of us. However, Andreas was going to need some closet space, and this had prompted a purging frenzy.

"Mom, you can't just—*achoo!*" I sneezed from the dust she'd stirred up, pulling all of her opera paraphernalia out from the back of her closet. There were programs, playbills, cast photos, review clippings, musical scores, tiny opera house–shaped chocolates from who knows when. "You can't just throw all that out—not the *Carmen* program, not—come on, I remember most of these shows. Wait!"

Mom paused to open a score and run her index finger along the notes, then she swore in some exotic language and threw it on the pile.

"When they cut off your leg, do you keep it to take it out and look at?"

"Eww. What?"

"Precisely."

"A leg would smell, Mom."

"Well, this smells too, and I don't want Andreas to find our house smelly. It goes."

"It's not a leg, Mom. This is your life. Our life. Your legacy. It's important."

At this she tilted her head toward the ceiling and growled.

"Oh my God," I said. "Fine."

"And we do not speak of it to him. Ever."

We'd been over this and were not in agreement, not that it mattered since 90 percent of the time in the case of a disagreement, I would lose. My being thirteen had not changed that fact.

The craziest thing was that Mom, even after almost two years with him, had still not told Andreas about her life in opera. Yes, he knew she'd been a singer and that she "didn't like to sing anymore." She'd told enough of the truth—that she'd drifted around Europe in her early years, hoping to make a living as a singer, that she'd taken bizarre jobs all over the place and sung wherever she could, but I could tell he had the impression she meant she was singing in bars, or even on street corners, and that maybe she hadn't been very good.

"All this time I thought you were just waiting for the right moment to tell him," I said.

"There is nothing to tell. That person," she said, pointing to a stunning photo of herself, "is not me. Not now. And it is me he is with. Me of right now. I don't want to talk about it, I don't want to relive it, I don't want him feeling sorry for me, and I don't want him wishing I were still that woman. He loves me now."

"So you're *never* going to tell him."

"No. And neither are you."

"But . . ."

"No!" she roared. "No, no, no! I would rather break up with him. Is that what you want?"

"Fine." I sighed and got back to the depressing task at hand. Margot-Sophia was in a *mood*, and even the old photographs, which we didn't have digital copies of, went in the pile. There would be no dissuading her. And so I helped: holding the garbage bag open, sorting recyclables from nonrecyclables, making runs outside to the bins.

My heart hurt with every bit that was tossed. It was my life too—the best part of it. Even things that had happened before I was born were part of who I was, and how we got to this place in time, with or without possibly odiferous metaphorical limbs.

Not all of it made it outside—some of it, as much of it as I could manage, made its way to the very back of my closet, from which I could produce it later on, if and when she regretted tonight's actions.

Chapter Fifteen

On Day Seven, after another night of restless sleep—due to Peace's ongoing snoring, and my own too-awake mind—I begin to lose it.

The tears start before I'm even out of my sleeping bag, then I am crying too hard to speak at breakfast, although of course Bonnie and Pat try to get me talking. I cry as we hike, and through every break, through lunch, and all the way to camp that night.

It's hideous. Embarrassing. Ally and Seth and Melissa all try to help, but I don't want help, and I can't talk. Won't. I'm so angry to have lost control of myself like this, to have cracked open, broken down.

"Ingrid, you need to tell us what's wrong," Bonnie says at circle that night.

I'd tried to get myself excused and just go to bed, but of course she and Pat wouldn't let me.

"All I know is what I already told you—that I don't want

to be here," I say finally. "It's not fair."

"Why not?" Bonnie says.

"I keep hearing the phrase 'at risk' from you and Pat," I say, through a quavering breath. "I guess what's not fair is . . . this is a boot camp. Right? For kids who are 'at risk.' Well, obviously I'm not the soul of stability at the moment, but . . . generally speaking, the only thing I'm at risk of is becoming something my mom doesn't want me to be."

"Which is . . . ?" Tavik asks.

My drippy gaze swings over to him. "None of your business."

"What's the big deal?"

"It's not a big deal, I guess," I say, deciding he's right. "Except to me. I want to be a musician. Specifically, a singer. And my mom . . . doesn't want me to."

Tavik snorts. The other campers look confused.

"And this is supposed to talk you out of it?" Jin says, incredulous.

"Well, you see, a few months back, I auditioned for the Ayerton School—this incredible music school. I didn't think I had a chance. Your grades have to be good and you have to be hugely talented. They take three people from North America per year, from thousands of applicants. Anyway, shock of my life, I got in. I'm supposed to do my senior year there, and then, if I do well, join their conservatory program after that. But I need my mom's permission because I'm underage, and obviously my saved allowance isn't going to be enough to pay for it. It's not the money, though. She doesn't want me to have a career in music. She wants me to do something . . . stable and sensible."

"Why?" Bonnie asks.

This is obviously her favorite question.

"She just thinks anything in the arts is too hard. Plus it's in England." I swallow. "Maybe she just wanted to make me prove how much I want it. I don't know. But those were the conditions she set—I do this program, she gives permission and finances for me to go."

"So, you're a super talent," Ally says. "Meanwhile, the rest of us are . . ."

"Badass messes and criminals," Tavik says with a wicked grin.

"I'm not mess-free myself. It's just . . . It doesn't seem fair."

"But to send you to this without giving you the right details about it," Harvey says to me, "I mean, dude, you must be pissed."

"Well, I'm not surprised," Peace sneers from the other side of the circle, where he's been observing with a nasty smile on his face. "You obviously expected a five-star resort."

"That's not true!"

"On your way to your five-star school with all the other 'special' five-star musical snowflake people."

"Peace, please," Bonnie says. "We were having a very positive, productive—"

Peace ignores her and gets up and advances on me instead. "You're nothing but a spoiled, capitalist, elitist—"

I haul myself to standing, and glare up at him. "If it's elitist not to want to see your hairy ass in my face and then lie on the ground, listening to you snore all night, then sure, I'm an elitist."

"I have a breathing condition! I'm tired of being discriminated against by people like you."

"I'm not talking about your freaking *breathing condition*, Bob, whatever the hell that means. You weren't even part of this conversation until just now, but since we're into it, I'm pretty tired of your agro-granola bullshit."

Peace growls.

Bonnie and Pat are on their feet, looking like they're ready to jump in and intervene.

"It's fine," I say, motioning to them to stay cool, and taking a step away. "Why don't we just agree to stay away from each other?"

"Fine by me."

The good news is that the argument has temporarily stopped the crying.

But now I have to go sleep in the tent with Peace. I stop Tavik on the way there, with a touch on his arm.

"I need your help," I say.

"Yeah?"

"Could you . . ." I swallow hard. "I know it's the worst spot, but could you sleep . . . in the middle? Tonight? I just . . ."

"Need a buffer?"

"Even two feet would make a lot of difference."

"Sure," he says. "Knight in shining armor, that's me."

"Thank you," I say, exhaling a relieved breath.

"He tries to hump me though? Deal's off."

We hike for two more days with me breaking down almost every time we stop walking. I cry and fight the crying, and while I'm walking, somehow find a way to shore up the walls and bridges I put up and have been maintaining the past few months, only to have them washed out and overrun every time we stop.

Every damn night we arrive late and eat bugs. My clothing and sleeping bag—everything I own— reeks and feels damp and slimy.

I am still weeping on the morning of Day Ten when Pat pulls me aside, hands me the master map, and tells me I'm going to be leader for the day.

"Are you kidding?" I wipe at my face with the back of my hand. "I'm a basket case."

"You'll be great," he says.

"Ha," I say.

This is the first time the leader hasn't been chosen via volunteering, and it doesn't take a genius to figure out the psychology—put a person who feels powerless in a position of power.

"It's going to be a looong day," Peace says. "Keep in mind, we don't have time for lunch at the Ritz. Or a stop at the therapist."

"Want me to take him out for you?" Tavik asks, coming up beside me.

"Thanks, but I'm guessing parole officers take a dim view of murder."

"You need help with the map?"

I look at it, tracing the route with my finger.

"I think I'm good."

I may be in the midst of a total meltdown, but if I have to lead, I'm damn well going to get us to the next campsite while it's still light out. For once.

"Okay, everybody!" I say, turning to the group, wiping at my face and tapping my watch. "I want to see you with packs on and ready to go in ten minutes sharp."

Tavik chuckles, Peace mutters, the girls grin and get to work packing up their tent, and Bonnie watches me with a bemused look on her face.

"And you know what we're *not* having for dinner?" I call out.

"What?" Jin calls back.

"Mosquitoes!"

Maybe no one thought I could lead. Maybe I didn't think so. I certainly didn't want the job. But once I have it? I'm all in.

Our route on the master map is mapped out with mileage and kilometers, and the estimated time each day's hike should take. So far we've never made time. Not even close. This has caused the two things I'm hating more than almost anything— (1) eating bugs and (2) never ever having time to wash and dry my clothes, and therefore feeling like a walking cesspool.

Hence, even though I am still battling weepiness, I am suddenly filled with purpose.

We leave on time, I have no trouble finding the path or spotting the cairns, and I set a good pace. When someone has to stop to go to the bathroom, I give the group five minutes, time it, and get us moving again as soon as the time is up. Lunch is twenty-nine minutes and we're on the move by the thirtieth.

I am not messing around, in other words. We are on the march and I will get us there. And once there, I'm going to get myself and my things clean and set out to dry, and I will re-group—patch up all the holes in my walls, fill the potholes on my psychological road, build some newer, stronger bridges, and finish with this ridiculous breakdown.

Needless to say, we get there. We don't just get there; we burst onto a stunning white beach at 2:00 p.m., having beaten the map by 1.5 hours.

A cheer goes up from the group behind me, and for a few beautiful moments, staring at that beach, I feel awesome. I feel like a freaking rock star.

"What was that you said about not having leadership quali-ties?" Bonnie says, coming up beside me with a slightly smug grin. "Nice job."

"Thanks."

Unfortunately I am only the leader for the hiking portion of the day, and we've scarcely set our packs down when Pat sum-mons us.

"Okay, everybody! Meet me down by the water. Don't bother with the tents yet—there's something I want to do."

"What is it?" I look at Bonnie.

"Oh, you'll see," she says, and winks.

That wink makes me think it's something good. Like on those reality shows where suddenly everyone is whisked off to have dinner in Hawaii, or whatever. Dinner in Hawaii would be awe-some. Or maybe there's a secret hot springs out here that also has showers and laundry facilities. With elves to do the laundry.

I saunter over, still feeling proud of myself, and willing to go along with whatever it is Pat has planned. Circle on the sand, maybe. Early circle. Fine.

Once we're all there, Pat claps his hands enthusiastically and says, "All righty, guys, I want you to stand in a circle."

I was right! We stand obediently in a circle, and then Bonnie passes out lengths of black fabric—one for each person—and instructs us to put them over our eyes. Next, we're each handed a bit of rope to hold on to, and then another for the other hand.

"All right, group. I've wrapped a rope around you twice," Pat says. "Your mission is to get yourselves out of the double circle and into a straight line. You may not let go of or slide along the rope. You may not take your blindfolds off. Go."

Of course it's not something good. Duh.

My brain wobbles and bends and hurts as I try to envision a solution to this puzzle, but I've got nothing.

No one else does either, but that doesn't stop them.

"Everyone!" Peace shouts. "Just do what I say! Take the right hand—the one that's holding the rope behind you, and step over it."

"No, no, dude, you have to switch places with the person to your left!" Harvey (or Henry?) says.

"No, no, I already did it, and I'm partly free!" Peace insists, and I can hear that he's on the move.

"You can't just start before we all agree," Tavik says, on my left.

"I don't hear you coming up with any solutions," Peace says.

"Dude, stop pulling me," Henry (or Harvey?) says.

It goes downhill from there—sand flying everywhere, people shouting and going off half cocked to try their own thing. Before long we're hopelessly tangled.

The sun bakes us from overhead, sweat rolls down my face and back, even my eyes are sweating, and eau d'inferno drifts up from my shoes, shirt, and pants.

I move when I have to, but I'm not playing.

Instead I am mourning my brief moment of happiness, of personal power. I'm realizing it was an illusion, and knowing, understanding deeply, fully, and for the first time, that I am stuck in a trap within a trap, here and in my life. I am trapped in this twisted circle, in this punishing sun, with these people, with no way out. I am trapped in a puzzle that there is no answer for. I am trapped in this wilderness hell, trapped in my own stinking body, even with a crystal-clear, glistening lake ten feet away. I am cut off from joy, unmoved by beauty, chased by grief, trapped under this sky, in this life, in my own head and heart, where everything, almost everything, has gone to hell.

Standing here in total darkness under the blazing sun, I see it:

I could set things on fire, take an ax to whatever edifice, inside me or out in the world, and it wouldn't make a damned bit of difference.

I am totally, dazzlingly screwed.

And I am going to lose my mind for real, standing here on this beach.

Then . . .

It occurs to me there is one part of this trap, one small part, that I *can* escape from.

Bonnie and Pat are obviously doing their usual thing—

standing around watching us fail, and not helping.

"I know the answer," I say, projecting my voice so it's loud enough to cut through the chaos.

"You do?" Bonnie asks.

"Yeah." I take my blindfold off. It's soaked from sweat, and more tears because my eyes are leaking again, but I can't bring myself to care. "The answer is, there's no answer. It's a trick. Or you two would probably prefer the word *test*. Like the tents. Like the riverbed. Like this whole trip, in my case. There's no solution. It's all just to see what we'll do. To see who's stubborn enough or stupid enough or sheep-like enough to stand here roasting in the sun all afternoon while we get skin cancer, and black flies and mosquitoes feast on us. I'm thinking, who is that stupid? To stay in this stupid trap just because you"—I point accusingly at Bonnie and Pat—"told us to? And the sad answer? All of us, I guess. But not me. Not anymore."

By this time everyone's mask is off, and the entire tangled rope is on the sand.

Pat smiles like he thinks he's the freaking Dalai Lama.

I round on him. "You're an asshole for smiling like that. You think this was fun? Capture the flag is fun. Volleyball is fun. This is hell. This is pure manipulation, day after day. This is Lord of the freaking Flies. You just wasted my afternoon with this garbage when all I ask for is a chance to sleep in a dry sleeping bag and have clean underwear that is not smoke scented, and a life where I can be my actual real self without thinking it's going to break someone's heart, or kill them."

And with that, I throw down the ropes and blindfold, and stomp off across the beach, sand flying in my wake.

Chapter Sixteen

LONG SILENCE

(Age Fourteen)

It was nice having Andreas live with us, and I had been quite sincerely thrilled for him to move in, but I had a hard time with it too. Andreas couldn't stop himself from going into coach mode sometimes, when all Mom or I wanted to do was vent about something. I tried to play along, but Mom couldn't—she wasn't used to people getting into her business, and it made her cranky. In addition, I was continually anxious about Mom hiding her past from Andreas, which was in fact not just her past, but mine. From the beginning, this caused me to feel we were not on solid ground, not in good faith.

Also, for a long time it had been just Mom and me, and I hadn't realized how accustomed we were to each other's habits and quirks until we had a new person in our midst.

A person who was cheerful in the mornings, and loudly so.

A person who might leave dirty dishes in the sink, or eat all the ice cream.

A person who liked to improve people, sometimes even

before the person being improved had had their coffee.

A person who, quite simply, took up space in a way that I wasn't used to.

Not to mention, I didn't know much about his past either, besides the business part. He loved to talk about his move from being an unfulfilled corporate guy to running his own business, where he now coached and advised corporate guys, sometimes about how to become more fulfilled. He loved his job.

He loved my mom.

I thought he might love me, too.

I appreciated that he was a very in-the-present person, and he was good to my mom, and to me, and he didn't try to parent me (I don't count the unsolicited advice on how to more efficiently pack my backpack in the morning, or on dressing and eating mindfully), which was probably wise. But part of me worried we were all just playacting, and that any minute, everything would fall apart.

One Saturday morning about a year after he'd moved in, Mom was doing her usual weekend sleep-in, and he and I were both up.

"Ingrid, would you like to come on a secret mission with me?" he asked.

I said yes, and we took the subway to Yorkville, where he bought me a fancy brunch.

I ate my gourmet waffles with ice cream, and watched him carefully as he made small talk, wondering what was up, because this wasn't standard procedure, and he was acting strange.

Finally, he clasped his hands under his chin, and said, "Ingrid, do you think your mother would marry me?"

My jaw dropped.

"You're surprised," he said.

"That's just . . . not what I was expecting!" I had, from force of habit, I suppose, expected something bad.

"Maybe I should ask, first, if you would be happy about it," he said, seeming to sense something off in my reaction.

"I . . . yes. I mean, of course you have to ask her, and . . . probably she would say yes. We're all living together after all, and she's happy."

"But . . . ?"

"But nothing. Except . . ." I shrugged, looked away, then back at him. "Have you ever been married before? It feels like a weird thing for me not to know about you."

"You never asked," he said.

"No, I guess I didn't," I said, swallowing down my own guilt about my part in keeping Mom's past from him. "I don't mean to be interrogating you. . . ."

"I was married once," he said. "When I was very young—in my late twenties. It did not work out."

"Why not?"

"This is a very grown-up conversation we're having," he said.

"I'm a very grown-up teen."

"All right," he said, seeming to come to a decision. "She became pregnant. I was happy; she was not. Then she miscarried. . . ."

"Oh, I'm so sorry."

"Thank you," he said, his expression solemn. "After, she told me the experience showed her she did not want to have children, and in fact did not want to be with me at all, and that was it. I understood something then—she did not need me. She had never needed me. Loved me, maybe, but . . . she was not a person who could be held on to, and all my plans for us—a home to settle into, children, long years together, and my plans to fix things between us . . . she didn't want those things. She didn't want things fixed. For a long time, I was heartbroken. But I worked, and traveled, and moved here to Canada, and eventually I healed."

"Did you have girlfriends?"

He laughed. "Of course! I was not a monk. But until I met your mother, I had simply never met another woman I wanted to be with in a serious way. I have known her for years now, and still I feel I do not know everything. She is fascinating. And you . . . perhaps I should speak with your mother about this first but . . ."

"But what?"

"If I ask her, and if she says yes," he said, suddenly looking a little nervous, "and if you would like the idea . . ."

"Yes . . . ?"

"I know you never knew your father," he said. "Your mother told me the story . . . ."

I nodded.

"It seems perfect to me. I never had the child I wanted; you never have had a father . . ."

"Yes . . . ?"

"I would like to adopt you, officially, and be . . . not your stepfather, but your father. Only if you and your mother agree, of course. And you have time to think about this, obviously . . . but . . . maybe you have been a long time without one and this would be too much?"

"No, not too much," I said. I could barely speak, and I'd been biting my lip to keep from crying. "No one has ever . . . I would like that."

His smile held so much relief and so much warmth that it lit me up from the inside.

"Then perhaps when you are finished with your waffles, you would come along and help me choose a ring?"

The (hopefully) impending engagement thrilled me, but also filled me with even more worry and dread of things coming crashing down than I'd been filled with before. Andreas liking my mother for being mysterious was great, but I didn't think he'd be very understanding of the two of us having hidden such an important part of our past, and I felt increasingly guilty about it. The stash of secret history in the back of my closet, I decided, had to go.

So, one night I crept out of bed, put slippers on, and retrieved the two garbage bags of memorabilia. Out in the hallway I tiptoed past Mom and Andreas's slightly open door and then down the stairs, wincing at every creak.

I continued through the house to the kitchen, where I quietly unlatched the side door, opened it, and stepped out into the darkness.

Even though it was the side of my own house in a mostly safe neighborhood, there were things to fear in the city besides burglars, drug addicts, and potential rapists. Like raccoons, mice, rats, feral cats in heat, skunks.

And so I stood for a few moments, listening and waiting for my eyes to adjust, before taking the twenty-odd steps to get to the recycling bin. Once there, I hugged the first bag to my chest before opening the lid and lowering it carefully into the bin.

I was starting to feel relieved and about to put the second bag in when a large shape rose up out of the darkness, flashed a light in my face, and spoke my name.

I screamed my head off for about two seconds, then stopped abruptly.

"Andreas!"

"Ingrid!"

"You scared the crap out of me! What are you doing out here?"

"Me?" he said, shifting the light of the flashlight upward so it no longer blinded me, but instead illuminated both our faces. "I am out here wondering what *you* are doing out here. I was thinking we had a thief!"

"Ha-ha . . ."

"Then I was thinking we might have a runaway. And so I came quietly from the front to see . . ."

"Oh."

A moment of awkward silence followed as I floundered, nothing but the truth coming to mind, and the truth being the opposite of my late-night goal.

Andreas waited, solid and patient in the small pool of light.

"I . . . I decided to clean up my room a bit," I said, and swallowed. "Get rid of some stuff. Clutter. You know the old stuff you never use . . . Those organizing experts on TV always say if you haven't used it or worn it in a year, you should get rid of it, so that's what I figured I'd do." I was talking too much but I couldn't seem to stop, and worse, the second bag was still at my feet, and any investigation would prove it wasn't clothing.

"Anyway!" I chirped. "You don't have to worry; we're not being robbed and I'm not running away, just getting organized, and I wanted to follow through and . . . get it out the door! I'll just chuck the rest of this junk and we can all go get a good night's sleep, okay?"

I started giggling like a lunatic and felt my cheeks hot in the cool night air and wanted to run but instead hoisted the second bag. It was rather heavy and required two hands, and unbeknownst to me had begun to rip.

"Please, Ingrid, allow me to help," Andreas said, and reached for the bag.

"No, no! It's fine!" I jerked it away.

"Don't be ridiculous, Ingrid, it's—oh!"

I saw it in slow motion: the tear, the sharp edges of Mom's photos, the soft, fast sliding of the newspaper clippings, all of it cascading out; the way everything landed and settled faceup, laid out perfectly for Andreas to see when he turned his flashlight on it. Which he did.

I had not been able to let these things go, and now I was going to pay the price.

For there was Margot-Sophia Lalonde in her publicity shot for *La Bohème*, a review with the headline "Soprano Margot-Sophia Lalonde stuns in *La Traviata*" and then another similar for *Troilus and Cressida*, a beautiful card from a fellow singer, and finally, one of the autographed head shots she used to give to fans.

Perhaps I could have scrambled to pick it all up before Andreas had the chance to really look. Or I could have thrown myself bodily onto the pile to block his view.

But it was too late and I knew it.

And so I sank to my knees beside him, gazing into the beam of light . . .

And let him see.

And died a little, in the long silence of his looking.

"Lalonde?" he said finally, his velvet voice coming out as a rasp. "Is Burke . . . not her last name?"

"Lalonde was her stage name."

"But . . . why? Why hide this?"

I braved a look at him but quickly turned away, the confusion and pain too hot on his face to bear.

"Please . . ." I said. "Please . . ." But somehow I could not manage anything else, because all I could see, all I could feel and imagine, was him leaving and how we would be gutted by his absence. And how it would be all my fault, for being such a sentimental fool.

"Please, what? What the hell? I always knew there was something, but I didn't think . . . She is a . . . not just a so-so singer . . ." He picked up a photo. "An opera singer?"

"Was," I said. "Yes. But please . . . she . . ."

"What?" He was in my face now, the anger taking over.

"Can't," I whispered. "Can't sing. She had . . . They're called nodes. Like blisters on the vocal cords. Her voice went crazy, then disappeared. After that . . . the singer part of her voice didn't come back. Not well enough, even with surgery. And so our whole life just . . ." My arms lifted to the side, palms up, as if to show life falling away like sand through my fingers.

Like it was about to again.

"Surely something can be done. For her voice."

"No. Trust me, we tried."

I started to cry and tried to hide it by crouching down to clean up the mess, but he got down to help me and I couldn't contain the telltale sniffles or the shaking of my shoulders.

"It's painful for you," he said gently. "I see it must have been."

"N-no," I said, shaking my head. "I mean, yes, but that's not why I'm . . ."

He was studying me with intensity, open like always, waiting for the rest of my sentence.

"That's not why you're crying?" he said. "Ingrid, talk to me. Why?"

"B-because n-now . . ." My lower lip was quivering and I felt about five years old, but what did I have to lose? What more? "N-now you're going to leave us. Leave me. And I don't blame you. But I wanted . . . Maybe it's stupid but I wanted . . ."

"Yes . . . ?"

"I so wanted you to be my dad," I said, voice coming out a tiny wail, and then broke down completely. "I never missed having one, never wanted one until I met you. But now, especially since we talked about it . . ."

"Oh," he said, and it was more of a sound than a word. "Oh, Ingrid. Sweetheart." And the next thing I knew, he'd scooped me up into the tightest hug.

We sat there in the driveway on the pile of splayed-out memorabilia, in the middle of the night, hugging each other as he let me cry, all the while making reassuring sounds and telling me everything would be okay. I didn't believe it, but I knew for sure then, that he really loved me. It was the best feeling in the worst moment. I was glad to have felt it. When I was finally cried out, I tried to soothe myself with the thought that maybe he would still agree to be my friend—come and take me to movies now and then, act like a kind of uncle.

"Come," he said finally, and we finished picking up the mess.

I started toward the recycling bins to put everything in there with the first bag, but he said, "No," and instead pulled out the unopened bag that was in there, and led the way to the front porch, and then inside, where he laid it all out on the dining-room table.

"I wanted to tell you," I said, speaking in a hushed voice so as not to wake my mom, even though I was sure he was going to do it soon enough. "But I promised her. I'm sorry."

"No, no," he said. "I am sorry that you should be asked to keep such secrets."

"I'll tell you now," I said. "I can tell you the whole story."

"No," he said, with a grim glance toward the stairs. "Your mother is the person who will tell me."

"Andreas, she might not be . . . very into talking about it. I just mean . . ." I reached for him, then dropped my hand. "She might freak. But also . . . she's fragile. About this, she's fragile."

"I understand." He picked up a program with her picture on it, then met my gaze. "Go to bed now, Ingrid. Try to sleep."

"But what . . ." I swallowed. "What are you going to do?"

I was used to him being decisive, leaping into action. But I could tell that this had shaken him too deeply for any of that.

"I am going to talk to her," he said. "And then we'll see."

And then we'll see . . . was not an Andreas kind of phrase, but at least it was honest.

"What else can I do?" he said, the question and his uncertainty piercing my heart.

"Okay . . ." I started toward the stairs, then looked back.

The fear and desperation must have been right there in my eyes, because he came to hug me one more time. "I won't disappear," he said into my hair. "No matter what happens, I promise you that."

I swallowed, nodded, tore myself away, and then tiptoed up the stairs into my room, shut the door, and lay, barely breathing, on the bed, waiting for the domestic apocalypse that was obviously coming.

It didn't take long. Footsteps on the stairs and then in the hall, the sound of their door opening and closing, murmured voices, quiet at first, which lulled me into a false sense of relief, and then . . . *boom*.

Not a physical crash; a wail, a roar.

I sat up fast, grabbed my pillow and clutched it.

"Get those out of my face!" came Mom's holler, crystal clear through the walls of the bedroom.

"I want to talk about it." (Andreas.)

"No."

"If we are to be together, we must. *Listen to me: we have to trust each other, Margot-Sophia!*"

The sound of paper ripping, of sobbing . . .

"I cannot be that person. *That person is dead and I have moved on.* You understand nothing—"

"Because you have not let me understand, because you have lied to me and shut me out and because you don't trust me—"

"Don't talk to me about trust." She sounded like she was spitting.

"And you haven't really moved on if you feel you have to keep it a secret. You've only buried it. Buried it alive, Margot-Sophia *Lalonde*."

"You didn't lose everything—not just your way to make a living, your way to say something to the world, to be connected to something better, to access joy . . ."

"I—"

"You didn't lose the one thing that made you sane, or the only thing that made you special!"

"That's not true, Margot-Sophia; you must—"

"I must nothing! I will not be lectured about what I must or must not. I'll have you out of my house, instead! You think you are going to tell me who I am and what to feel, and dictate what I must disclose to you about my past, and force me to take out my scars for you to drop salty tears onto? I will not."

"Margot-Sophia, please—"

"Out. Outoutoutout out of my house!"

"You don't get to just turn this around on me, Margot-Sophia."

And then there was shuffling and stomping, and I, oh so still with my heart crashing, hiding in my bed, heard their bedroom door flying open, and imagined Margot-Sophia standing there, all fire and wildness, commanding this very good, dear, beautiful man to leave us.

Because of me. Because of her, too, but most directly because of me.

I would have moved if I could, but I couldn't; I was braced too hard against what was coming, despite what he promised me. How could he stay in my life at all after this?

"You see here is the door, open!" Margot-Sophia shouted. "Now, go."

A beat, two . . . and then . . .

"No, I won't."

"You won't . . . ?" The incredulity was apparent in her voice. "What do you mean, you won't? You just want to stay here and fight?"

"Yes, if that's what we have to do. Or I could stay here and . . . not fight."

Andreas stayed.

There were tears. There was more yelling, and then, finally, they talked. They talked and talked. I heard enough of it to know that Andreas was relentless in his need to know everything, that he was furious and hurt, but once again working toward solutions. In the predawn hours their voices softened and slowed, and finally I slept.

All of this was good, was great.

Except after their big talk, Mom went to bed.

Days passed.

Seeing Mom spiral down brought back the old fear, and the old fury. Here we were with this fantastic man who wanted to be part of our family, and she goes off to bed. Like some overly delicate Victorian woman in a too-tight corset, with vapors and smelling salts. Nothing wrong with her except what was in her head.

Although, of course, what was in her head was real, and serious.

At first I reverted to my former behavioral mode from the last time this had happened—tiptoeing, whispering, wringing my hands, begging her to eat, standing silent in her doorway watching her breathe. It felt awful—like the time that had passed between then and now had been a dream, a bittersweet, fairy-tale daydream. I felt eleven, not fourteen.

But this time I wasn't so alone. Andreas and I had numerous hushed conversations, in the kitchen or out on the front porch.

"Why won't she just . . . get up? I can't do this again. I can't handle it."

"Ingrid . . ." Andreas leaned forward. "You must be patient, and you must understand . . . there is a sickness of the soul, a grief, perhaps, over the loss that cannot completely be processed, because she doesn't know how, and maybe doesn't want to. Because to process is to forever give up on it. And I think it is obvious your mother suffers from depression. From what you've told me recently, she's battled this her entire life. And music is what she used to battle it. Now she needs to find something else. And all of this is horribly tangled up and entwined, and it is not so easy to just 'get up' as you say."

"You still love her?" I asked.

"Yes," he said fiercely.

I believed him. In fact, I would almost say he loved her more. This crisis seemed to bring out the best in Andreas, and maybe knowing the whole story also made him feel more connected, more invested, more useful, even. It brought out the best in him, and called on his skill set. He quickly rearranged his schedule so he could work from home while I went to school, hung out in bed with her in the evenings, watching Netflix or coaxing her to talk. He gently harassed her until she ate/showered/sat up, and in the meantime he got on the phone and convinced her doctor to make a house call, which led to getting Mom onto an antidepressant much sooner than the last time this happened.

Still, I was angry, and scared. I wanted to say, *Get up! Nobody did anything to you. You lie to this amazing guy and he still wants to be with you, and then you huddle in the dark like the world is ending. Get. Up.*

I thought it, but I didn't say it. I got myself up instead, and went to school every day, stayed late at the library, and tried to pretend it wasn't happening. Juno did notice something was wrong and asked me about it, but all I told her was that I was fighting with my mom. She could relate to that, since she fought with her parents constantly, mostly about things like her curfew and how much time she spent with Toff, who had become her boyfriend, when they weren't fighting.

"I'll bet you've been setting her expectations too high," Juno said, with a sage nod.

"Huh?"

"You're too well behaved, obviously," she said, and then threw an arm around me. "I'll bet you sit around the dining-room table talking about world events and stuff, and I already know you hardly go out. Here's my new strategy: I am setting the expectations low. I'm never on time, even if I have to wait outside an extra twenty minutes to make sure I'm late. Plus, every time I have Toff over, I make out with him constantly, right in front of them. That way they don't dare come down to the basement when we're watching a movie. They're terrified of walking in on us fooling around. And just generally, I don't talk to them, don't tell them anything or warn them about my plans ahead of time, and I throw a few dramatic crying fits per week, slam my door, shout about them not understanding me—the works."

"How . . . does this make anything better?"

"You have to make them grateful for every crumb! At least that's my theory. And honestly, this is what they expect."

"What?"

She laughed at my confusion. "My mom has read at least eight books about teenage behavior, the teenage psyche, et cetera, and even earmarked sections that I'm guessing she's read to my father. I just had to read those sections to see what she was expecting."

"Oh my God."

"Seriously. They're anticipating problems, and they'll be looking for them even if I act totally civilized. So instead, I'm training them to expect the worst from me, which means when I'm not the worst, they'll be happy. Already, they're so relieved when I act normal that they've stopped interrogating me about every little thing. And if I actually ask them nicely for something? Bam—they're all over it."

"Wow," I said, "that sounds . . . tiring."

"But I'm not going to ask them for much, because I'm saving it for something big," she said. "I'm being like that character in the Shakespeare play we saw on the school trip. Remember the dude that was actually a prince?"

"Oh, you mean Prince Hal from *Henry IV*."

"Yeah, him. He inspired me, the way he was hanging out and drinking and robbing people, and he made that speech—the one we had to study beforehand about how he was basically being a shit so he'd look all the better in comparison, once he reformed."

"'Yet herein will I imitate the sun,'" I said, starting to laugh.

"Yes, exactly! I'm going to imitate the sun coming out from the clouds, and then my parents will be right where I want them."

"I'm not sure that was the lesson we were supposed to take away from the play."

"You should try it."

"Er, my situation is a little different," I said, but she had moved on to talking about Toff, which was just as well. Juno would have tried to help if I'd told her—I knew she would—but talking about my problems wouldn't have solved them, and it was much more fun to let her entertain me, most of the time.

Within a month, Mom was back to normal. Everything Andreas had done had worked, except that she'd refused to go to a therapist.

We packed the opera memorabilia away in storage boxes in the garage, and promised her we wouldn't talk about it.

Still, she seemed to have let him in more, after that. They held hands all the time, she would lean her head on his shoulder, and when she wasn't looking at him, his eyes followed her with adoration, relief, and a tinge of sorrow.

"Someday I will find her a doctor," he said to me. "A specialist who can fix her voice."

"Been there," I said. "Don't bother."

"New technologies and methods are invented all the time," he said. "Even if it didn't bring her voice all the way back to the professional level . . ."

"Andreas, trust me: leave it," I said.

But I wasn't sure he would.

In the midst of her recovery, Andreas once again did the opposite of what I expected, and proposed.

She cried, and said yes.

Two months after that, the three of us went to City Hall, where they got married.

She wore a long Japanese-inspired dress, in black, red, and blue, hair up, as stunning as she had ever been on any stage. He wore a tux. I wore a crazy vintage orange and sky-blue Lilly Pulitzer that I found in her closet, and threw a belt on with it. We took a helicopter to wine country and had a private dinner in the cellar of a famed vineyard.

I had a dad. An extravagant, sweet, determined one.

And obviously a crazy one, if we were what he wanted.

Chapter Seventeen

PIT

(Peak Wilderness, Day Eleven)

I continue as leader on Day Eleven, the second-to-last day of the hiking portion of the trip.

This time I'm not taking any crap or playing any stupid games, on the beach or off, when we get there. I have stepped out of that trap for good. This many days in a damp sleeping bag and wearing clothes so stinky, they're ready to hike on their own, is enough. I am so disgusting, I want to climb out of my skin, and I am getting that dealt with. Today.

Order on the outside will bring order to my insides.

We break camp with precision and get on the trail. As the morning goes on, I realize that I tend to stop crying when I'm hiking because . . . I like it. I might even love it. There's a visceral pleasure in finding my footing over tree roots and flexing my quads and glutes and hamstrings to climb a hill; there's satisfaction in having to fight, relief at having something *to* fight, with each step. And there's a rhythm to the whole thing—heartbeat, steps, breath—that's challenging and soothing at the same time.

And unlike the tangled, humid, bramble-and-bug-filled, oppressive section of the forest we started out in from the original beach, this part is populated by tall, majestic trees, with most of the leaf cover being higher up, so the effect is almost of walking in an outdoor cathedral, multiple dappled shades of light filtering down.

I'm a wreck, but it's beautiful.

And so we march on.

Then, from behind me, comes a loud whisper. "Hey, Ingrid . . . ?"

It's Tavik, who doesn't usually talk on the trail.

"What?"

"Are you really keeping your shitty TP in the bag?"

My jaw drops in surprise, then I glance back to see a look of positively evil glee on his face.

"Are *you*?" I ask him.

"You tell me first. Worst case, you're not and I tell on you and . . . what are they going to do—make you go back and get it?"

"Okay, no," I say quietly. "Wait, lemme rephrase that: no way."

"Me neither. I'm just burying it."

"As your tentmate," I say, "let me be the first to thank you for that."

"Are you always such a rebel?"

"Ha," I say, the question bringing up all kinds of thoughts I then have to shove aside.

"No?"

"No," I say. "More like never."

Dear Mom,

What they didn't say on the map—you know, the one where there was the direct route and the scenic route— what they didn't say, and what is nowhere in evidence on that map?

The mud pit.

The massive, unsurpassable mud pit, maybe a hundred feet long and six feet wide, with two long ropes suspended above it, presumably for use while attempting not to sink into the mud and die.

Oh, and on both sides? Rock wall.

We are taking a short break in order to assess.

Correction: we are taking a short break while I, because I'm so lucky to be the leader today, assess, and decide what to do. Perhaps they think that's what I'm doing here—writing down the brilliant plan that I do not have.

If I end up leading us all to a watery grave, I hope some-one finds this journal and shoves it down Peak Wilderness's collective throat.

Love. Ha.
Ingrid

I put down the journal and stand to look at the mud pit again.

"Is there a way around?" I ask Bonnie.

She shrugs. By this time I know the game all too well, and I want to grab her by those shrugging shoulders and shake the truth out of her.

Peace and Henry, meanwhile, get some sticks and start poking into the mud to check its depth—one of Peace's better ideas, actually.

I move closer to Bonnie and Pat. "Guys, we've been over this. You know whether or not there is a way around, and I know you know. Cough it up."

Nothing.

"Ahem. As today's leader, I am *asking you to please* share whatever information you may have that can help us. I know it's part of the 'thing' to keep us in the dark," I continue, my frustration now barely in check. "I think that's crap. As you know. And I think it's wrong because time after time you're basically tricking us. Like the natural hardships and dealing with all these personalities isn't enough. Trust me, it *is* enough. So. Is there a way to get around this thing?"

"There's no way around," Bonnie blurts out finally, ignoring Pat's sharp look. "Only through."

"Great," I say. "Thank you, Bonnie."

"There's no way around, only through," Pat repeats.

"Oh my God, yes, Pat, I'm making the fridge magnet already," I say, then ask Bonnie, "Is it quicksand?"

"No, just mud," she says.

"Bonnie!" Pat frowns hard at her.

"What?" she says. "She's right; some of this is a bit unreasonable."

"Thank you," I say pointedly to her.

A few minutes later, when I've had a chance to study the terrain (i.e., potentially deadly bog), and after doing my own depth check with a stick, and then asking the group for suggestions, I have a plan.

The mud is at least waist-deep, possibly chest-deep for some, which means we can't wear the backpacks without everything getting (more) soaked and filthy. So, we take our packs off and put them in a tight pile near the "entrance" to the mud.

"Everybody," I say, when the group has gathered around, "hold the rope at all times with at least one hand, whether you think you need to or not. Get to your spot, which hopefully will be reaching distance to the next person. The goal is to be lined up, evenly spaced, from one side to the other, and then to pass the packs along, person to person, to the end. Then we climb out. Sound good?"

"We'll have to let go of the rope to pass the packs," Jin observes with a smirk.

"Good point. Make sure your footing is solid before you let go."

"Why doesn't each person just carry their pack?" Harvey asks.

"Because I don't wish the permanently wet sleeping bag and clothes situation I've been dealing with on any of you, and this would be worse because it's mud. I'm taking my boots off for the same reason," I say, trying to sound confident even though I feel like I might throw up. "Plus I think this way is safer—for balance. Do we need to vote?"

Apparently not. I take my boots off and attach them to the top of the pack, and everyone else does the same.

"I'm also going to suggest . . . everyone tuck your pants into

169

your socks, and your shirts into your pants. Don't leave your skin exposed."

"Why?" Ally asks, though she's already doing it.

I wince in advance of my answer, then Jin saves me the trouble by saying, "Leeches."

"Yeah."

Ally looks like she's going to faint. I don't blame her.

Seth also looks extremely pale as he gazes at the pit.

"Great." I eye the mud with ill-concealed dread. "Since I'm the leader and it's my plan, I guess I'll go first."

The first step in, I'm up to my knees. I'm carrying one of the long sticks, and with it I poke the mud ahead of me, trying not to think of snakes, snapping turtles, deadly algae, live or dead amphibians. I test each step with the stick, then move. Five steps in, the mud is up to my thighs. Midway, having obviously misjudged with the stick, I go down fast, stopping chest-deep. I muffle a shriek, swear, then grip the rope above me with both hands and call out the obvious, "Guys, it gets deep here!"

"Got it," Tavik says. "How's the water?"

"Awesome. Just like a spa," I say, and hear more than one person chuckling. "This is what we paid the big money for."

The mud is rank up close. Revolting.

Forget washing my clothes—I'll just burn them.

I start moving again, slower now, pulling through roots and other unidentified stringy things that graze me at ankles, thighs, and waist. I grit my teeth, and eventually make it to the far side, where I stop, four feet or so from the edge, still thigh-deep in the mud.

"All right," I call across before the next person starts, "the deepest part is in the middle."

"No shit," Peace calls back.

I ignore him. "If you guys can figure it out, you should arrange yourselves by height—so the tallest people end up in the middle section. Yeah?"

Half an hour later we're lined up, more or less evenly spaced across the mud pit, when Seth lets out a high-pitched yelp.

"Something touched me! Something just touched my leg!"

Everyone freezes. Seth moans.

"Get me out of here, get me out of here, help me, God . . . ." He's making terrible sounds in his throat and hyperventilating. Any second he might let go of the rope and bolt, which will be a disaster.

"Seth!" I shout. "Are you hurt?"

"N-no . . ."

"We have to get the packs across, so hang on."

"What if it's a snake? It's probably a snake! Ahhhhhhhh," he cries, "I think I felt it again!"

"It could be a root," says Ally, who looks pretty spooked herself.

"Come on, you wuss!" Peace says.

"It's not a root! I don't want to die out here. Oh God, please get me out of here . . . ."

Suddenly everyone is yelling—some at Peace, some at Seth, some at me, some simply because they're freaked. If this doesn't stop, everyone's going to start stampeding out of the mud, and then we'll have to start all over to get the backpacks.

"Ally!" I holler through the cacophony.

Her head snaps toward me. "Yes?"

"Help him!"

Ally is just ahead of Seth, and now she turns back and reaches one hand out to him. She's talking to him. I can't hear what she's saying, but eventually he stops screaming and takes her hand.

I call out to Henry next, because he can whistle really loud. I motion to him with two fingers in my mouth, he nods, and a couple of seconds later, he whistles. It's loud, and it stops everyone.

"Passing the first pack, now!" I call into the momentary silence.

Bonnie sends the first pack across, and we pass it, one person to the next, all the way to me, and I take two steps out to set it on dry land, before heading back into the mud. We repeat this ten more times, with many breathless, dodgy moments where people start to lose their minds and/or balance. Three times, a pack almost goes in. We are sweating and filthy and wigged out, and I can guarantee that not one person is having a good time.

But it works.

It works!

When the last pack is across, we haul ourselves one by one through the rest of the pit and out the other side. A raucous cheer goes up for Seth when he makes it out and collapses on the path, looking green.

We are staggering, and some people are crying, including me. Seth crawls into the bushes and throws up. Jin starts laughing a hysterical laugh as she rolls around on the ground, pounding on it with her hands. Peace makes roaring sounds and, I'm not kidding, flexes his muscles. Harvey and Henry, in a currently rare moment of brotherliness, start spouting out lines from the Star Wars trash compactor scene.

Melissa, Bonnie, and Pat all begin, very sensibly, to use sticks to slough the mud off their clothing. Melissa has remained quiet over the last few days, and she did through this, too. I can't figure out whether she is just super tough and good at being stoic, or if she's in some kind of post-traumatic comatose state.

Everybody starts trying the stick method of mud removal, but it only goes so far, and before long we're all just trying to get our feet clean enough to put on fresh(ish) socks so we can get in our boots and press on toward camp.

I have a few brief moments of that same rock-star feeling from yesterday—proud of myself for getting us across, amazed that we survived—but it doesn't last. I am soaked through, filthier than I've ever been in my entire life, grossed out, starving, and now completely out of hope that I will ever get myself or my things clean and dry. The goal of Peak Wilderness is obviously to crush us entirely. And to make us hate the people who sent us.

Chapter Eighteen

✦ ❋ ✦

OH, BOY

(Age Fifteen)

It was a regular school day in tenth grade, fall, with dried leaves on the wind, the start of iced breath in the air. Juno and I burst through the front hall doors, arm in arm, flushed from our lunchtime walk, laughing and talking.

And then I saw him across the foyer—a golden-brown-haired boy standing outside Rhea's office. He was in profile, studying what looked like a class schedule, and something about him caused me to stop in my tracks.

It wasn't that he was cute.

It wasn't that he was obviously new.

It was that, as he turned, and as my eyes registered the facts and details of this well-groomed, well-dressed boy, my mind superimposed another vision, that of a gangly, blemished, geeky-looking boy with bad hair and ill-fitting clothes. The glasses were gone, the skin was clear, everything was different almost to the point of unrecognizability . . . but I knew him.

Isaac.

My insides lurched and tumbled.

I was so incredibly happy to see him, and see him looking so well. I had wondered, all this time, what had happened to him. Worried about him. And here he was, looking just fine. Better than fine.

I was astonished to find him standing there in the foyer of my school all of a sudden, and floored by his transformation. And at the same time that I was trying to process his presence, the physical fact of him brought everything back, and there I was, drowning in a flood of unwelcome memory, feeling again the isolation, the misery of being locked in that closet every single lunch hour, the embarrassment of being forced to kiss in front of a jeering crowd, and the horror of seeing Isaac go down, blood on his face.

And so maybe that's what Isaac saw, when his eyes met mine—not the happiness I felt at seeing him, but my sudden and sharp reaction to those memories.

Because he'd started to smile, the same smile I'd felt coming when I realized who he was, big and warm and delighted, and then he stopped. His expression changed, darkened. I'd recovered by then and was walking toward him, smiling back, arms open for a hug, even, but he turned abruptly away, headed up the stairs, and disappeared.

I stood there, reeling, feeling like I'd been punched in the stomach.

After that, I didn't know what to do. Every time I came anywhere near Isaac, he turned away, pretended I didn't exist. When we were introduced by his "official buddy," who happened to be Toff, he wouldn't meet my eyes. It shouldn't have mattered so much, shouldn't have hurt me, but it did.

The awkwardness became mutual, and I decided to try his method and just forget about him, pretend he didn't exist. He obviously didn't want to be my friend, or even talk to me. Fine. But I obsessed. I got it that he'd seen a funny expression on my face, maybe. But his reaction seemed over-the-top, and I couldn't even get near him to explain, and anyway I would need to be near him *and* alone with him, which seemed doubly impossible.

Finally I couldn't take it anymore. One day I heard him say he was staying late to meet with the algebra teacher. I told Juno to leave without me, parked myself in front of his locker, and sat with a book, pretending to read. Half an hour later the school was quiet enough that I heard his footsteps before he came around the corner, heard his sharp intake of breath when he saw me.

I waited until he was right in front of me to look up.

"Ingrid. What are you doing?"

"Sitting in front of your locker, looking at a book, Isaac."

"Yes," he said, his voice careful. "That's evident."

"Evident. Nice word. Wanna sit?" I patted the creaky wood-planked floor beside me.

"No, thanks, I'm good."

"C'mon, Isaac," I said, getting to my feet. "Are you just never going to talk to me?"

"I have no idea what you mean."

"Don't be obtuse."

"Nice word," he said, and then did a shoulder check. "I don't want to talk here, Ingrid."

"Okay, then where?"

"I don't really want to talk at all."

"Look, either you talk with me, or I'm going to keep showing up at your locker."

"That's going to give people the wrong idea, don't you think?"

"I don't care."

"Oh, sure you don't," he snapped.

"What?"

"Can I get in there, please?"

I moved aside, watched him with narrowed eyes as he shoved stuff into his messenger bag and grabbed his coat, put it on, closed and locked the locker.

He started down the hallway and I followed.

"What was that supposed to mean," I said, "that I would care if people got 'the wrong idea,' whatever that is?"

"You care," he said, not looking at me.

I kept pace with him down the main stairs and into the lobby, where a few students were still loitering. I could tell he wanted to ditch me but there were a few people still around and he couldn't do it without making a scene. He headed to the front doors and I leapt ahead, pushing them open for him.

"We can talk there," I said, pointing across the street to a large field surrounded by a running track.

Isaac glanced at me, then frowned. "You don't have a coat."

"Sweet of you to consider my comfort," I said with an edge of sarcasm.

"It's just a logical fact. No coat equals you will be cold."

"I'm fine. I'll go back for it later."

We crossed at the light and headed through the gap in the fence.

"All right," Isaac said, starting to walk counterclockwise on the track. "You wanted to talk, talk."

"I just want to know what . . . I mean first, honestly I want to know how you *are* and what happened to you, because we went through something and it feels weird not to talk about it. Not to mention that you refuse to talk to me at all, or even acknowledge my existence."

I stopped, turned to face him, but he looked down at his feet, over my shoulder, anywhere but at my face.

"See? You won't even look at me. You seem to have this problem with me and it doesn't make any sense."

"It's you who has the problem." His angry eyes suddenly, finally, locked on mine. "You've become one of them."

"One of . . . ? What? I have not."

"You have. You're one of them—"

"Oh, is that so?" I cut in. "You see me calling people names, then, and locking them in closets and humiliating them and beating them up? Really?"

"No, but you've become a popular person," he said, with a sneer that didn't suit him.

"I do have friends, if that's what you mean."

"Yeah, and you can't be hanging around with a guy like me."

"That makes no sense. That's absurd."

"Okay, a guy like the old me. Who is still me, in fact."

"So . . . you think if you still were . . . what—looking like how you did when you were twelve, I would arbitrarily decide not to be your friend? That's a ridiculous conclusion, Isaac, based on zero evidence."

"I have all the evidence I need!" He was almost shouting. "I saw the evidence, Ingrid, and you can say what you want and you can lie your ass off now, but I saw it in your eyes my very first day here. I saw you standing there with your giggling friend and I saw the look in your eyes when you realized who I was."

"Isaac, I was happy to see you."

"You weren't!"

"I was. But I—"

"*I saw it!* In your eyes—like I was a ghost, or some unwelcome relative who showed up to take a dump in the middle of your new life." He turned away, started walking so fast around the track, I had to jog to keep up with him. "After all the time I spent remembering you as this brave, ass-kicking girl, and meanwhile all you did was *hide*; all you did was *assimilate*."

I grabbed his arm, forcing him to stop again, and got in front of him.

"Listen," I said, right up in his face, "having friends is not a crime. Having a chance to be a normal teenager is not a crime. And the friends I have now are nothing like the people who did that to us, and you've been at Godark long enough by now to know it."

"But you haven't told them—"

"Told them what?"

"That you were . . . that you were like me."

"You know nothing about what I've told them or not told

179

them, Isaac. And you know nothing about what you saw in my eyes, either."

"So you have told them?"

"It's not like it's a disease, Isaac. Or something to be ashamed of. They were assholes. Bullies. They're the ones you should be mad at, not me."

He gaped at me, and I continued.

"You expected me to be some kind of banner-waving advocate, is that it? I don't see you telling everyone all of those sad details either. You don't want to bring that along with you any more than I did. You want a chance for people to look at you as something other than a victim. You want to be able to look at yourself as something other too. You say I'm hiding? You've had a full body *makeover*, and don't think I don't know you're enjoying every second of being the cute new boy at Godark. I don't see you refusing to 'assimilate' as you call it, or refusing to make friends, so what the hell is your problem with me?"

"I—"

"You want to know what I was thinking, what I felt when I saw you? Yeah, you saw something there. Because just in case you've forgotten, we had an awful time, and seeing you brought it back all at once. So excuse me if it took me a millisecond to start jumping for joy, Isaac."

"Okay, okay."

"No, not okay. You want me to tell everyone? I can tell them. I happen to believe they're real friends and nobody would turn on me, or you. Personally, I don't feel the need to dwell on or share every terrible thing that's ever happened to me, but if you want me to, I will."

He kept his eyes trained on some point in the distance.

"C'mon, just say the word."

Isaac's eyes met mine then, and held for a long moment. "You mean it," he said, finally.

"Duh."

"It's . . . okay. I mean, you don't have to."

"You mean *you don't want me to*."

"No, go ahead."

"All right, I will," I said, and started to walk away.

"Okay, I don't want you to," he said, and I stopped, turned back to look at him.

"Well, maybe now *I* want to."

"I . . . whatever. Do what you want. Just . . . warn me first, if you don't mind."

"Fine."

"Great. Fine," he said.

My fury started to fade, and suddenly I noticed the wind, felt the cold on my arms, and crossed them over my chest. He looked shell-shocked. He was more fragile than I'd realized, more damaged, maybe, from his experience than I had been from mine. He'd had it worse, and for longer, certainly. I should have been gentler, but I was angry about how he'd treated me, frustrated at how he'd jumped to the worst conclusions about me, and confused by the ache I felt as he held my gaze.

"Next time, Isaac? Before you make assumptions about me based on something you think you see in my eyes?"

"Yes?"

"Why don't you save us the drama and just ask me?"

And with that, I turned and walked away.

Chapter Nineteen

PEACE

(Peak Wilderness, Day Eleven, Continued)

The moon is out (again) when we stagger into the campsite. It isn't quite dark, but it certainly will be by the time dinner is being made.

I don't wait for anyone to give me a job to do. I don't even worry about getting the tent up. I set my backpack on a rock near the shore, take my boots and socks off, dig out my bar of soap, and walk into the water fully clothed.

Most of the group follows suit, with the exception of Peace, who strips down first, and runs back and forth in the sand, giving the rest of us a prolonged (should we desire) view of his genitals bouncing in the glowing pink last light of day.

At least he's going to bathe.

It's a long beach, and we each find our own spaces in the water to shimmy out of our clothing and try to rub the mud off. Once my pants, shirt, and socks are done, I dash out of the water in my underwear and bra (another thing my mom would freak over, but how can I even care?). I wring the clean-ish clothes out and put them on the rock next to my pack, then go back into the water.

It's cold—really cold—but I want desperately to be alone, and the cold feels so good on my sore feet, on the hundreds of bug bites, on my sore muscles. I kick back and forth in a futile effort to warm up, then pull my bra and panties off, looping them over one arm so I don't lose them before I can get them washed.

Before long it's just me, my dwindling bar of soap, the reflection of the rising moon left in the water, and my miserable, angry heart beating against the cold.

I am too tired to cry.

I am so tired of everything, *about* everything, that I can imagine allowing the cold to take over, letting myself sink under the surface, and staying there, releasing my hold on the world and everything in it. I'm so tired, I'm not even shocked by the thought.

Then I hear splashing and turn to see Peace coming back into the lake.

I sink farther down into the water, hoping he somehow doesn't know I'm here, and/or will get the hint that I don't want company.

But no.

He comes right over to me.

And there I am, horribly aware, suddenly, that I am naked under the water, and *not* too tired to care about that.

"Hey, fearless leader," he says, giving me a splash.

"Hey, Bob," I say, with a deliberate lack of enthusiasm.

"Peace."

"Right. Um, no, thanks."

"No thanks for what?"

Another splash.

"For the splashing game invitation."

"What's the matter, afraid to drop your soap?" he says, with a yucky waggle of his eyebrows.

"I'm just trying to enjoy the peace, Peace."

"Yeah, me too."

"Alone, if you don't mind." I drift sideways.

He follows. "Free country."

"What, are you five?"

"Hey, hey, it's all love, baby. All love."

"Riiiight."

"You don't like me," he says.

"I don't know you," I reply. I've hunched as far down in the water as I can, and now I have to step backward into deeper water to keep him out of my space.

"But you don't like me. Admit it."

"Why do you care if I like you?"

"I don't."

"Then why are you asking?"

"I just want you to admit it."

"Look, sometimes people don't hit it off. It's normal." I inch backward again.

He follows again, towering over me now—his height and the fact that he doesn't care that he's naked and I do care that I am are both to his advantage. Because clearly he knows, and knows I know he knows, and he's enjoying my extreme discomfort.

Since backing away isn't working, I plant my feet on the lake bottom and cross my arms over my chest.

"I think, Peace, we should just agree to disagree."

"Yeah? About what?"

"Everything."

"I dunno . . . Maybe we should talk about it." His hands come down on my shoulders, and he starts massaging. "Maybe I can help. You seem very tense around me."

"I don't need your help. And I don't want a massage. Take your hands off me."

"Come on," he says, hands gripping me harder, and bending down into the water so we're face-to-face. "I think I know what this is about. It's tension."

"Let go of me," I say in a more assertive voice.

He pulls me closer.

"Sexual tension."

"Eww."

"I knew it."

"Let. Go. Of. Me. *Now*."

I struggle backward, but suddenly there's no sand under my feet.

He still has me, and he's stronger than I am, stronger than I expected. And he's managed to get me in a position where he can still touch the bottom and I can't.

"I know how to take care of that kind of tension," he continues, putrid breath in my face. "We're far enough out we could take care of it right here, right now."

I start kicking hard—not at him, but to get away.

But he just laughs and yanks me right up against him so I can experience his disgusting hairiness and be revolted by his erection.

"I don't think so," I snarl, but I'm scared. And worse, I can see by the satisfaction flaring in the depths of his eyes that he likes it.

Now I kick him, but it's hard to kick underwater and have any effect, and it lands with a whimper.

He grins like a maniac and dunks me, holding me underwater for a few long, terrifying moments, as I try not to panic, not to waste energy struggling, and it becomes very clear to me that this is not how I want to die.

Peace yanks me back up and, while I'm sputtering and gasping, makes a grab for my butt.

"I could fuck you and drown you at the same time," he says. "That would solve all my problems."

Chapter Twenty

LOCAL ORGANIC AUTUMN
(Age Fifteen)

My conversation with Isaac cleared the air between us, somewhat. He stopped avoiding me, I stopped obsessing about his avoiding me, and I made a (possibly exaggerated) point of saying hello to him, particularly when I was with my friends, to show him I really wasn't "one of them" as he put it. Everything was friendly.

Friendly-ish.

There was still something awkward between us, though. He would catch me looking at him in class, usually when he'd said something particularly smart, which was often, and I would turn away, my face feeling hot. Or I would notice him hovering at lunchtime or recess, acting like he wanted to talk to me, but then he'd wander off once he noticed me noticing.

I was curious and disturbed by him, and filled with a kind of . . . expectancy.

And then he fell into the clutches of Autumn Robarts.

Became friends with her, I mean.

Autumn was perfectly nice . . . in a perky, overly positive, possibly secretly evil sort of way. It was just that she always had to be the person to point out that your jeans were probably made by a child laborer, or that the cheese in your lunch wasn't real cheese. Whatever you had, or thought, or did, she had/thought/did it better/cleaner/more ethically/ecologically. She gave up coffee and sugar and wheat and dairy and nightshades (what?) and television and her phone and found it *transformative*.

"I'm so much more *present*," she said.

Was I the only person who considered this a bad thing?

But we were a tolerant school, and if someone wanted to spend their spare time in conspicuous meditation and/or proselytizing, fine. Some people even joined her.

It galled me to see Isaac hanging out with her. They were in music together (a subject I did not take, due to the not-subtle discouragement of Mom, even though it would have been an easy A for me), and I noticed him helping with her campaign to get rid of the school vending machines—a campaign Juno was campaigning against. In fact, suddenly Isaac seemed involved in everything—band, rugby, basketball, fund-raising, track-and-field, good cause X.

"You've become quite the joiner," I said in early November when I saw him putting up posters outside the theater. This came out a little more acidic than I'd meant it to, and his eyes narrowed.

"Why not?" he said. "College applications aren't far off. And it's a good way to make friends."

"Plus you'll be saving the world," I said, unable to

help myself. "You know, with your friend Autumn."

"You don't like her."

"I never said that."

"Then why are you being such a bitch all of a sudden?"

"Why are you still not talking to me?" To my surprise, this came out almost a wail, which was embarrassing.

"I'm talking to you right now."

"I know, but it's still . . . it's not . . ."

"Look, Ingrid . . ." He stood in front of me, flustered now and gripping the stack of posters tightly in both hands. "It's . . . I don't know. I recognize it's still weird. But . . . it's not like we have to be friends. Maybe that's the problem—we're both working on the illogical hypothesis that we should be. But we weren't friends before."

"We didn't have a chance to be friends."

"We wouldn't have been, though. If you'd stayed. You'd eventually have risen to a higher social circle, and we wouldn't have been friends."

"Okay, you have to forget about that. Neither of us has any idea what would have happened. It's done. But . . . just come with me." I gestured to the posters. "Put those down and come with me."

"What? You want to drag me over to the track and argue again? It's cold out."

"No, I just . . . want to talk to you. Don't you feel like . . ." I looked up and down the hall to make sure we were alone, and then felt awkward because he'd seen me doing it.

"Like what?" he said, and took a half step closer, then took the same step back again.

"I just have this . . . I keep having this sense that you and I, that we *know* each other." I paused, waiting for him to say that we did or that we didn't, but he was just watching me, waiting, so I barreled ahead. "I realize we don't, actually, but I feel like one of these days we're going to start talking and . . . it'll be crazy because we won't be able to stop. We have things to say, both of us, and I think we can say them to each other."

"Don't you have Juno for that?"

"Yes, but . . . no. Juno's awesome. Very fun, very loyal, and she's hilarious, but . . ."

"Nothing bad has ever happened to her?" Isaac said. "That's how she seems to me. Not that there's anything wrong with that."

"That you just said that is exactly what I'm talking about. You get it. We're meant to be friends, Isaac. Like, we already *are* friends, but just haven't . . ."

"Activated our friendship program?" he finished for me, a funny smile tugging at the corners of his mouth.

"Yes!"

"You're a weirdo, you know that?"

"Why?"

"You go from shy to persistent to bitchy back to shy, and now you're this tornado of intensity."

"So . . . what are you saying? You don't feel it?"

"I'm saying you confuse me. Yes, I have a similar feeling of knowing and yet not knowing you and being . . . curious about you. But we might find each other boring and stupid and nothing alike. What happens then?"

I shrug. "Well, I know you're not stupid at least. And neither am I, so we've got that part secure."

"You're very all-or-nothing, Ingrid."

"I just want to be your friend, Isaac. No big deal." It was a big deal, though. "I'm sorry if I'm being a freak."

"Well, why don't we start by doing something normal?" he said, and held out the posters. Autumn had made them, to advertise auditions for *The Wizard of Oz*. "You can help me put these up."

"All right," I said, taking them.

"Awesome," he said, and handed me a roll of tape. "Just give me a poster, then hand me pieces of tape. Easy."

We focused on the task for a few minutes before I asked him what he'd been up to the past couple of years.

He checked to see if anyone was around before answering, and then did so in a low voice. "I stuck out another year at school. Then things got a little worse. My parents—they're professors and . . . idealists."

"What, like, professionally?"

"Ha-ha. Professional Idealist." His eyes brightened for a moment, but then he turned serious again. "But really, idealist in the sense that they wanted me to hold my head up and be proud to be different, and somehow, you know, overcome all that stuff with the force of my intellect, and differentness."

"Yeah, that always works," I said, rolling my eyes.

"They meant well. They tried. Put me in Tae Kwon Do, bought me all kinds of biographies of brilliant people who'd been through the same thing and survived and gone on to win Nobel Peace Prizes. And I got lots of free

191

lectures about individualism, Darwin, social constructs, the hormones of the teenage human brain."

"Oh my God."

"They wouldn't let me leave, though. Until finally . . . well, let's just say they clued in. The school wasn't going to help; nothing helped. So they let me homeschool for a few months, and then my aunt offered to take me traveling with her. She works for the Red Cross, and goes to South America and Asia to train people. I got to go with her. Kept up with school via computer, which is what I was doing anyway. Did that for a couple of years, and then came home, got in here, that's it."

"How did you like traveling?"

"Loved it. Whatever I do with my life, travel has to be part of it."

"Me too. I spent most of my childhood living all over Europe with my mom."

"Really?"

"Really. So . . . are you happy? I mean, is it hard to stay in one place, after all that? Do you miss it?"

"Did you?" he asked.

"It was a long time ago," I said, looking at the floor, then back up at him. "I was . . . pretty preoccupied with our new life and didn't think about it at first, but yes. I missed it. I still do."

"I miss it," he said, holding his hand out for tape, reminding me that we actually had a job to finish. "But, uh, my parents thought I needed what they call 'normal teenage social interaction.'"

"Oh, that!"

"Yeah, that. Not sure where 'normal' comes in, though, or whether I'll even know it when I see it."

"You could just go for 'not horrible' and consider it done," I said.

"Aim low?"

"No, I mean—"

"You mean in the context of my previous experience."

"And mine."

"Speaking of social interactions," he said, "am I living up to your big expectations? Do I have enough to say? Am I brilliant and funny and your soul mate already?"

I started to laugh, and he laughed too, and before I knew it, the posters were up and we were finished.

"You cut my time in half, I bet," he said.

"You're welcome," I said.

We were back where we started, in front of the theater doors.

"So . . ." he said, shoving his hands into his front pockets. "You going to audition?"

"Not my thing. And anyway, as my mother would say, it's not practical."

"Not practical?" He gave me a skeptical look. "In what sense?"

"You know, for life."

"This isn't life; it's the school play," he said. "It's for fun."

"What's for fun?" Autumn's high, bubbly voice announced her arrival as she rounded the corner and turned her big blue saucer eyes on Isaac.

"This," Isaac said, pointing at the poster.

"Oh, we have so much talent in this school," Autumn

said. "We're going to have a *real* orchestra so the music will be *live*. Isn't that wild?"

A real orchestra didn't exactly seem wild to me, but I refrained from saying so.

"You both going to play?" I asked. Isaac played trumpet and guitar, and Autumn played oboe.

"Probably," Isaac said.

"Actually . . ." Autumn said, "a little bird told me I have a good chance at being Doro—ahem—in the cast. And didn't you say you wanted to stage-manage, Isaac? Since you already have music on your résumé?"

"I've got to go," I said, irritated that she'd horned in on my time with Isaac, and even more irritated at how she was making plans on his behalf.

"Ingrid," Isaac said with a pointed look, "they need singers."

"Oh," Autumn said, wincing. "You wouldn't know this, being new, but poor Ingrid is . . . not musical, Isaac."

"Really?" he said, with a quizzical glance.

The thing is, to prevent people from asking me to join choirs, et cetera, I always mumbled my way through any necessary singing at school, and gave the general impression of being a musical dunce.

"Plus you have to be able to act," Autumn continued, with a smile so sweetly pitying, I wanted to smack her. "But we'll need help with props and costumes and painting the set if you want to get involved."

It was suddenly obvious that she did *not* want me to get involved.

"Maybe I could audition just for kicks," I found myself

saying. "Not all the parts are singing parts, right?"

"Yes, but everyone sings as part of the ensemble!" She moved close to Isaac. "Everyone has to sing at the audition!"

"So? I'm not allowed to try?"

Isaac, all this time, said nothing. He just leaned against the wall, eyes sliding from one of us to the other.

"It's not for kicks, Ingrid!" Autumn was really getting into a lather. "It's serious! You can't just audition like it's a joke. You can't—"

"Oh, I can't audition according to you? I can do whatever I want, Autumn."

And that is how I found myself signing up to audition for *The Wizard of Oz*.

Remorse set in immediately.

I would die of a combination of mortification and stage fright at the audition, if not before. I would suck. Or I wouldn't suck, and I would land a part and then my mom would kill me. Or go to bed for the next five years.

I hadn't told her about it yet.

Meanwhile, Autumn could be heard practicing "Over the Rainbow," complete with the extra intro that she told us with great self-importance is *not* in the movie, but *is* in the play. She practiced in the hallways between classes and every recess and lunch hour. She'd started wearing her curly blonde ringlets in freaking *braids*. These actions, combined with her false modesty about whether she'd get the part (resulting in people reassuring her that she was awesome and would totally get the part, even though her voice was mediocre at best) made her more annoying than ever before.

"Good news," she told me the day before the auditions. "I just heard there's another non-singing part available—there's the Wicked Witch, of course, but you're a bit short for it, and it's a major acting challenge. But Rhea's changed her mind about bringing a real dog onstage. They're going to cast a student as Toto! So . . ." She sidled up close and whispered, "You could be my dog!"

"No, Autumn," I said, seething. "In no way could I be your dog."

"Listen, it's not too late to change your mind," she said, fake sympathy all over her face.

Oh yes, it was.

Beyond a couple of low-volume run-throughs in the shower, I did not practice.

Call it denial, call it pure terror, but I basically pretended it wasn't happening.

And yet the day came and there I was, sitting outside the theater with everyone else. The worst thing, besides the gut-gripping fear, the sweating, and the racing heart, was that the theater's acoustics were excellent and the place was not sound-proof, even with the doors closed. This meant everyone waiting outside to audition could hear everyone inside when they went to sing.

Awful.

Juno had decided to audition too, so I had her for company, but still I nearly bolted. Fortunately, Autumn's presence (conspicuous vocal warm-ups, pretending unsuccessfully not to listen and judge every audition) helped to anchor me to the spot while I waited for my turn.

It took forever and still came too quickly.

Godark had kept the larger of the two theaters that were in the old church when the school took over the building, and it was constantly in use for various school activities. The theater was a faded beauty, with about two hundred rubbed-thin velvet seats, a balcony held up by Corinthian columns painted deep blue with gold leaf, real lights, and a thrust stage.

Inside, it was lit up as if for performance. To one side was a piano with Mr. Krauss—the music teacher—sitting behind it, and on the other was Isaac in a chair with his stage manager's clipboard. Halfway back, in the audience, was a table with muted red lights, where Rhea sat.

"Miss Burke," Rhea said, her voice booming out of the semidarkness as I reached center stage, "I'm pleased to see you auditioning."

I heard her shuffling papers, and squinted, trying to see her.

"You did not specify a role," she said. "Is there anything particular you're interested in?"

"Well, this isn't the kind of thing I usually do. I just signed up because . . ." I glanced at Isaac, and then quickly away. "Um. Because I thought it might be . . ." *Fun* would be the wrong word, I realized just in time. Rhea's vibe was dead serious.

"Yes . . . ?"

197

"Actually, I love the story. There's something about it. . . . The movie is iconic, of course. But also there's *Wicked*, which I saw years ago, and I've read the original books a bunch of times. There are so many big themes—learning that you carry what you need within yourself, learning to be careful what you wish for, embracing where you come from, friendship, good and evil . . ."

I'd gone from unable to speak to unable to stop.

"Anyway, if there's something I'm right for and you want to cast me, great. I'm short, but I might make a good witch, or . . . whatever part. Except . . ."

"Except . . . ?"

Autumn's dog. Please God.

"Nothing. Any part."

"And do you sing?"

"I . . ." I glanced at Isaac, thought of Mom, then shrugged. "I can sing a bit."

Surely I could sing well enough for a chorus part. It was just the high-school play.

"Fine, we'll try a few things," Rhea said, then came forward to the foot of the stage and handed me a couple of scenes. "You'll read with Isaac."

I read for various parts—Glinda, the Wicked Witch of the West, the Scarecrow, and Dorothy. I hadn't worried much about the acting part, but it was flustering and weird, and I only settled down by focusing on Isaac, who, thank God, was a good reader.

"Very nice," Rhea said when we were finished. "Now, did you prepare a song?"

Not exactly.

"Which, um, which one do you want?" I said. "I kind of know them all. I think."

Mr. Krauss put his hands to the keys and played the opening notes to the intro of "Over the Rainbow."

Oh crap.

I stepped forward, clasped my hands in front of me, unclasped them, stepped back. Realized if I'd had sheet music at least I'd have something to do with my hands. Realized maybe I looked unprepared not to have it. But the opening notes were coming to an end, and I needed to take a breath because there was no turning back now. . . .

What was I thinking, signing up for this?

Somehow I was singing. It was a miracle I'd even managed to open my mouth. Damn, it had a big range, this song, and here came the first high note, the one we kept hearing from the hallway in all the auditions, coming out flat and/or screechy: the wince note. I would be no better, probably worse. . . .

But no, I wasn't flat or screechy. I'd had a shaky start, but I'd hit that note no problem, and no way was I going to screw this up with Autumn outside the door, listening.

When it was done, I stood there blinking, pulling myself atom by atom back into the present. I had gone to Oz, and it took some time to return. People were talking and I was answering on autopilot . . . and then it was done, and Isaac was escorting me, flashlight in hand, off the stage, up the aisle, and to the door. There, he paused.

"Why are you giving me such a funny look?" I whispered.

"I'm just happy you auditioned. If that's making me give you a funny look, so be it. Get ready for more funny looks."

"Why?" I said, panic starting to rise in my throat. It had felt so good, but that didn't mean it *was* good.

"Ingrid," he said, shaking his head. "You just blew the roof off."

"I did? Like, in a good way?"

"Seriously? Yes. Now go—I have a job to do."

And with that, before I really had a chance to register his words, he pulled the door open and ushered me out into the bright light of the hallway.

Juno started cheering and clapping when she saw me, and other people did too.

Not Autumn, though. She was staring daggers at me and was quite pale—so pale that I actually felt sorry for her. I gave her an encouraging smile, and said, "Break a leg, Autumn."

I am such a bitch, I thought. *But I'm a bitch who can sing.*

When the cast list went up, my name was on it. I was playing Dorothy.

The news hit me like hundreds of tiny explosions going off up and down my spine. How had I gone all these years without knowing how much I wanted this?

Only a high-school play, as I kept telling myself, but still . . .

I hadn't told Mom yet.

Andreas had been away coaching some executive in Ireland, and I'd been hoping to have him there if/when it became necessary to tell Mom about the play. But finally it was giving me too much anxiety, and so one morning I decided to tell her over breakfast.

"Mom?" I cleared my throat. "I'm . . . trying to add some extracurricular activities so I look more . . . well-rounded on my university applications."

"Smart idea. What is it—debating? Soccer?"

"No, I thought I'd . . . That is, someone suggested I try out for this little . . . play."

"Try out?" Her eyebrows climbed up her forehead.

"Audition."

"I'm aware of the meaning. You are auditioning for a play?"

"Y-yes," I said, making the lightning-fast decision to save the part about how I'd *already* auditioned and landed a role, *the* role, for another conversation.

"Why is it little?"

"Huh?"

"You said a 'little' play. What is little about this play?" she said, her diction becoming crisp as her attention fastened on to the subject. "Because it's a bad play? Or an insignificant one?"

"Nooo . . . it's not a bad play. Not insignificant, either. It's just the school play, Mom," I said, then stood up and started clearing the breakfast dishes. "Anyway, it would mean staying late for rehearsals . . . for a few weeks. But I won't get behind on homework or anything, and it would look good on my résumé."

She gazed fixedly at me and tapped one long nail on the tabletop.

"What play is it?" Her tone was light, conversational.

I mumbled the answer, "Wizardofoz," while making a bee-line for my coat and shoving my feet into my boots.

I don't know quite what I expected when I finally met her gaze, but what I found there was sympathy.

"Oh dear, you think you can play Dorothy."

"You don't think I can?"

"Ingrid . . . we've been over this. You are not a singer and that is not the life for you. You deserve stability. Respect. Something where you can't be thrown away like yesterday's trash. I don't want you to be disappointed if you are not cast, or they give you one of the smaller parts. There *are* small parts."

"You don't mind if I audition, though?" I said, grabbing on to the small window of opportunity I could see open. "Just to give it a shot?"

"If you must," Mom said with a sorrowful gaze. "I'll be here for you."

"Oh, Mom, thanks," I said, and then we stood and hugged in the entryway while, in my head, I began to re-create my timeline for auditioning and landing the part . . . that I was starting rehearsal for that night.

If only I'd had a time machine, it wouldn't have been lying at all.

A week later I burst into the house, on a high from a great rehearsal, and told her.

"I got a part!" I said, trying to recapture and re-create the crazed and amazed feeling I'd had when I first found out. "*The* part. Dorothy!"

"Oh!" She'd been so sweet and solicitous over the past few days, I was convinced she'd be happy for me. "Sweetheart. Ingrid. Well, that's . . . Well, isn't that . . ."

"Great?"

"Yes. Great. Congratulations, darling. That's wonderful," she said, then hugged me and kissed me on both cheeks. "Magnificent!"

It was exactly what I'd wanted her to say.

So I should have felt fantastic.

Except she looked like I'd just dropped a house on her.

Chapter Twenty-One

COURAGE

(Peak Wilderness, Day Eleven, Evening)

Peace lets go as soon as I start yelling.

I kick backward then sideways so I don't have to pass too close to him on my way to shore, where I can see Bonnie and a couple of others gathering.

He turns, follows me with his beady, creepster eyes, then starts laughing.

"Hey, I'm just kidding around," he calls out between chuckles. "Don't be such a pussy."

"Get away from me!" I shout back at him. "Don't talk to me, don't touch me, don't even think about me!"

"Ingrid?" It's Pat at the shore, Bonnie beside him. "Everything all right?"

"I will get you when you're sleeping and castrate you!" I continue.

I'm in the shallow water now, crouched down because of course I've lost my underwear and bra (and soap) in the tussle and now after everything, that bastard is going to see me naked, too, though, in the balance of things, this is the least of my worries.

"No, everything's not all right," I say, making the decision to stand up and walk over to them, all the while fighting the urge to try to cover myself. "Bob here thought he'd have some fun trying to threaten, harass, and assault me."

Bonnie pulls her jacket off and covers me with it.

"Oh, come on, I told you I was joking," Peace says, coming out of the water after me.

"Was that when you were holding me underwater, or when you were groping me? Which part was the joking part, Peace?"

Bonnie gasps, and Pat sucks in a breath. The rest of the group, almost all here now, gathers closer.

"Oh, that part? That was the part where I was trying to help you because you were having trouble swimming," he says with an exaggerated scoff. "And this is the thanks I get."

"Help me? 'I could fuck you and drown you at the same time'—I believe that's what you said, right after you held me forcibly underwater."

Ally hands me a towel, which I happily wrap around myself, under Bonnie's jacket. Then, shivering, I head to the fire.

"You lie," Peace says, hot on my heels.

Pat holds his hands up. "Okay—obviously we have a problem here. Two versions of the same story and two very upset people. As a group we're going to sit down and talk this out. But first, I'm going to suggest each of you goes your separate ways and gets dressed."

I can see my body shaking, but I feel hot, not cold. And there's a roaring in my ears—a roaring that's almost a screaming, because it can't be possible that I'm going to have to defend myself in a nightmare battle of he said/she said over this.

When everything happened in the dark . . .

And underwater . . .

Out in the lake where no one heard us or saw us.

Which was exactly how he planned it.

"Wait!" someone calls out, the female voice cracking slightly. "I have something to say."

It's Melissa, with Jin next to her, holding her hand.

When everyone's attention is on her, though, she seems to shrink.

"After what I went through . . . it's hard for me to . . ." Her eyes flick fearfully up, then back down. "I get so scared. But I have to . . . It's even more important for me to . . ."

"Do it," Jin says, squeezing her hand. "It's okay."

"I heard him say that," Melissa says, looking to Bonnie and Pat. "About . . . how he could f-fuck her and d-d-drown her at the same time. I heard the whole . . . I was out on the rock just, you know, thinking. The sound . . . their voices carried. It wasn't just that one comment. I heard her asking him to leave her alone a bunch of times and then asking him to let her go, and splashing, and the thing about the drowning. . . . I was about to come get someone when Ingrid screamed. She's telling the truth."

Dead silence.

In my peripheral vision I see Pat moving quietly back and around to stand behind Peace, and then Tavik closing in on the other side of him. Peace twigs to it and twists around, glaring at them, like he's daring them to jump him. Which they will, obviously. Tavik looks deadly, and Pat's eyes are filled with steely determination. Bonnie is suddenly running, heading to her tent and zooming inside.

Peace snarls and looks like he might lunge at someone, but can't decide if it'll be me, or Melissa, or Pat and Tavik. Ally moves close to me, as do Harvey and Henry and Seth. Jin steps forward, glaring at Peace.

"This is bullshit," Peace says finally. "I'm out of here."

He wheels away like he's going to set off into the forest in the dark.

I almost hope he will, except then we'd have to worry about him being out there where we can't see him.

He doesn't get far, though. Pat, surprisingly fast and strong, grabs him around the chest, and in about five seconds, Tavik is on him too, and they've taken him down and are holding him in a wrestling lock. He swears and yowls like an animal, and kicks and punches, one hit landing on Tavik's shoulder. Tavik retaliates, hard and fast, kneeing him in the stomach and then getting him in a stranglehold until Pat's shouts penetrate his fury, and he stops, shifting to another hold Peace can't escape from.

Peace has stopped struggling, but continues with verbal abuse and demands that they release him from their "capitalist bullshit."

"Relax, Peace," Bonnie says, striding up, a cell phone in her hand. "You're about to get your wish."

Forty-five minutes later I'm grateful to be dressed in my wilted, stinking clothes and standing on the beach. Duncan, with the aid of massive spotlights on his end, and flares on ours, is pulling the ferry into the cove.

"That was fast," I say to Bonnie, who's standing next to me.

"We have measures in place," she replies.

"For emergencies of the nonemotional variety?"

"Uh-huh," she says. "For the emotional ones, well, *we* are supposed to be the measures. This is different. I'm so sorry. Are you all right?"

"I'm fine." As much as I ever am, anyway. "What'll happen to Peace?"

"We'll be writing up an in-depth report and he won't be getting his money back. Also . . . you could press charges against him. You should. You don't have to decide on that now, though."

"I'll have to think about it."

"Listen . . . I know you never wanted to be here . . . ."

"True."

She hauls in a breath like she's bracing herself for something, and then says, "You could go."

"What?"

"Leave. On this ferry. I . . . have some idea that you've been through some rough times lately. Up to you whether you ever want to talk about it or not . . ."

"Not," I say.

"But my point is, I don't feel good about your lack of emotional preparation for this trip. About your being misled about what you were getting into. It's hard enough without being blindsided. And it sounds like a lot for your mother to have asked of you, and a lot for you to handle, considering."

"You would just let me go? Now?"

"I would give my permission, recommendation, and approval. I believe your mother would understand."

"Don't be so sure," I say.

"Regardless, I'm saying you can leave."

"With him?" I say, gesturing up the beach to Peace, who is sitting, guarded by Tavik, Jin, Harvey, and Henry. "I don't want to leave that badly, actually."

"No." Bonnie puts a hand on my arm. "I mean, you can go first. Now, with Duncan, and he can come back tomorrow. We can handle Peace until then."

Now what she's saying finally sinks in, and I take a few moments to imagine going home.

Home, where there would be hot showers, clean clothes, my own bed to crawl into . . .

Normal food, no mud pits or mosquitoes or zillion-pound backpacks to carry, no one trying to insert themselves into my business or messing with my head . . .

Well, there would be lots of Mom stuff that would mess with my head. . . .

But surely I'd feel much better, much stronger, once I was clean and warm and dry, and had had a decent night's sleep. I'd stop feeling like crying all the time, and I would deal with Mom just fine.

And yet, is my mental health actually the most relevant factor in this decision, or is it the principle of the thing?

"No pressure," says Bonnie, breaking into my thoughts, "but you need to let me know right now."

"Oh . . . okay . . ."

I'm not having a good time.

I dislike almost everything about Peak Wilderness, I resent having had it thrust on me like this, and I'm a blubbering wreck most of the time.

But . . .

Although I appreciate Bonnie's offer, and would love to take her up on it. I can't leave. I made a promise, and I have to keep it.

"Thank you," I tell her. "But I'm going to stick it out."

We don't exactly cheer when Peace-Bob leaves. In fact we gather at the shore to watch him float away with Duncan, in a collectively somber mood.

But once he's gone, the vibe shifts. Bonnie and Pat don't wait to start us talking about what just happened, so dinner is intense, and morphs straight into circle.

I don't know if it's because I'm numb, or because I'm so bone-deep exhausted, or because Peace's departure is such a relief, but Melissa is way more messed up than me right now, or at least more able and willing to talk.

"Everywhere I go, there's someone like him," she says, huddled with her sleeping bag around her shoulders, in front of the fire. "Like our cult leader. Psychos, narcissists, control freaks, liars. I knew he was like that. Days ago I knew it."

"And you distanced yourself," Bonnie says, softly.

Melissa nods. "I felt him watching me, though. And Ingrid. I saw him. It sent me . . . into myself. I was scared. I'm still scared . . . that I'm going to have to spend my life on guard. Bob would never make it as a cult leader, though," Melissa says. "He doesn't know how to do the charming part, the bomb-you-with-love, be-everything-you-ever-dreamed-of part. Be the rescuer."

"He just knows how to be an asshole," I grumble.

"The worst part," Melissa continues, "is that the first stage of someone brainwashing you—the amazing part? They're so good at it. They figure out every one of your secret needs and somehow know how to meet them. It's . . . amazing. And the whole rest of the time, when you've lost yourself and you're afraid to even go to the bathroom without permission, and you're blaming yourself for everything going wrong . . . all you want, all that time, is to get back to how that person made you feel, at the beginning. And you somehow believe that you will."

"That's messed up," Jin says.

"I'm sorry I'm taking over the conversation like this," Melissa says, looking at me. "You're the one who was assaulted. It's just . . . this took me back. I was such a fool, for so long, and such a coward."

"Not tonight, you weren't," I say, reaching across to squeeze her hand. "Thank you. And honestly, talk all you want. I . . . have things to think about, but not much to say. At least not tonight. I'm okay. I'm much better now that he's gone."

Bonnie and Pat are thorough, helping Melissa sift through the issues confronting Peace brought up for her, and then checking in with everyone else, one at a time. Of course they do eventually come back around to me, and I know I have to say something because they won't feel they've done their job otherwise.

"When I say I'm okay," I tell them, "I really am. It was scary, but I fought back, and Melissa supported me, and . . . in a way, Peace gave me a gift."

Everyone is silent, obviously surprised at these last words, and waiting for me to clarify.

"I was out there by myself thinking about death," I say, having decided I don't care if they know. "My own death. I had this moment where . . . I saw how sometimes it seems like it would be easier to just . . . drift away."

Jin becomes very still, eyes sharp and on me. Melissa is nodding; Seth is looking at the ground. Ally looks like she might cry any second, and Tavik watches me with a fierce expression that I can't read.

"And then Peace came along and threatened me and held me underwater, and I discovered really quickly that my melodramatic notion of drifting away is garbage. I hate my life sometimes, but I want it. So, in fact, I almost feel better than I did before it happened. I know that's weird. . . ."

Everyone is silent for a few moments, and then Ally goes, "Wow."

"Yeah," I say, ready to shrug off my seriousness. "So, yay, Peace."

Jin starts laughing, and then most of us are laughing, and then I'm yawning.

"Can we go to sleep now, please?"

Pat finishes off by teaching us a centering meditation to step out of dangerous emotional thought loops.

"Step out of the thought loop, the emotion changes. Change the emotion, the behavior changes," Pat explains. "Or vice versa. In fact, if you shift any part of it, that will cause a chain reaction of change."

"Also," Bonnie continues, "even if you can't change the external situation, you can change how you're experiencing it."

A few minutes later, when I've just finished brushing my teeth, Tavik ambles over.

"Bonnie's moving into our tent," he says.

"What?" I frown. "Why?"

"Ah . . ." He looks away. "Just in case you're feeling . . . you know . . ."

"What? So horny that I decide to jump your undefended bones in the middle of the night?"

"No." He cracks up, then goes abruptly serious again. "In case you're feeling vulnerable . . . you know, after what just happened."

"Oh, for goodness' sake . . ." Just then I spot Bonnie, her sleeping bag slung over her shoulder.

"Bonnie!" She changes direction and heads over to us.

"I'm not afraid of Tavik," I tell her.

"According to procedure I am supposed to—"

"I actually feel much safer with just Tavik than I did with Peace in there with us," I protest. "And honestly, I was looking forward to the extra space. . . ."

"The rule is three in a tent. With everything that's happened, I'm taking every precaution," she says, and then goes to our tent.

"Oh well," I say, and swat at a mosquito—mosquito number million and whatever; I've given up counting. "Hopefully she doesn't snore."

Chapter Twenty-Two

GLINDA'S AGONY
(Age Fifteen)

Andreas came home, finally, arriving just ahead of a big winter storm.

"Did Mom tell you?" I asked before he even got his boots off.

He frowned. "Tell me what?"

"About the play?"

No, she hadn't. She was pretending it wasn't happening.

I told him.

"Congratulations," he said, and lifted me up in a huge, swinging hug. "You're going to be fabulous!"

"What's going to be fabulous?" Mom asked, coming down the stairs.

"Ingrid in *The Wizard of Oz*," Andreas said.

"Mmph," she said. "I only hope she doesn't neglect her schoolwork."

"This is a big deal, my love," Andreas said. "Once in a lifetime."

"I certainly hope so. I would like her to spend her time getting ready for the real world, not playacting."

Up to this point I'd been hoping she'd come around. I'd even secretly imagined her coming around so much that my playing Dorothy helped her in some way, like that she'd offer to help with the songs, or just find herself so proud of me that it would help make up for the loss of her own voice.

But I was about out of patience.

"'I certainly hope so'?" I repeated back to her. "Do you even hear what you sound like, Mom?"

"The voice of reason, I believe," she said. "And the voice of experience. You know as well as I do what can go wrong."

"*It's the school play*. And anyway, just because something bad happened to you . . . How can you act like this experience can have no possible value for me? Or me to it? I'm not you, in case you hadn't noticed. And while in the grand scheme of things it's not such a big deal, it's a big deal for me. Why can't you just be happy for me?"

"Don't make assumptions about what I feel."

"I don't have to make assumptions; I live with you. I have eyes and ears and I'm not stupid, Mom! I don't even feel like I can practice my lines in this house, much less sing a single note."

"Practice, then," she said, glaring. "God forbid you fail to learn your material and then make a fool of yourself and blame me for it. I doubt my benefits will cover the therapy."

"You don't want me to do it, but you do want me to practice?"

"My wants are evidently irrelevant, as is any wisdom I've gained over the years. But since you are going to do it, you had better do it well. I don't want to be sitting, ashamed of you, in that audience."

She turned to stalk out of the room.

"Wait!" I said.

She turned back, giving me an icy gaze. "Yes?"

"You're . . . planning to come?"

"Of course."

"I will never understand you."

Her eyes narrowed and she allowed herself a very slight smile. "I hope not," she said, and sailed up the stairs . . .

Leaving Andreas and me blinking after her.

So I started rehearsing at home. Not the songs, but the scenes at least. I even did it while Mom was home, albeit in my bedroom with the door closed. I felt horribly self-conscious at first, and worried because she continued to be moody—silent some days, affectionate others.

Meanwhile, at school, the great news was that Juno was playing the Wicked Witch of the West.

The bad news was that Autumn was Glinda, and she kept trying to make her part bigger.

"I feel like Glinda would reappear here," she said when we were working on the poppy-field scene. "Like she could appear off in the distance, showing her anguish at not being able to help."

Showing her anguish.

"I don't think this scene is about your anguish," Juno said, glaring at her.

"Let's talk about this during a rehearsal you're actually called for, Autumn," Rhea suggested diplomatically.

I was, with great effort, refraining from sarcastic commentary when my eyes met Isaac's.

He smirked.

My lips twitched, and I had to look away to keep from laughing.

Later, when Juno had taken off to hang out with the Tin Man and the Lion (Toff was going to be jealous), Isaac found me backstage near the props table.

"I have it," he said, coming up beside me. "Forget the play that's written; we need a *duel*. A Glinda–Wicked Witch of the West duel. In the sky above the Emerald City."

I covered my mouth, trying not to laugh.

"Or they could do it in a mud-wrestling pit," he added, grinning.

I snorted. "Perv."

"Exactly. They'll be lining up to ref," he said. "We'll sell a ton of tickets. But seriously, Autumn—"

"Shh."

"Don't worry; she's gone and Rhea's packing up. And Rhea told me she's going to ask her to stop coming to rehearsals she's not called for."

"Well, it is getting irritating, the way she tells everyone else when they've missed their cue or screwed up their blocking," I grumbled. She was hovering around Isaac nonstop, looking over his shoulder at his notes, and acting like she owned him. I could tell he felt awkward about it too. "That stuff is supposed to be your job."

217

"Yeah," he said. "Sorry about that."

"Why should you be sorry? She's the one doing it."

"I just . . . I guess you're right. But I should probably tell her to . . . tell her not to . . ." He looked down, shrugged. "I'm not great at . . . I don't want to hurt her feelings."

I picked up Glinda's wand (a fancy one covered in glitter—Autumn was so method, she'd made it herself) and twirled it around. "She just needs to put her energy into something else. She should get to work on the companion play: *Glinda's Anguish*."

Isaac snorted with laughter. "Or we could just change it so that she plays all the other parts—Oz, Wicked Witch of the West, everything."

I spun the wand like a baton and chuckled, then stopped abruptly and looked at him.

"Are you two still friends?"

"Oh. Um." His own amusement disappeared as fast as mine had, and he actually blushed. "Yeah, I . . . We are. But, um, not hanging out so much lately . . ."

"I'm not saying you shouldn't be."

"I'm a jerk for talking about her like this, though. That's what you're saying."

"Look, she's being a legitimate pain in the ass, Isaac. And I have to admit, she's always rubbed me the wrong way without even trying. Her perfection is irritating. Her earnestness is irritating. And now, in these rehearsals, she's making me crazy. At the same time, it's not like she's evil. And I just . . ."

"Don't want either of us to turn into someone who'd lock somebody in a closet during lunchtime?" he said.

I gaped at how close he'd come to what I'd been thinking.

"It's a fine line," he said. "Right?"

"Hey, we're just talking. Venting our frustrations. And I'm an equal participant here, so, you know, don't take me too seriously."

"I always take you seriously, Ingrid."

"Well, complaining about Autumn comes naturally to me. But also? In no way could you become that."

"You say that," he said, gazing steadily at me. "But it's human nature, Ingrid. *Lord of the Flies*, *The Road*, any dystopian novel you pick up, survival of the fittest. People get out of civilization, they're not so nice. They turn into animals."

"Or they find friends, band together," I said. "Like Dorothy."

"Oz is a fairy tale."

"Maybe we need more fairy tales."

"Maybe."

"But how about we not talk about Autumn," I suggested.

"Yes," he said, and exhaled forcefully. "Let's not."

"We'll talk about something else."

"Agreed."

And then there was a pause in which we both tried to figure out what to say next.

"Listen, actually . . ." he said, finally. "I know we're past it, but . . . I keep wanting to say I'm sorry about how things . . . went . . . between us. You know, when I first got here."

"Oh, that," I said. "It's fine. I'm sorry too."

"Regardless, I just wanted to officially say it," he said, drawing himself up as if for a formal speech of some kind. "I am truly remorseful."

I was struck in that moment, with the formality and the mussed hair and the sincerity in those big eyes of his, by the fact that he was adorable. And because there was apparently zero filter between my brain and my mouth right then, I burst out with, "Remorseful? Isaac, you are the cutest," and then I stood on my tiptoes and hugged him.

To my surprise, Isaac proceeded to turn a shade of pink that made him even cuter. Then he cleared his throat, cleared it again, coughed, muttered something about making sure I was on time for rehearsals—I had never been late so far—and bolted.

"Do boys not like being told they're cute?" I said to Juno on the way to rehearsal a couple of days later.

She turned to study me, surprised. "You told someone he was cute?"

"Yeah. Just. Not cute-cute, just cute."

"Like stuffed-animal cute? Is that how you said it?"

"I dunno. Kind of. And now he seems, like, offended."

"Who'd you say it to?"

I looked around, lowered my voice. "Isaac."

"Ahhh," she said.

"What?"

"He *is* cute."

"Not like that."

"Really. Well, what makes you think he didn't like it?"

"He stopped talking to me."

"I didn't know he'd actually *started* talking to you. You know, more than normal. I didn't know you were even friends, particularly."

"Yeah. I think we were. Are. I don't know."

"Okay, you better give me the context. I am the boy expert of the two of us, as you know."

I told her. Not the whole story, of course, just the part where he was being sweet and it occurred to me that he was adorable and I called him cute.

"And then you hugged him like a teddy bear?" she asked, studying me closely.

I nodded.

"Well, see, teddy bears don't have penises," Juno said.

"*Juno!*"

"No, listen: maybe he found it emasculating."

"Shhh. No."

"That, or he just liked it too much."

"No, no, no, no, no."

"Really . . . ? Because you? Are thinking about it way too much for it to be nothing."

"Crap. You have a point."

"Trust me, it all comes down to the penis. He has one. You don't. You either acknowledge that or you don't. You're not friends, you're just friends, or you're something else. Which is pretty interesting to me, considering I've never seen you with a crush on anyone."

"I didn't say I—"

She bulldozed right over me. "The only one of those options that doesn't involve a decision about you both being heterosexual—I assume—and having different body parts . . . is the not-friends option. You wanna not be friends?"

"No."

"Okay then. Deal with the penis."

"Oh my God."

I was half an hour early for the stumble-through, which is exactly what it sounds like—the first attempt to get all the way through (even if stumbling) the play. I had claimed a sort of walkway in the wings backstage; it was stage right, away from the props table, and long enough for me to be able to pace back and forth in either direction.

With opening night approaching fast, tension at home, and Isaac avoiding me as much as possible, I was finding the need to pace often.

"Hey."

I half shrieked, stopping once I realized it was Isaac.

"Sorry," he said, "I didn't mean to—"

"No, I'm sorry. I'm just jumpy. Uh, so . . . what's up?"

"I . . . have some notes for you," he said. "Blocking notes."

"Oh, okay." I stood up, grabbed my script and a pencil from the floor, and stood waiting.

Isaac had the script with him at all times, in a big book. It had the schedule, the cast and crew contact info, all the blocking and lighting calls and so on, and it was where he wrote his notes for the actors. He looked down at his arms, as if noticing for the first time that he didn't have it.

"Oh . . . um . . . ." he fumbled, then looked up at me, meeting my gaze for the first time since the hugging incident. "Guess what. I lied. I don't have any notes. You're fine. Exceptional, in fact."

"Ah . . . thanks," I said, closing my script and hugging it to my chest. "But . . ."

"But what am I doing here pretending to have notes for you and then saying I don't?"

"Yeah. That."

"It could be the wrong thing," he said, then took a deep breath and blew it out. "And if it's the wrong thing, then definitely I should wait until the show is over. And considering our history, it might really be the wrong thing or feel too complicated and in that case, before or after or during the show, maybe I'll regret it. At the same time, I want to erase the thing that happened before, or at least replace it with something better, and really almost anything would be better, in which case maybe it would be good even if it *wasn't* good, per se, because it would be better than terrible, and then we could laugh about it . . . ."

"Isaac, what the hell are you talking about?"

"Ingrid . . . I can't stop thinking about—and maybe I'll regret it, but I think I'd regret it more if I didn't try, so . . ."

At this point, based on the high level of awkwardness and my frenzied heart rate and my own confusion, I figured I had some idea of where he was going with this, and I would have loved to help him out, but I was paralyzed, and hearing Juno's voice saying, *Penis, penis, penisssss.*

"Ingrid . . ."

"Yes?" I croaked.

"What I'm trying to say is that it's gotten awkward between us—and I think that this is because of . . . an unanswered question that's arisen. . . ."

Penis . . .

223

"Uh, so to speak—"

"Oh my God, Isaac—"

"—between us."

Penis, penis . . .

Oh my God.

At this point my entire body must have been blushing, and I felt I might, at any moment, break into totally inappropriate and hysterical laughter. Or possibly tears. And then I would die on the spot.

"I thought it might help, um, resolve the situation . . ." Isaac said, looking none too comfortable himself, "if I, ahem . . ."

"Yes . . . ?"

"If I kissed you."

"You think that would resolve the situation . . . ?" I parroted, incapable of anything else.

"If I kissed you. Yes," he said, dead serious. "How do you feel about that? What do you think?"

"How I feel is . . . like I'm going to pass out from embarrassment, Isaac."

"I'm sorry."

"And what I think is," I said, recovering somewhat now that it was out in the open. "Two things. One: you talk too much sometimes."

"That's definitely true. I'm so sorry; it's just that I—wait, what's the second thing?"

"Yes."

"Yes?"

"That's what I said," I said, holding his gaze. "The second thing is, yes, I think you should kiss me."

"Okay, good," he said, nodding vigorously.

"And third: thank God that's what you said—I was afraid you were going to say we should have sex," I blurted out.

"Sex?"

"I mean, not that that's . . . uh, permanently out of the question, but ah, it would be a rather big . . . Oh, I should just not talk at all. Forget I said it."

At this he threw his head back and laughed.

Meanwhile, I was one huge head-to-toe body of steaming mortification.

"How about we save sex for future awkward conversations?" he said.

"Agreed!"

"Phew."

"So . . . did you mean now?" I finally asked when he didn't move.

"Sure. Now-ish," he said.

"In that case we need, um . . ."

"Closer proximity?" he said, and took a step.

"Yeah, that," I said. "Come on, let's get it over with."

"That's the spirit."

"Ha-ha."

There was still a significant gap between us.

"All right then," he said, "because—"

"Isaac! Seriously? Shut up."

"I'm not the only who keeps stalling us by talking," he said, then came forward, took my script away from me and placed it gently on the floor, and then put his hands on my shoulders.

"Maybe we should . . . count to three?" I suggested.

"Good idea. You start."

"Why do I have to start?"

"Why do you have to argue about it? It was your idea!" he said. "Now you're stalling again. You count, I'll kiss."

"Okay, fine. One . . ."

I looked up at him, saw his Adam's apple bob down and then back up as he swallowed.

"Two . . ."

Fighting nerve-induced paralysis, I took a half step forward.

"Th—"

I didn't get through three.

And our lack of collective experience wasn't a problem.

But I am not sure anyone has ever stumbled through a stumble-through like I did after that.

Chapter Twenty-Three

KILLER
(Peak Wilderness, Day Twelve)

Day Twelve I wake with my shin aching, and all my muscles so sore, I can barely move.

"Well, it's easy to forget," Bonnie points out when I groan about it, "that in addition to everything that happened last night, we walked through a mud pit yesterday. That uses different muscles."

I nod in agreement with her, but what's hard to explain is how my insides, my emotions, feel the same—overused, sore, sluggish. Every day out here is like a lifetime, in terms of what we're going through, and it's all a bit much.

I don't feel like crying; I feel like sleeping.

But I'm leader again, so there's no chance of that happening. And hey, maybe today is the magical day I get us to camp early and nothing messes up our free time.

Tavik is directly behind me again on the trail, and twenty minutes in, when everyone has spread out a bit, he starts asking me questions, starting with, "So, you were suicidal?

Is that what's wrong with you?"

"What?" I whirl around to stare at him, and almost shout, "No!"

"Don't get mad. You're the one who said it last night—that you were thinking about death, and all that."

"I would never," I snap. "Thinking about death and pondering the meaning and potential ease of it . . . are not the same as being suicidal. I thought about it for a minute, about what it would be like, but I wasn't going to do it. God. And everyone wonders why I don't want to talk."

"Hey, I believe you," he says. "I mean, you don't seem the type. But on the other hand, you've spent a lotta days out here bawling your eyes out."

"Crying a bit," I correct him, and then turn and start walking again.

"All right, crying a bit, all the time."

"I'm not in the mood for this, Tavik," I say. "Can we change the subject?"

"Sure," he says, and goes on to ask more questions.

Lots of questions.

They're just the usual questions now, the kind people ask when they don't know each other well. But for Tavik I suspect this isn't "usual." He fires questions, listens with an almost palpable hunger, follows up with more questions that show he's been paying close attention to my responses, all of it giving the impression of his being truly and avidly curious.

I'm not in the habit of divulging swaths of information about myself, but I somehow end up launching into the story of my life, from the beginning . . . which alarms me enough that after the first break, when he shows no sign of getting bored with talking to me, I try to shift the focus to him.

I haven't asked Tavik a lot of questions. Neither has anyone else, aside from Bonnie and Pat, who've gotten almost nowhere. To me, "Gee, how did you end up in jail?" seems like an awkward place to start, and "Where did you grow up?" seems like just a cloaked way of asking, "How did you end up in jail?" Also there is his abrasiveness—still present—and the feeling that he's always mocking me, which has admittedly lessened.

"So . . . you seem to have really calmed down," I say as an opening gambit.

"You didn't think I was calm?" he asks.

"Maybe you finally got enough sky?"

"Head out of my ass."

"Same thing, maybe."

He chuckles.

"What, ah, what did you do before? Before your . . . incarceration, I mean."

"I was running tables at the casino. And in my basement. Illegal ones."

"Ah. Is that . . ." Crap, here I am at the question, and I can just feel it, that he knows I've been trying not to ask, and knows I've been wondering.

"Nah, it wasn't that," Tavik says with a dry laugh. "I killed someone."

I managed not to gasp, or trip and fall on my face. "Really?"

"Yeah."

"Huh," I say, trying to sound cool. "Did they, um, deserve it?"

"No one deserves it."

"I just meant—"

"You scared of me now?"

"If you were going to kill me, I think it would have happened already."

He snorts.

"And you don't seem crazy or anything. Angry, maybe, but not crazy."

"Ha. Thanks."

"I'm the one who's crazy, feels like. Crying one day, grumpy the next, numb the day after that."

"You seem homesick," he says.

"You think?"

"Kinda. And you're angry, too. Different angry from me, though," he says. "There's a frequency—different frequencies, that anger vibrates at. Like a clue where it comes from. You gotta learn to read the frequency. You know, in order to get by."

"In jail?"

"Everywhere. Like our former roommate, Peace? He pretends to be all about the world and injustice, but his anger is all narcissism, 'poor me.' Mixed with some psycho rapist mojo, obviously."

"Okay, let me try," I say, brave considering I'm talking to a murderer. "Yours has a defensive vibration. Like, 'stay the hell away from me.'"

"Sure. Probably. Works, too."

"What about mine?" I say. "Since you're such an expert?"

I look backward at him, and he grins like he knew I wouldn't be able to resist.

"You? Angry about injustice, about being here especially.

But under that you're, like . . . screaming mad, like you're a little kid and somebody took your teddy bear, or your ice-cream cone."

"Oh, so I'm a petulant child?"

"Not that, exactly. It's more than that. Deeper. I'm still trying to figure you out, but you're more than what you say. You're here for more than what you told us."

"You calling me a liar?"

"We're all liars about something."

We're silent for a while then, because he's surprisingly hard to lie to, and I therefore can't think of any answer to give him. Little threads of heat shoot up my leg from my shin, and I imagine myself telling him about how good it felt to swing the ax. He'd love it. He'd get it. But he'd never just leave it at that, he'd keep digging, and that would suck immediately.

No. I take deep breaths, but my insides are overrun with a twisting, squeezing feeling.

"Hey." A hand on my shoulder. I must have stopped walking, because he's right behind me, touching me, this self-professed killer, and his hand is warm and surprisingly heavy.

I turn. The group is a ways back from us—the rule is, we always stay in visual contact with the person in front of us, but throughout the day people naturally fall into pairs and groups and have conversations. The path is longer and straighter now, with more visibility, so we've gotten in the habit of spreading out.

"I'm okay," I say.

"Except not really," he says.

"I'm fine."

"Okay," he says, and shrugs. "FYI, I didn't kill anybody."

"What?"

He smiles, big and beautiful, no irony in it, and shakes his head.

"Why did you say it, then? Speaking of liars."

"'Cause that's what you expected."

"Untrue."

"Or, okay, because that's what you were afraid of."

"Or because that's what you're afraid I was afraid of, and you wanted to see what I would do."

"See if you would run screaming, you mean?" He studies me, eyes narrowed. "You took it pretty well."

I laugh.

He laughs.

"That means you'd be my friend, even if I killed somebody?"

"Are we friends?"

"Maybe." He tilts his head, looks into my eyes. "If you want."

"Sure," I say, but suddenly I'm pretty sure he's shipping a whole other option, which I am definitely not up for, even if it were allowed, even though he is sexy, in that scary-sexy way.

"Hey, I should have killed Bob for you and made it true."

"Very funny."

"No, I'm that good of a friend."

"I don't want that good of a friend," I say, not completely convinced he's kidding. "I just need a regular, straightforward kind of a friend."

"I'm only joking. Straightforward friend—I'm your guy."

"Uh-huh," I say. "Non-murderous."

"There for you," he says.

"So . . . if you're not a cold-blooded killer, what did you do?"

"What if I say it's none of your business?"

"You'd be right. But none of the stuff you've been asking me is your business, either. All this sharing of stories can just be part of being friends, regardless of whose business it is. Or so I hear."

"Fine, I'll share. I didn't hurt anybody," he says, dropping the innuendo and the jokes, finally, but still standing awkwardly close and looking into my eyes.

"Okay . . . ?"

"It's lame, actually. Breaking and entering. And such a waste, because me and my buddy . . . we were just messing around. Drunk, you know, and being stupid. Although, as I said, I was running tables, and I think the cops knew it, and that's why we got busted. They were watching."

"Wow."

"Yeah," he says.

"They're catching up," I say, gesturing toward the approaching group, and suddenly feeling like I don't want anyone to see us like this—having this long, weird series of intense, close-talking moments. "We should go."

He nods, steps away, and we start hiking again, this time in silence.

That night, despite being exhausted, I stay staring at the fire after circle, my journal on the log beside me.

Tavik joins me and adds another piece of wood to the fire.

"You mind some company?" he asks, though he's obviously already decided to stay.

"I don't mind. I'm not writing at the moment."

"This whole trip . . . gives you stuff to think about, huh?"

Suddenly I feel my throat tightening, and tears welling up again. I am so not up for it, and yet I know if he starts asking me more questions, I'll be crying again.

"What things . . ." I say, and then have to swallow. "What has it given you to think about?"

He squats in front of the fire and blows on the coals to make sure the new log catches on.

"Just . . . I gotta figure out a job," he says, then sits down next to me. "And a place to live. I can't go back to where I was. Too many people doing the same old thing."

"And you could get pulled back in?"

"Sure. Like those thought loops, but a life loop. I don't want that loop."

"What do you want to do? In life?" I'm feeling better already, with the focus on him.

"School if I can. I finished high school in the pen. With a pretty good GPA, actually," he says, grinning. "I like to read."

"Porn?"

We've been both looking into the fire as we talk, with just the occasional glance sideways at each other, but now he turns and really looks at me, still intense, but all traces of mockery gone.

"Hey, I'm sorry. That book, it's not actually . . . I was just being a dick. And after what just happened to you, well, not cool."

"That's okay. What's your book?"

"It's the Big Book. The Alcoholics Anonymous book."

"Oh. Are you . . . ?"

"I'm just reading it. For interest mostly, and because I know a lot of addicts, and because they had meetings in jail and it was something to do that was well regarded."

"Ah."

Jin joins us now, and sits down.

"I read a lot of stuff," Tavik continues. "I like history, literature, a good mystery. But in terms of life . . . I like fixing things too. And being outside, it turns out. So, I dunno."

"History professor, auto mechanic, engineer . . . Peak Wilderness guide?"

"These are your suggestions for what he's going to be when he grows up?" Jin asks.

I shrug. "We're just talking. Anyway, you could just go to university and figure it out while you're there."

Jin starts shaking her head.

"What?"

"Just . . . your privilege is showing," she says. "No offense."

"Um . . . okay, none taken . . . I guess . . . ?"

"I was on that track too, you know," she says.

"What track?" I say.

"Applications to good schools where my tuition would be paid."

"What . . . happened?"

"You know any Asian parents? Or students?"

"Students, of course. Lots."

"Okay, how much do you see them, say, having fun, or doing a not-required extracurricular, versus studying?"

"I . . . I don't know. Isn't that a stereotype?"

"Sure, but there's a reason for it. GPA is king. And you break your brain if you have to, but you get into a good school, and you go into engineering, or dentistry, or premed, because otherwise your parents will lose status."

"Status with who?"

"With their other friends who have kids going into good moneymaking careers, and with family back in Hong Kong . . ."

"Ah. Right."

"But in my case, it was way beyond that, because my dad is an abusive asshole, and totally obsessed with grades."

"Oh," I say, and she nods, visibly upset.

"Yeah," she says. "I could take music, but only because it's supposed to be good for math skills. I could do sports, but only because being athletic is good for the brain, and only until the athletics started taking too much time from my studying."

"My mom . . . has almost the same attitude," I say.

"She's going to let you go, though," Jin says. "To that school."

"It comes with a pretty big price."

"As did my so-called freedom," Jin says. "As will Tavik's schooling, and in his case, it's literally."

"Yeah, I can't just do a general arts or science program," Tavik says. "I like books and stuff, but I might be better in a trade. And there's gotta be a plan."

"Why?"

"Money, for one."

"Right. I get it."

"So, Jin," he says, "you saying you cracked? Ran away? What sort of abuse are we talking about?"

"I sat up past midnight fifty-five nights in a row, being yelled at and quizzed by my father on properties of matter and atomic theory. He wouldn't let me sleep. He hired someone to write my English essays for me, even though I actually loved English and wanted to write them myself. It was taking too much time from my STEM subjects, he said. Then I got caught for cheating—the essays, of course—and I was so humiliated, and it went on my record, and he blamed me, and I had to quit the volleyball team, which was basically the only good thing in my life, and I . . . It was too much. I left. So, yeah, I guess I cracked. And then, homelessness and my brief experiment with prostitution weren't much fun either, so I cracked quite a few times."

"Motherfucker," Tavik says.

"My God," I say.

"Yeah. So. That's why I'm not going to be one of those people melting down out here," she says. "This is the Plaza Hotel compared to living on the street. But enough about me. What are you writing in that book all the time, Ingrid?"

"Besides complaints about this trip?"

Jin smirks; Tavik laughs.

"It's a journal. My mom bought me a huge stack of them, all different covers. But in it . . . it's letters, mostly to her."

"To your mom?" Jin says.

"Yep," I say, hoping my tone conveys that's all I want to say about it.

"You going to give it to her when you're done?" Tavik asks.

I stare into the fire, swallow, shake my head. "No."

"Why not?" Jin says.

"Why do you do it, then?" Tavik asks

"I . . . It's a long story. It's complicated."

"So?" Tavik says.

And Jin just stares at me, like she's issuing a dare.

"Not tonight." I get up, shaking my head. "I'm way too tired. Nice chatting with you both, though."

I resist the urge to run as I step out of the firelight, and so I hear Jin loud and clear as I'm walking away.

"Chicken."

Chapter Twenty-Four

JUST LEAVE ME HERE

(Age Fifteen)

In addition to my mom being weird about the play, she and Andreas were having a problem—a fight, but a silent one. There'd been the rumble of late-night conversation after he got home, and strange tension, and she was taking sleeping pills, but still up pacing some nights. At first I worried it was about me, but I got the feeling it was something else.

Normally I would have jumped in to help, or at least tried to find out what was going on. But for the first time in my life, I didn't want to. If I got involved, it would take over, and I couldn't afford that with the play about to go up.

Plus, had my trying to help ever actually helped? Maybe I put myself through hell worrying and fussing and it made no difference. In which case, the only thing I'd achieved was making myself feel terrible. Maybe enough was enough and maybe . . . *maybe* I could be happy, even when my mom wasn't. A revolutionary thought.

And I was happy. I was living intensely, running on an

energy I'd never tapped into before. I was full and vibrating—with music, with words, with Dorothy, with the heart-tripping breathlessness of Isaac, and the million tiny, secret moments happening between us.

We went for long walks when we had time between the end of school and rehearsal, drinking lattes and talking. Isaac had ideas about everything—his brain wheeled and darted from art to music to international politics, to science, ethics, psychology, even sports. He could see something in a store window or the byline of a newspaper article, connect the two, and then reel off three or four ways of looking at them. He could look at me and know immediately what mood I was in, and whether to try to make me laugh, or give me a hug, or both.

Like me, he tended to shy away from anything too deeply personal, to have no-go zones in terms of talking about his past, most particularly the years he'd spent being bullied. He didn't have to say it; I just knew.

Isaac was many things all at once, was a person who could, like me, hold on to many contradictions, simultaneously. It's not an easy way to be, because it means you live with paradoxes, with conflicts between things that are true and yet diametrically opposed. It means, sometimes, that you are the bridge between those things, and also the battleground.

So we talked about the world, but not ourselves. And then, in the theater, he would pull me behind curtains and into dim corners backstage, and run his hands up my back, and kiss me until I felt like I was full of liquid fire.

"You must be over your claustrophobia," I murmured one time, between kisses.

"We're not locked in anywhere," he said. "No doors."

"Mmm."

"But hey, if you want to try a closet . . ."

"No, I'm fine like this."

We didn't talk about "us" or what it meant. And we hadn't told anyone, or let anyone see us holding hands or making out. Juno had given me a few inquiring looks, but she was too distracted by her most recent drama with Toff—which she had clearly created by purposely making him jealous—to really notice. Keeping it private for now felt right, felt necessary.

The morning of dress rehearsal, Mom and Andreas erupted into an actual shouting match over breakfast.

He was scanning the news online, and mentioned something about a medical breakthrough for Alzheimer's. I have no idea why it set my mother off, but it did.

"Stop right now," she said.

"Pardon me?" He looked up in surprise.

"I see what you're doing."

"I'm not—"

"Don't treat me like I'm stupid, Andreas. I don't want my life tinkered with! And, by the way, you are not a subtle as you think."

"But, Margot-Sophia, let's talk about this," he said, either not reading the signs that persisting was a bad idea, or choosing to ignore them. "If you would only—"

"The subject is closed!" she exploded, and then burst

into tears. "It's closed and I won't tolerate any more of these hints, any more of this campaign of yours."

"I am simply . . . making . . . conversation over breakfast!" he protested, raising his voice too.

"No, you are trying, again, to make your point, and you've made your point multiple times, and *my* point is you are not listening to me! You are simply working your way up to trying again, and I said no already. No, no, no, no."

"All right!"

"Because it hurts me! Every time, it hurts me, Andreas, and I don't like being hurt and so then I get angry, so very angry . . . !"

I stood up, and they both looked at me as if just realizing I was there.

"What the hell is going on?" I said.

"Nothing you need to worry about," Andreas said.

"Is it a nothing I can do something about?" I asked.

"No," they both said together.

"Fine. Look, I have to go to school. It's a big week for me, and a big day today, and this problem you two are having . . . is stressing me out. Can you stop?"

Mom looked up at me with haunted, exhausted eyes, and didn't answer.

Andreas cleared his throat.

Mom turned away and muttered, "I am not the one starting."

"I'm sorry," Andreas said, to her and to me.

I left them like that, fraught and unresolved, and stomped my way out of the house, then shoved it to the back of my mind and told it to stay there.

Dress rehearsal went how they supposedly always go; it was terrifying, exhilarating, and awkward in places because of missed cues, nerves, prop malfunctions, line flubs, et cetera. Rhea and Isaac gave copious notes but sent us straight home after, with the rationale that a solid night's sleep would do more good than anything.

While everyone else was packing up, and Isaac was resetting the props and chatting with Rhea, I got back on the stage with my script and started quietly and carefully working through my entrances and exits, checking my marks, whispering my lines, singing the songs in my head. I remembered Margot-Sophia's work ethic, and mine would be as good, if not better.

After a few minutes Rhea appeared stage left, and I paused.

"Go home, Dorothy," she said. "Sleep."

"Oh, that's funny," I said.

"It's not meant to be funny."

"Are you going to be able to sleep?"

"Yes, I am," she said, then relented. "But I suppose that's because I'm older than you and can't do without it. Also, I don't have to perform."

"I'll go soon. I wanted to practice the songs one more time," I said, my eyes going to the door, where the rest of the cast and crew had congregated and were joking and laughing.

I wished I could laugh, but I didn't feel like it.

"I can lock up, Rhea," Isaac said, coming up beside her. "And I need five or ten, so that should give Ingrid the time she needs."

Rhea looked from him to me, and back to him, raised an eyebrow in a way that made me think she'd read our situation with perfect clarity, and then shrugged. "All right."

The rest of the cast cleared out along with her.

Isaac rummaged around in the wings while I stood on the dimly lit stage and sang "Over the Rainbow" six times. My voice was getting tired, but I was thinking about Mom and Andreas again, and I just didn't want to go home. Personal revolution aside, the fact was that anytime Mom wasn't stable, I was freaked. The only solution was to fully immerse myself in what I was doing.

I was ready to start going through all the other songs, just at a hum, when Isaac stepped onto the stage.

"Time," he said.

"Okay," I said, not moving.

"What's wrong? Are you nervous?"

"Sure. But. It's more . . ." I looked out into the dark space. "I just want to stand here. I just want *this* to be my life."

"You want to be Dorothy?" he said, cocking his head to the side.

"No. I want to be in this theater. Playing Dorothy. Rehearsing being Dorothy. This . . . what's happening here, even with a messy dress rehearsal, it's . . ."

"A world."

"Yes," I said with a sigh. "And most things in this world are simpler than in the real one."

Isaac went to sit on the edge of the stage, legs dangling off the front, and patted a space next to him.

"What's not simple, Ingrid?" he said once I'd sat down. "Do you mean . . ." He gestured from me to him.

"No, not that," I said with a smile. "I just mean . . . putting on a show, the job is very clear. And in the show, the problems Dorothy faces . . . Yes, she has to learn the whole 'no place like home' thing. But her obstacles and what she has to do and how she needs to feel about it all—that's clear. She wants to go home. She needs to get to the wizard. She needs to stay alive. She needs to kill the witch."

Isaac nodded. Waited.

"Sometimes you can't kill the witch," I said. "You know, in life."

"Why not?"

"Because there is no witch? Or because the wicked witch is also the good witch, or because the witch is inside someone you love, or inside you. Or the witch is an unsolvable problem between two people you love. And then . . . you can throw as much water as you want to, but you can't kill that witch because she's not yours to kill and even if you did, she just comes back."

"Ingrid . . ." he said, covering my hand with his, "what's going on?"

"Oh, I'm . . ." I could have talked to him. I knew he'd have understood, grasped the depths and the difficulties, cared. But I couldn't talk—not with him, not with Juno either, because if I talked about it, I would be the one melting. And I needed everything I had, to do what I needed to do tomorrow and the next day and the day after. And anyway, I rationalized, Andreas and Mom and I had been through the wringer before. It would pass. And pass faster and less painfully for my keeping it to myself.

"Just some stupid family stuff," I said to Isaac. "Too long a story for tonight. It's fine."

I kept hold of his hand while sliding off the stage, and

tried not to see the hurt in his eyes.

At the door, right after he flipped the last light switch, I pulled him close and got on my tiptoes to kiss him.

My backpack slid to the floor, then his.

"You know it's not just about this," he said, breathing between kisses. "You can talk to me."

"I know." I pulled him closer, pressed myself tight against him, feeling better by the second. . . . "We've been talking. Lots. There's time for more of that later. But we're busy right now, right?"

All the way home I carried the feel of him on my lips and the warmth of his arms around me, the push of our bodies against each other.

And in my mind the music played and the stage lights shone.

Isaac and Oz, like touchstones.

I tried, as I walked the last half block toward home, to pull all of that into me, as if I were a bottle and could keep these feelings, to be taken back out whenever I needed them, like an antidote, or a buffer.

But nothing could buffer me from the awfulness of finding Andreas sitting in his car, windows down, in front of the house while Mom shoved armloads of his clothes through the back window.

She was not crazed or screaming, but silent, hair in a severe ponytail, and decked out in dangerous-looking high-heeled black boots over black leggings, with a beaded black tunic. In the brief moment when I saw her face, I glimpsed red lipstick. The look was opera singer/ballerina/ninja/vampire, and all diva. Like she had dressed for drama.

Then the front door closed and she was gone and I ran to the car.

"Andreas . . ."

Oh God, why had I ignored this? Why hadn't I tried to help?

"Ingrid," he said. His cheeks were wet, and the backseat of the car was full. "I wanted to . . . talk to you . . . calmly . . ."

"No. No, no, no . . ." I said, insides roiling, reaching down to open the door and pushing more clothing out of my way so I could sit in the passenger seat. "You can't leave."

"I wouldn't, but she says she needs me to," he said in a ragged voice.

"What she says and what she needs are— How could she do this?"

"I have made mistakes."

"You? What? What mistakes?"

He dropped his head for a moment, then looked back up at me.

"She told me, very clearly, that she did not want me searching for a cure for her voice."

"And?"

"I did not believe her."

I groaned, unfortunately not surprised, and getting a sense of where this was going.

"I thought . . . if I could find someone," he continued, "if we could fix it and she could sing again, she would be . . . Things would be . . . easier for her."

"What did you do?"

"I found a specialist," he said softly. "I thought, in the time since it happened . . . there must have been medical advances. And there have been, which means maybe she could get her singing voice back—some of it, anyway. Maybe all. I know . . . she told me she did not want this, but I thought I was bringing her the greatest gift, this possibility. I thought she would change her mind. Instead she's furious. She feels betrayed somehow. She doesn't want to try, and she thinks it means I don't love her as she is, which is obviously not the case."

I gripped the windowsill of the car, wanting to hit something, wanting to smash my head against a wall in frustration.

"You always want to help people," I said to him. "You want to help them, solve them . . . but she doesn't want to be solved."

"I understand that now. I was . . . foolish."

"No," I said. "I mean, yes, you sometimes go overboard wanting to fix things, and you are guilty of . . .not listening, or not believing what she told you. But she . . . Honestly it pisses me off that she would rather hang on to her misery, that she would choose it over hope. And then blame you for it. She is the foolish one, to lose you—the best thing that's happened to us."

"Perhaps she is just too frightened," he said. "Too scared to hope."

"That's fucking stupid."

Andreas gasped.

"It is. And it's so depressing," I said, anger moving in and pushing aside my shock and despair. "Seriously, I'm sick of it. Let me come with you. Or you come in with me and I'll fight for you."

"She has changed the locks, Ingrid."

"What?"

"And right now trying to fight will only make her more resolute. Trust me. For now I have to leave, and you need to go inside."

He pulled me in for a hug and squeezed me hard.

"You're supposed to be my dad," I said, blinking back tears.

Four months ago, he'd filed the papers to adopt me. We were waiting on the next step. But how could it possibly go through, if he and Mom were broken up? Why would he even want it to?

"I am," he said. "Sweetheart, I will be at the play tomorrow and I am always going to be there. I promise. But you must stay with your mother tonight. Even if she won't say it, she needs you."

"What about what *I* need?"

Mom had seen me after all, and left the door partially open.

Inside I found her at the dining-room table, spine erect, a glass of red wine in front of her, the open bottle in front of it.

"Mom." I wiped at my eyes. "What the hell?"

Her gaze stayed on the glass.

"Is he gone?" she asked.

"Yes. And that's about the shittiest news I've had, ever."

"Watch your language." She swallowed, pushed forward a key. "Here is your new key. Have you done your homework?"

"My homework? Are you kidding?"

Finally her gaze sliced up to meet mine. "I am never kidding about your education."

"I don't have any tonight. All the teachers, unlike you, are sympathetic to the fact that we have a show opening tomorrow night. Half the population of the school is involved one way or another, Mom."

"Ah yes. The show," she said wearily.

"But forget that. This thing with Andreas—"

"There's no happily ever after, Ingrid," she snapped, then took a sip of her wine, swallowed. "It's better to know that. Expect pain. Expect disappointment. And then, once in a while you will be pleasantly surprised."

"Wow. Is that really the parental wisdom you want to pass on to me?"

"Yes."

"That's really warm and fuzzy, really reassuring, in the middle of our life here falling apart. Thanks."

"I think you should be reassured that I don't lie to you."

"He is our family, Mom. Do you get that at all? All he did was try to help you, because he loves you. And you kick him out? Change the locks?"

"Are you taking his side, then?"

"Side? I am on the side of 'we have a family and I want it to stay together.' That's my side."

She snorted, took another drink. Her arm was shaking, and I knew she was a mess behind that brittle mask. She was being honest with me? Fine. Maybe I could get through to her with my own honesty.

"Okay," I said, putting my hands on the table and leaning toward her. "Maybe I am on his side, because his side is reasonable. Compassionate. Generous. He loves you and wants to help you."

"He doesn't understand."

"I don't understand either. It seems to me you'd rather just be miserable, and make everyone else miserable too. Live your little safe half life, and encourage me to do the same," I said, standing up, volume rising. "God forbid anyone should *hope* or think big or try something scary. Better to hide in a freaking *hole* the rest of your life. Better to ruin everything good that happens to you and do the same for your daughter, just in advance, in case she starts to be happy. You know what? That is hard to understand, Mom."

"Now this is about you, is it? I am here, reeling from this betrayal, and it's all about how I'm trying to prevent you from becoming a star. Forgive me for wanting you to have solidity in your future, for not wanting you to live a sordid, heartbreaking life of poverty."

"A sordid, heartbreaking life of poverty? Do you hear yourself?"

She turned pale, gripped the edge of the table, pushed herself up to face me.

"You know nothing," she said. "You know nothing of what I've been through. What I struggle with."

"Oh, that's right. I'm not the one who's been here by your side my entire life. None of that has affected me whatsoever, and I don't know anything. And solidity? Really?"

Mom pressed her lips together, breathed in and out through her nose, and just when I thought she was going to start screaming, a single tear slid from her eye and down her cheek.

"I don't want to hear another word from you," she whispered. "Go to bed."

"And what are you going to do?" I said, torn now between fury and concern.

"I'm going to sit here and get drunk."

"Great. Enjoy," I said, starting toward the stairs, then pausing.

Part of me wanted to stay, wanted to apologize and comfort her. To be there to catch her in case she fell, especially because it was unusual for her to be drinking, much less getting drunk, and at the best of times she was very delicately balanced. But she had done this on the eve of my opening night, and no, their argument wasn't about me, but it would affect me.

If I'd hurt her, fine. She had hurt me too.

And I was tired of this, tired of being hurt, tired of walking on eggshells, worried that any little thing I did might send her into a downward spiral. It was too much responsibility. Too much worry, too much putting her before me, and all the while leaving her the power to just . . . ruin my life, dismantle everything, and stop me from doing things I loved.

Yes, right at this moment she looked like a strong wind might blow her over.

Like a bucket of water would melt her.

Like she was going to drown herself in that bottle of wine.

But I had my own problems.

And so I went to bed and tried to open my own bottle, that bottle where I'd trapped the feeling of Isaac and the dream of Oz. . . .

Too few hours of sleep, and then the early hours brought thunder and pummeling rain, and I realized I must have been sleeping through some of it, because Margot-Sophia had climbed into bed with me and wrapped her body tightly around mine.

For a few minutes I just lay there, imagining I was a little girl whose mommy had crawled into bed with her to banish the bad dreams, instead of the girl whose mom had basically told her to expect life to be shit.

I cuddled closer, she tightened her arm around me, and I fell back to sleep.

She was still there when my alarm sounded. I turned it off, disentangled myself, and slid out of bed. Mom moaned, rolled the other way, and kept sleeping. She wasn't much of a drinker, so she was going to have a rough day.

I gently kissed her cheek. She reached up sleepily, with the saddest eyes, and touched my face.

"I love you no matter what," she murmured softly, and in that moment I just wanted to crawl back into the bed with her, because I loved her no matter what too. Loved her with everything I had. It was something I couldn't block, couldn't shut out.

"Sure," I said, instead. "Me too."

"See you tonight."

"You're still coming?"

"I am Margot-Sophia Lalonde," she muttered, a hint of her regular, fierce self showing through. "Of course I'm coming."

My phone buzzed: a text from Isaac.

Look outside. East.

I headed to the window, pulled back the curtain, and saw it . . . After a terrible night and in the face of no sleep and a life full of uncertainty on this day in particular, there it was: a rainbow.

Chapter Twenty-Five

TRY NOT TO KILL IT

(Age Fifteen)

All day I felt like I was balanced on a wire.

People patted me on the back in the halls between classes, wished me luck, asked if I was nervous. Nervous, yes. If only that were all.

Autumn showed up at my locker after French.

"Juno told me you were looking unwell," she said. "She's right."

"Oh, thanks. I'm not going to keel over, if that's what you're hoping."

A look of wounded surprise came over her face and she took a step back.

"I was just going to offer you some aromatherapy, Ingrid," she said. "And I bought you a smoothie because I noticed you didn't eat lunch and you look like hell and you happen to be our Dorothy. And a good one, too. But never mind."

She started to walk away, stomping, and now I could see the smoothie in her hand.

"Autumn, wait!"

She turned partway back, even her ringlets bouncing with indignation.

"I'm sorry. You're right, I do feel like hell. What's in the smoothie?"

"Spirulina, whey protein, blueberries, banana, pumpkin seed butter. It's a meal. And it'll give you energy, but calm energy."

"That's . . . sweet, Autumn. Thank you."

"You're welcome. It's Isaac's favorite."

I felt a nasty jealous twinge at the way she said that—like she had ownership of him. But she was trying so hard to be nice, so I pushed it away.

"And in my locker I also have—"

"Sure," I said, falling into step with her, "hook me up. The aromatherapy, the smoothie, healing crystals . . . whatever you've got."

"You wanna meditate, too?"

"Why not?"

"You smell like a health-food store," Isaac said, coming up beside me on the way to the theater.

"It's cinnamon and orange for energy, lavender for relaxation. I've gone to the dark side. I hear you did too."

"What?" he said, stopping outside the stage door.

"You have a favorite smoothie . . . ?"

"Oh." He shifted his weight from one foot to the other, then laughed. "Yeah. She's very persistent, pushing those smoothies."

"Yeah, well, I'm weak today, so I took everything she offered."

"Uh-huh. I saw you meditating."

"It's in lieu of sleep."

"You okay?"

"Sure."

"I don't believe you, but I'll let it pass."

"I loved the rainbow. It was almost like you gave it to me."

"If I had rainbow-making power? Every morning, there'd be one outside your window."

"Whoa, Isaac. That was . . . kinda romantic."

He blushed. I blushed back.

"Shh," he said.

We were ridiculous.

"Anyway," he said, after a few love-dork moments, "you ready?"

"No. But I don't think I'm supposed to feel ready."

I peeked out through a gap in the curtains at the gathering audience. The goal was to locate Margot-Sophia and know in advance where she was sitting, so I didn't make the unprofessional move of actually looking for her when I was onstage—something I've seen happen in every single student production ever.

I found her in the middle—halfway back, where she must have figured the best acoustics would be. Andreas was out there too, in the front row of the balcony.

My heart hurt for them, but I was nearly collapsing from

nerves. Forget the rest of the audience—my mother was about to hear me sing, and that made me want to hide under the stage. And yet I had this ridiculous fantasy that they would both be so moved by the play that it would fix everything somehow. Sure.

Before I knew it, we were in Kansas, and suddenly I understood in a new way what all the rehearsing was for: it was so that even when you feel like you're going to have a heart attack and pee your pants and throw up and keel over all at the same time, your feet, when you hear your cue to go on, will still move.

They will move onto the stage and take you with them.

And your mouth will open and you will say your lines . . .

. . . and you will not have a heart attack or pee your pants or throw up or keel over.

Still, even by the time I got to the song (why was the song so early in the show? Such a big song!) being onstage was still an out-of-body experience.

There I was, blinded by my spotlight, alone in front of two hundred people, thinking, *Shit. Shit, shit, shit! My mother did this in front of thousands, hundreds of times, and made it look like no big deal. How the hell did she do it? Why did she do it?*

The opening notes played, and good God, she was out there and I would never be what she was and I would never even . . . get . . . this . . . song . . . sung.

I started. My voice was wobbling. Terrible. Nearly inaudible. It was a worse start, even, than in the audition, and all I could think was, *Noooooooooo!*

Then into my mind came the picture of the morning's rainbow.

Better . . . and now I breathed . . .

Rainbow, rainbow, Isaac . . .

Deeper breath. And . . . I was in it, on that magic lane, if barely.

In didn't mean it got easy; it just meant I was on a tightrope and thankful not to fall off. But once I hit and held the final high note, I knew I'd survived, and when the wave of applause hit, the relief was so intense, it was like a high.

And the rest of the show . . . whoosh . . . was a pure and taut kind of joy.

I learned that night that, in a live performance, everything, every facial expression, every cue, motion, note, every moment you're on the stage, all that you have is called forth and used in order to make it happen. Everything else fades as you grapple with something essential: telling the story to the best of your ability to those very specific people who have come to have it told.

As the final minutes came and then we were standing for the curtain call, I was electrified and high, and never, ever wanted to get off that stage . . . .

That was when I finally understood, finally knew why she did it, why anyone does. And I understood what she'd lost. How it had been everything. Through the noise and lights I found her eyes, dry and fierce as she stood clapping for me . . . .

And then I wanted to weep.

There was a party in the greenroom after, Juno playing music on speakers she'd set up, and dancing around in her Wicked Witch costume.

There were flowers—lilies from Andreas, who hugged me tight and told me he was so very proud. Gerbera daisies signed *I* were obviously from Isaac, who'd already told me he thought roses were cliché.

Mom, inarguably magnificent in a black-and-gold beaded dress and a floor-length black velvet cape, made her way over after Andreas moved off, and presented me with an orchid—a flower notorious not only for its beauty but for being easy to kill.

"Try to keep it alive," she said, with a rather devilish smile.

Typical.

I nodded. Gulped. People were swirling around and congratulations were flying and there was squealing and laughing and all I could do was stare at Margot-Sophia, and try so hard not to ask her what she thought.

"So, Mom, what did you think?"

And try so hard not to *care* what she thought.

She put her hands on my shoulders, kissed me on both cheeks, then said, "Your voice . . . is nothing like mine, but you are my daughter."

"What's that supposed to mean?"

"It means . . . not bad."

"Not bad?" I repeated. It had been better than not bad. From the audience reaction, I'd felt it. Deep inside I felt it. And I knew that she felt it. I thought she did. But maybe she didn't. Maybe it wasn't.

Over her shoulder I saw Andreas. He winked, blew me a kiss, mouthed *Proud of you* again, and left.

Oh, the thing I wanted, but not from the person I wanted it from.

I turned back to Mom.

"Well," I said, "two more performances. Hopefully I'll be a little less nervous."

"You won't," she said. "Not much less. Unless you're doing it wrong."

We exchanged a few more words and then she announced she was heading home, leaving me to enjoy the backstage party.

Isaac watched her go from where he'd been hovering—not too close, not too far—waiting for me. He'd dressed up in slim, dark pants and a black-and-navy button-down shirt—dark for being backstage, but also a whole other level of style and cuteness.

God, it was a relief to have something so good in my life.

Someone.

Without letting myself think about it too much, I slid and pushed my way through the people between us, and went straight up to him, and kissed him.

There. No more secrecy. Now was as good a time as any to come out as a couple.

A few people whooped, and I heard Juno suddenly cheering.

But Isaac . . . didn't react well.

He flinched and took a rapid step back, almost falling over in the process.

I gasped, and then in seeming slow motion, saw his eyes go to Autumn, who looked shocked and dismayed and hurt, then back to me.

It was only a few short moments, but they were enough. He came back and put an arm over my shoulders and started leading me away from everyone—away from her.

I shrugged him off. I was purple with humiliation, furious, confused.

I was ablaze.

I grabbed my backpack and coat, then headed in the direction of the least resistance, which was into the empty theater. I crossed the stage, went down the front left stairway, and started up the aisle.

"Ingrid!"

I turned. "What?"

"Come back."

"Oh, now you want me?"

"Sorry, I just . . ."

"Humiliated and rejected me?"

"You could have warned me, that's all. I didn't know we were about to go public."

"I guess we're not."

"We can. I just thought you didn't want to, so I . . ."

"So you what? Kept seeing Autumn on the side? Or was I the one on the side?"

"I'm not seeing Autumn . . . exactly."

"Exactly?"

"I'm not. I just . . ."

"You just what?"

"I . . ." He looked everywhere but at me, then mumbled, "I guess we were, sort of . . . but I wasn't serious about it. I wasn't really into it at all, but she seemed to really like me, and I . . . went along with it for a while. I was flattered, you know? Then you and I started hanging out, and I tried to sort of . . . send her the message . . . that I didn't want to continue."

"I don't think she got that message, Isaac."

His shoulders slumped. "No, I guess not."

"How exactly were you trying to send it? By ignoring her and talking behind her back?"

His eyes met mine, full of shame and guilt.

"I kept planning to call her, or go see her and talk to her, but . . . I didn't know what to say, Ingrid. I admit it, I was a coward. But I also . . . I couldn't tell what this was—between you and me. I thought maybe we were just having fun. That maybe it would be over once the show was done."

"So, what, you were keeping your options open? So you could go back to her?"

"No! I just mean, I didn't want to be with her no matter what, but I also didn't want to tell her about you unnecessarily, because that would make it worse for her. I didn't want to hurt her feelings."

"What about my feelings?"

"I couldn't tell what your feelings were! I still can't!" he said, almost shouting all of a sudden. "Because you don't want to talk about feelings, except in the abstract. And you keep things from me—I can tell. You have a whole bunch of . . . I don't even know what going on, but all you want to do is make out with me."

"Excuse me for not spilling my entire soul in the three weeks we've been together," I spat. "I didn't know that was a condition."

"I'm sorry. Maybe that's not fair."

"Damn right it's not. But go on with your explanation. I can't wait to hear the rest."

"Look, I felt guilty about her, okay? I felt a responsibility toward her because I . . . because I let it go as far as it did, and let her maybe think that I was more into it than I was, and so . . . I was all screwed up and hoping she would get the message without my having to make a big thing about it, and that everything would sort itself out just . . . over time. I realize that sounds idiotic."

He was a picture of dejection, but I was too wretched and hurt and furious myself to feel any pity for him, especially as I started to see the full picture.

"You had sex with her," I said, feeling an ice-like pain in my chest.

For a second he looked like he was going to deny it, and I hoped I was wrong, but then he met my eyes and gave a sharp nod.

"Damn it, Isaac!"

"It was only a . . . few times."

I felt like I might vomit.

"When?" I said, voice like steel.

"What does it matter?"

"I don't know. Why don't you want to tell me?"

"Fine. The . . . about two weeks before I . . . before you and I kissed . . . was the last time. And before that . . . it had been a while. Like, two months. I'd been avoiding being alone with her and I was honestly thinking way too much about you, and I went to see her, intending to tell her, officially, that I didn't want to be in a relationship with her . . . but I was sick about it because I hate hurting people. . . ." He swallowed. "And she was already upset when I got there, and, like, didn't really want to let me talk at all, and I just . . . didn't know how to say no."

"You bastard."

"I wasn't with you yet when it happened," he said. "I promise you there was no overlap—none!"

"That's not even the point!" I said. "What about her? You slept with her and then didn't bother to break up with her? Expected her to just figure it out? You're a coward, and an asshole. And now you've made me into the homewrecker. What the hell is the matter with you?"

"I'll talk to her," he said, coming up the aisle, hands reaching for me. "I'll explain everything. Tell her everything."

"Don't touch me," I said, backing away from him. I couldn't stand the thought of him telling her about us, everything about us, when what we were had been so precious to me, so beautiful, and so private. And when it had felt like something so new, like something neither of us had ever experienced, and meanwhile he had already had sex. Had sex with *her*, of all people. And not bothered to tell me, and acted like there was nothing between them. "I don't want you to say a word about me. In fact, I'll save you the trouble of having to tell her anything at all, because there's nothing to tell!"

And then I turned and ran the rest of the way up the aisle and out of the theater and all the way to the subway, where I clenched my fists and pressed my lips together and squeezed my eyes shut, trying to keep the tears in and thinking about how my mom was right: there are no fairy-tale endings and you can't trust things to turn out. You can't trust anybody. Not your friends, not your family, not the nicest, smartest, and most interesting guy you've ever met, who turns out to be a coward and a liar. Especially not him.

Chapter Twenty-Six

SERVE

(Peak Wilderness, Day Thirteen)

Dear Mom,

1. (I love you forever but) fuck you for doing this to me.

2. After two days of feeling relatively normal, I started my day by screaming myself (and everyone else) awake from a nightmare, and I am a wreck again. Months and months like this. How am I supposed to keep going, Mom?

Bonnie, Tavik, and I were there in our sleeping bags, her and Tavik groggy and probably still full of adrenaline from the horror-movie wake-up, while I was curled up in the tightest ball I could make, and crying.

"Is this related to what happened with Peace?" Bonnie asked.

"That fuckface," Tavik murmured.

"No," I said. Although being assaulted by him certainly hasn't been a help, either.

"All right. I realize this is a personal matter, Ingrid," Bonnie said, "but . . ."

"Yes . . . ?"

"It's obvious to all of us that you've suffered . . . some trauma."

For some reason this comment helped shut the tears off, and suddenly I found myself laughing.

"What's funny?" Bonnie said, looking confused.

I kept laughing. I couldn't stop. But I didn't have an answer for her, Mom.

Trauma. Such a small word, only two syllables.

I can't go to bed for a year, if that's what's supposed to happen next. And I can't cry my way through school when I get to London, either. I am not giving up the one thing that can give some meaning and purpose to this crazy life of mine. Which means somehow I have to pull myself together. Again.

Love, et cetera,
Ingrid

Tavik, I suspect, thinks I'm crazy.

And kind of likes it.

And wants to confirm it.

I first realize this when we set out for Day Thirteen's hike, which is the last before we start canoeing, and he lines up right behind me, and says. "I think you might have a multiple personality disorder."

"Very funny," I say, starting onto the path behind Melissa, who has taken over as leader.

"No, really," he says, following. "You started the day screaming, then you were crying, that changed to laughing, and now you're not talking at all."

"I'm talking to you, aren't I?"

"Not because you want to."

"Those aren't personalities, Tavik; they're expressions of emotion. I'm messed up, sure. But it's not like I turn into someone who calls herself Betsy."

"If you say so . . . Betsy," he says.

And it does cause me to smile, a little.

"So . . . ?" he says a few minutes later as we head up the side of a long, steep ridge overlooking the lake.

"So what?"

"It's pretty here."

"Yes," I say, keeping my face forward, mostly because I don't want to fall on it.

"You crying?"

"No."

"You going to tell me the rest of that life story of yours?"

"Not today, Tavik," I say, reaching up to rub my temples, which are aching, and pausing to catch my breath. "Why don't you tell me about some bad guys instead? Or, no offense, but I wouldn't mind just . . . hiking."

"What—you want to listen to the trees? Or, you know, the voices in your head?"

"Ha-ha."

"That's cool," he says, like he totally doesn't care.

But I can tell he's offended, because when we set off again, he goes way to the back of the line, and that makes me feel like crap. More like crap, that is.

The good news is that this final hike is only four hours, and we therefore arrive at camp in the afternoon. Even better, neither Bonnie nor Pat forces us into any organized group activity, which means we finally have the day I've been wishing for—one in which I can wash my stuff, lay it out in the sun, and try to regroup.

Harvey lends/gives me his bar of soap—he's clearly doing his best to go feral, though not in a creepy, Peace-Bob sort of way—and it takes me over an hour to get everything lathered up, scrubbed, rinsed, and wrung out to my satisfaction. When I'm finished, I climb onto one of the heaping stretches of orange, pink, and gray granite that surrounds our beach, where I lay each piece of clothing out, and anchor it carefully with stones I collected and set out in advance. The rock is warm, the sun is hot, there's a gentle breeze . . .

And I am screwed if it rains, because I washed everything except the bikini I'm wearing.

As it is, getting the sleeping bag completely dry is a dodgy proposition.

Below me, a few other people are also washing clothing or airing it out; others are playing cards, swimming, or sitting around having earnest-looking conversations.

I consider joining them.

But then I'll be expected to talk, and Tavik is only biding his time before coming after me again for my life story. I should never have started telling it to him. What is it with people anyway, expecting me to want to talk about things, as if talking will make them better?

So, instead of rejoining the group, I lie back on the warm stone, my clean clothes drying around me, close my eyes, and stare at the inside of my eyelids, pretending to be asleep so no one will bother me.

Seven more days. I only have to survive seven more days of this.

Serve them, more like.

And then, everything will be perfect.

Sure.

Chapter Twenty-Seven

TRY TO KEEP IT ALIVE
(Age Fifteen)

The night of the Isaac breakup, the second night of *Oz* performances, I woke in the wee hours to something I hadn't heard in many years: Margot-Sophia, singing.

She was singing low, really just above a hum, rich and full and beautiful.

It wasn't a song; it was a vocal warm-up—a string of ascending arpeggios, like scales, but prettier and more complicated. I remembered it well. And for a few moments, there under the covers in the dark, I was filled with warmth and wonder and a longing that made me ache, but ache so sweetly.

I had lost that voice too. I never knew until that moment how much I'd missed it, how much I needed to hear it.

But lest I be transported all the way back in time and forget reality, Mom stopped midway up the scale, not venturing into the higher notes—the ones she couldn't sing, or couldn't sing well anymore, and went back down the scale instead.

I lay there, afraid if I got out of bed, she would hear me and stop. And I wondered why—why she was singing now, after all this time? Of course it had something to do with me, and *The Wizard of Oz*. But was it also because she was reconsidering going to Andreas's specialist? Or did she just miss it, like I did? Or was she trying to let it go?

Or was she drinking again? It wasn't a great sign, her being up all night like this.

But whatever the reason, the sound was soothing to my aching soul and brought back such a palpable happiness, I could barely contain it. I squeezed my eyes shut and listened with everything I had, trying to take it in and hold it, until finally she stopped, and I drifted off to sleep.

By Saturday morning I'd received fifteen texts from Isaac, which I refused to read. Mostly refused. They were all variations of "let's talk" and "please listen" and I couldn't. It hurt so much, but many other things were hurting too, and I needed to just slam the door on Isaac and lock it behind me. I didn't want to sort through what was fair and not fair about my reaction, what was ego and jealousy on my part versus what was real and unforgivable. It all felt unforgiveable. And his weakness and confusion were deeply disappointing, because if I were ever going to be in a serious relationship, it would have to be with someone strong, someone honest, someone who knew how to make decisions. Not someone who kinda-sorta-accidentally fell in and out of relationships—or beds, for that matter.

I drank coffee with Mom, who must have taken my extra-miserable mood to be about her breakup with Andreas.

We spent a quiet day in the house, not talking. I didn't mention the middle-of-the-night singing. She seemed weary, fragile, and closed off. I knew from experience that trying to make her talk about anything she didn't want to was foolhardy.

She wasn't coming to the show that night—her plan was to come for opening and closing only, so I got ready, gave her a kiss on the cheek, and headed for the door.

"You were very good," she said to me when I was halfway out.

I froze for a moment, hearing it, then turned around and went back.

"What did you say?"

"I said you were very good. That's twice I've said it and I'm not in the habit of giving out praise like it's nothing. It's something."

"Oh, I know it is," I said, then reached out to hug her, throat tight. "Thank you."

"You are welcome." She hugged back, hard, and I could feel, despite the bite in her voice, that she was shaky. "Now you must go and do it again."

"I will."

"Better this time. Always better."

"Yes."

"For me."

"All right."

"I love you."

"You too."

"Merde."

We did the show, and again, despite everything in my real life really sucking, or maybe because of everything sucking, I loved it. And I was distinctly aware that without the necessity of performing, all I would be doing was wallowing in self-pity. Instead I had something to throw my emotions into.

I ignored Isaac, in the sense that I was perfectly civil and met his eyes when we needed to communicate, but that was all. Juno tried to get me to talk about him—she'd been texting me all day too—but I deflected her questions by asking for an update on her life.

"I see what you're doing," she said, rolling her eyes. "But okay, I'm not a masochist, to keep coming after you to get you to talk when you're like this."

"Like what?"

"The original Fort Knox."

"Juno, I'm sorry, I just—"

"'S okay," she said. "I accept you. Of course you do realize that by never, ever talking about yourself, you give me carte blanche to be totally self-absorbed?"

I shook my head, and laughed, and she took me by the elbow and led me over to where the Tin Man and the Lion were still in their costumes, making a hilarious behind-the-scenes movie on somebody's iPhone.

I hung out for a while after, needing the time to come down from the stage high, but Autumn was sulky and weird, and Isaac was doubly weird, and I quickly realized I couldn't be in the same room with either of them without feeling like I was going to either burst into tears or start throwing things. I couldn't stop myself from picturing them together, naked and probably bathed in an organic, kale-infused aphrodisiac.

Finally I decided to head home, where I could maybe take a page out of my mother's book and just hide in my bed.

Except I didn't get to.

I came trudging home, heart brooding over Andreas, over Isaac, over Mom's singing in the middle of the night and what it meant, and trying, with all this swirling around, to find a place of solidity inside myself—my Kansas, or my Oz; either would do.

I let myself in, took off my backpack and coat, put them on hooks, slid my shoes off and set them neatly side by side.

Even after only two steps in, there was no way to deny the house felt different without Andreas, with him not just on a business trip, but gone. Sitting awake in some executive rental apartment, or maybe a hotel, big heart undeniably broken, blaming himself.

I tiptoed upstairs, looked at my tired, over-made-up eyes and braid-kinked hair in the bathroom mirror, and gave myself a wan smile.

Padding across the carpeted hall to my room, my foot came down on a cold, wet spot. I looked down, then got on my knees, down close to it, and sniffed.

Wine. White wine. Spilled and just . . . left there?

That wasn't like Mom.

Then I was in front of Mom's bedroom door, knocking, and then trying the knob, and realizing it was locked.

"Mom?"

There was no answer and she wasn't okay—somehow I knew it.

"Mom, Mom, Margot-Sophia!"

Nothing.

A louder nothing than I'd ever heard.

The loudest nothing.

I panicked. Suddenly I was screaming, and kicking the door, pounding, throwing my body against it.

Maybe it was illogical, maybe I was acting like a crazy person, but since I couldn't get through the door, I ran through the house, looking for something to break it down with. On my way I grabbed a phone and called Andreas and told him, in a hysterical rush, that something was wrong, and he didn't act like I was crazy at all, but said he'd be right over, and to leave the front door unlocked for him.

I checked the rest of the house and didn't find her, then my eyes landed on a fire poker and I took it upstairs and knocked again and when nothing happened, I swung the fire poker at the door until there were holes and gashes in it, but it was such an old and solid door, I still couldn't get in.

Then I thought I heard something from the inside of the room, so I begged and cried and shouted through the door, willing myself to be through the damned door or for it to open and for everything to be okay, even if it meant all of this was just my overactive imagination. I would be happy to play that particular fool all day long, if she would only be okay.

But the door didn't open.

I had to do something.

I ran down the stairs and outside and turned on the porch lights and pulled a recycling bin—the massive ones with the lids—under the porch and climbed up on it, and jumped from it onto the porch roof. I landed, but couldn't gain purchase on the roof tiles, and therefore slid all the way back down and fell onto the front steps.

It hurt, but nothing was broken. I moved the bin closer and managed to make the leap the second time, with only a small amount of sliding and scrambling, and soon I was standing at her bay window.

The curtains were closed. I decided not to bother knocking, because why would she let me in the window when she hadn't let me in the door?

There were three casement-style windows, each with screens on the bottom. I soon managed to pull off the one on the far left. I then tested the window, which was locked. Could not catch a break. Could have used the damned fire poker at this point, but of course I'd left it inside.

I had to break the window.

I tried first with my elbow, thinking it would be the sharpest, but I didn't have enough force, especially balanced precariously as I was on the roof.

Next I tried my fist.

Bruises only.

Then I kicked the window, and kicked it again, and finally threw my whole self into the kick, which meant my foot and much of my leg went halfway through, with a magnificent smash.

I pulled my leg and foot carefully back out so as to avoid further wounds (there were wounds by now, but I still couldn't really feel anything—I was in my socks, more poor planning), and then I punched the remaining shards of the window through.

Andreas pulled up in his car as I was wriggling my body through the broken window, legs first.

"Ingrid!" He ran up the path. I told him to go in and I'd let him in the bedroom from the other side.

And then I was slipping down onto broken glass, squinting in the dim light of one candle she had lit at her bedside, its flame almost out.

Mom was crumpled on the floor in front of the bed, two empty bottles of wine lying on their sides nearby. And in her hand was a bottle of pills, open.

I'd had lots of practice looking at her to see if she was alive, but this time she was so pale, and I couldn't see her breathing.

I came closer, cautious now despite having tried to break the door down and subsequently smashing the window. I was thinking of all the nights she'd been awake recently, pacing, drinking, singing, about how fragile she'd seemed, how strange. Thinking about how certain medications were not supposed to be mixed with alcohol.

I clicked on the overhead lamp . . . saw her chest rise, ever so slightly. Breathing, thank God, but barely.

Something was pounding, and at first I assumed it was coming from inside me, but then I remembered Andreas, and heard his shouts in the hallway—I'd forgotten to let him in.

I ran to the door, opened it. "Ambulance!" I shouted, running back to her. "Call an ambulance. She's breathing but she's passed out. And I think she took something."

He came forward, cell in hand, already dialing. I slid the

bottle of pills from her grip and looked at the label. She had a few ongoing prescriptions, and these ones were for anxiety, and to help her sleep. Which meant, in combination with the alcohol, if I understood it correctly, taking too many could make everything just . . . stop.

Chapter Twenty-Eight

🍂 🍁 🌿

ON THE WATER

(Peak Wilderness, Day Fourteen)

Duncan arrives on the morning of Day Fourteen, pulling a flotilla of canoes and bringing new food rations.

"Just when the backpacks were starting to lighten," Ally groans.

"If they get too light, Pat and Bonnie will probably load us up with bricks," I say dully. "You ever canoe before?"

"Nope. I'll probably suck."

"Not with all the push-ups and stuff you've been doing with Seth," I say. "You'll be great."

"At least we'll be off our feet," she says, obviously unconvinced. "And hey, maybe it'll be easier. . . ."

Ally's feet have recovered somewhat, in the sense that her first round of blisters healed, and the second and the third set are sitting on top of tougher skin, and therefore not hurting her as much. But her boots are just a tiny bit too small, so they keep coming. She even walked barefoot one day.

Before we can speculate further, Duncan calls us over—

apparently he's giving us a canoe lesson.

Our first collective discovery is that it's easy to tip a canoe. Dead easy.

Second discovery? Getting back into it is hellishly difficult.

We start by learning (the hard way, of course) what, exactly, will cause a canoe to tip. Duncan doesn't relent until every one of us has taken at least one massive spill and managed to climb back into the boat—which often causes a second spill.

There is a lot of shrieking and laughing, and even Duncan cracks a few smiles.

I am pretty worried about drowning, though. Or about having the canoe capsize, along with everything in it, sometime when it's for real and there's no Duncan to help fish us out of the water. The life jackets make sense, but I'm trying to figure out why we need helmets, and instead of being excited, I feel skeptical and ill at ease. I have always been a bit like this— heavy when other people are light, trapped when other people feel free, and just . . . unable to catch the mood.

I'm not crying, though, so that's something.

When we come back onshore, most of us shivering and exhausted, a miracle awaits us: Pat and Bonnie have done most of the work breaking camp—the tents are down, the fire extinguished, and all we have to do is get our packs and divide the pile of fresh food supplies.

For this portion of the trip we're no longer each carrying food. Instead it's going in food barrels—waterproof barrels made of light, hard plastic—one barrel for every canoe. Apparently we can send the barrel down the river if we get into a "situation" and need to lighten our load. A twinge of anxiety lodges in my gut as I wonder what sort of "situation" would call for such an extreme measure, but I try to ignore it.

In addition to the barrels, we now have "dry bags," which are exactly what they sound like—waterproof bags to store our clothing and sleeping bags in, within our packs, so nothing crucial gets wet if the pack goes in the water.

"This is helpful," I say to the leaders, refraining from commenting that I could have used a dry bag the very first day. "Are you guys okay?"

Bonnie smiles. Pat kind of smiles.

I wonder if I've gotten through to them with my objections to the bullshit tactics.

Maybe this part of the trip will actually be enjoyable. . . .

I try to lift myself with a bit of optimism. The hike is over, and this is going to be a great new adventure. I have clean(ish), dry clothing and a waterproof bag to keep things in, and I never have to see Peace-Bob's ass again. Canoeing might not be better than the hiking, but it can't be worse. And I'm tougher than I was two weeks ago. Much tougher.

And maybe all that practice falling in the water was over-preparation and what we'll actually be doing is paddling peacefully along the shores of the lake, early morning mist rising, fish jumping, loons calling, all of us wearing preppy sweaters from outdoorsy catalogs.

Okay, we don't have the preppy sweaters, but I didn't actually hate the canoeing we did with Duncan.

I begin the afternoon feeling better, and even looking forward to starting out.

This, of course, is a mistake.

Because I am about to learn a new word: *portage*.

Portaging is part of canoeing, apparently. . . .

But instead of the canoe carrying you, you carry it.

"We're heading to a nearby river system, and we have ap-proximately one kilometer to cross," Bonnie says, pointing to the map. "Each person carries his or her own pack and then you divide up the other items—food barrel, paddles, helmets, life jackets, canoe."

Some of the canoes have two people; some have three. I'm with Jin and Ally. Bonnie and Pat are together, Tavik is with Harvey, and the other three-person canoe is Melissa, Seth, and Henry. Since we have three, this means one person takes the barrel and life jack-ets, another takes the paddles and helmets, and a third person car-ries the canoe. That's right—the third person carries the canoe. By themselves. Like this portaging thing doesn't suck enough already.

Jin, thank God, volunteers to be the first canoe carrier, and I end up with the paddles and helmets.

The group sets off, a bumbling caravan, into the woods. The people with only two per canoe look horribly overburdened, and at first it seems like I got off easy. But the trail is treacherous—root-riddled, overgrown, and winding—and before long I realize it's really awkward, carrying all this stuff. The paddles keep slip-ping out of my grip and falling, the helmets knock against one an-other and the trees, and the whole thing is totally out of balance.

All up and down the trail, people are having problems, and we're stopping constantly for someone to pick their stuff back up.

There's a lot of grunting, swearing, and sweating. Jin yelps and drops the canoe entirely in order to swat at a black fly that's attached itself to the back of her neck. Twenty minutes in, we're at a standstill, the trail littered with packs, barrels, paddles, and so on, all of us grumpy and frustrated.

Me and my "loons and preppy sweaters" fantasy.

I'm an idiot.

"So," Pat says, making his way to the middle of the line, "what have we learned?"

"Portaging sucks ass," Tavik says.

"Food barrels are heavy," Ally gasps.

"This is impossible," Henry concludes.

"Nothing is impossible," Pat says.

I don't even try to hide my eye-rolling.

"Ingrid?" Pat says. "We can usually count on you for some astute observations. . . ."

"Am I the only one experiencing déjà vu here?"

"Say what you mean," Pat says.

"Oh, okay, how about this sucks?" I say.

"And . . . ?"

"And you set us up to fail again and I shouldn't be surprised, but I still am?"

Pat stands there, still waiting for a better answer.

I look around, in spite of my irritation. What I see is a ton of impossible-to-carry crap.

"It's just too much stuff," I say. "But we need all of it."

"And the solution is . . . ?" Pat says.

I shrug.

And then I see.

"Oh, don't tell me," I say, barely repressing a groan. "We have to take more than one trip?"

"Bingo!" Pat's face splits into a huge smile. "Take what's manageable, leave the rest, and things will go much faster. It might take two trips; it might take three."

"You could have just told us, and we would have believed it," I say, throwing my hands up. "Instead you've just reinforced the fact that we can't trust you."

Bonnie has the decency to look ashamed.

Pat, though, just gives me his wiser-than-thou look, and says, "It's yourself you have to learn to trust, Ingrid."

I might hate him.

I would punch something if I had any arm strength to spare.

Instead, I join the rest as we heave our packs off to the side of the path and get ready to move forward. Ally keeps the food barrel, now with the option of swinging it over her shoulder. The rule is still one person for the canoe, as carrying it is an essential camping skill, and I volunteer to take over because Jin's fly bite is swollen and itchy.

The canoe isn't that heavy unless you get off-balance, but then it's awful. It's much harder than carrying gear, and harder than hiking, too, obviously. Well, it *is* hiking—hiking with a canoe. With all the ups and downs and turns and twists of the trail, I get thrown off-balance often. My shoulders and upper back start burning, and my arms start shaking. *I hate this. I hate my life.* I hate that I could have gone home three days ago and didn't. Obviously I'm insane, not to mention ridiculously stubborn. And now there's nothing to do but keep going.

The only good news is that this task takes so much focus that

I have no brain space left with which to dwell on my legion of other problems.

It takes three trips before we're at the river with all our gear.

We're all falling-down tired, but now we have to canoe for another three hours.

Most of us can't even lift a paddle right now.

Tavik comes up to me during the short snack break before we get on the water, and says, "How about we try it interview-style?"

"Pardon me?"

"Your life story."

"Tavik, I can barely move, much less speak."

"You have a boyfriend?"

"What? No."

"Someone trash your heart?"

"None of your business."

"I never said it was. But that sounds like a yes. Wasn't that easy? I ask, you answer. Nothing bad happened."

"Tavik . . ."

"You know, you're not going to get rid of me. I'm like an on-coming train."

"And I'm, what, tied to the tracks?"

"Possibly. But you see? We have a deep conversation going now. With metaphors 'n' shit."

I put my head in my hands and groan.

"I think you need to talk. Who tied you to the track? Or did you do it to yourself? What does the track symbolize? What does it mean?"

"Oh my God."

"And who was the boy?"

"I think we're about to go," I say, pointing with relief to where Bonnie and Pat are edging their canoe toward the water.

"You can tell me about him after dinner, if you want."

"Yeah, sure," I say, not meaning it, but too fried to argue.

Dear Mom,

Isn't it hilarious that I chose to stay for the portaging and canoeing? Can you hear me laughing from where you are? No? Let me try a little louder.

HA-HA-HA-HA-HAAAAAAAAA.

Now, here's a little life/nature lesson for you:

If you ever have to schlepp a canoe through the forest, then paddle said canoe for a zillion hours, and then you find yourself, at dusk, with arms and shoulders like noodles on fire, and wishing only for a simple dinner of bugs and rice followed by passing out in your tent . . .

And then you discover that your asshole trip leaders have taken the tents and given them to a giant Scotsman who has ferried them far beyond your reach, and that they expect you, instead, to build and sleep in your own lean-to . . .

Yes, in a lean-to . . .

for the rest of the bloody, rotten trip—that's seven more nights, by the way—

here's what you do:

That is, here's what you figure out, and do with the help of your fellow campers, because the lousy, manipulative leaders refuse to give any instruction, and don't even demonstrate, because guess what? They get to keep their tent. . . .

- Find two trees, not too far apart, that are on high ground and just the right distance from each other.
- Collect many long narrow straight sticks, plus three larger branches.
- Make the three large branches into a frame to lean against the two trees. Hopefully you will have rope for this. If you're lucky. (Note: if you're in this situation in the first place, you're probably not lucky.)
- Lay the long narrow sticks against the frame (lean them, actually—get it?).
- Set/weave evergreen branches on top of the narrow sticks, trying not to knock the whole thing over in the process. Then finish with a layer of large-ish leaves facing out and flat so they will funnel the rain, if it rains, down to the ground, instead of into the lean-to.
- Place your sleeping bag inside the lean-to.
- Cry a few hot, silent, and totally pointless tears while you ponder the lengths you would go to, what you would give, or give up, just to get your stinky tent back . . . .
- Hate everything.

Your wretched daughter who still loves you,
Ingrid

Harvey, Jin, and Seth all build solid-looking lean-tos.

Henry will only be able to crawl into his, because he's made it on top of a hollow. Ally's is dodgy, Melissa's looks like a beaver dam, mine is a deathtrap.

And Tavik—the person who generously helped us all figure out what to do—has a masterpiece. The branches are tight and even, it's almost tall enough to stand in, and he made it next to a large boulder, so one side of it has an actual wall.

"Unlike me, I'd say you have an excellent chance of surviving the apocalypse," I say to him, beyond caring if people notice the tear streaks on my face.

"When I was a kid, there was a forest—well, some woods, I guess. Me and my brother, when my dad was on a bender, we'd go build one of these in the woods, hide out for the day, or even overnight. We built one really good one that stayed up for years."

"Wow." Every time I get to feeling sorry for myself on this trip, I hear one of these stories so matter-of-fact in its terribleness that it makes me feel thoroughly unworthy of my own unhappiness. "Sounds rough."

But Tavik grins. "It was okay. We were safer that way, and we kinda had fun. Glad you like it. Yours is . . ." He surveys mine, a funny expression on his face.

"Look, I really can't even lift my arms after today, so it's a miracle I built one at all."

I am not keen on sleeping out in the open, so I actually worked hard trying to make the roof area dense, in case it rains. So the top is heavy and furry, but the whole thing sways slightly in the wind.

"It looks very . . . uh, artistic." He's trying not to laugh.

"Let's be honest; I'll be lucky if it doesn't collapse on me. And then, tomorrow, after it has and I have a concussion? That's when Pat will tell me what I did wrong."

"I'm just across the way if you need to take refuge."

"Oh, so you can fire questions at me about my nonexistent love life?"

"What happened?" he says. "Since you brought it up."

"There was a boy," I say. I don't know why the hell I'm saying it, but I am. "His name was Isaac." And then, standing there in front of our lean-tos, I start to tell Tavik about Oz—the Isaac part, not the Mom part.

It comes out calm and factual, and he just listens until we're called to eat.

Dinner is a quiet affair. Everyone except Harvey and Tavik is pissed about losing the tents, but no one is tired enough to argue, and anyway, what's the point?

Bonnie excuses us from circle, a reprieve that is met with a muted cheer.

The downside is bedtime comes much faster.

I had not realized how much the tent protected us not only from mosquitoes but also from the sound of them. And there are bats. We can hear them and sometimes see them in the moonlight, or firelight, swooping low across the sky. They must have been around the entire time, but of course tonight is when I notice them.

I wear the netted hat to bed. I tie it up at its base, around my neck, then climb into my sleeping bag, and pull it up over my net-covered head, so there is absolutely no skin exposed, and really just enough net exposed for me to breathe.

The temperature keeps dropping, and I start to shiver.

Every forest sound becomes, in my mind, a bat swooping down to bury itself in my sleeping bag, or a venomous snake slithering in beside me, or a rampaging bear coming to eat me one limb at a time. . . .

I see Tavik's reading light click on, and moments later I'm at the side of his lean-to, sleeping bag in hand, mosquito hat still on.

"Knock, knock," I whisper.

With amazement, I realize he has some netting hung over the open side of his structure.

"I heard you coming," he says, pulling the fabric aside and poking his head out. "You'd be a terrible tracker. Your lean-to fall apart?"

"Not yet. But . . . I'm cold and s-scared."

"Come in." He moves to make room for me.

I crawl in and scoot over to one side.

"Where did you get this?" I point to the fabric.

"Something I brought, just in case. Crunches up small. You okay?"

"No." I wriggle into my sleeping bag, pull it back up to my neck—even this little movement kills my canoeing-sore arms—and sit facing him.

"You're a freak in that, you know," he says, reaching out and touching the hat brim.

"Add that to the long list of things I no longer give a shit about," I say.

"Fair enough," he says with a grin. "You can probably do without it in here, though. I killed any mosquitoes that got in."

"Okay . . ." I pull the hat off and take a shaky breath. It's good to be in a superior shelter, and not alone. "I miss the tent."

"I know," he says, eyes on mine in the dim light. "The night sounds seem a lot louder, and I guess we were keeping each other warm. All of us, I mean."

"Uh-huh." I'm still shivering, and trying unsuccessfully to hide it. By morning I am going to be a frozen ball of lactic acid.

"Listen, you could . . ." He holds his arms out. "Turn around, and you can lean back against me. It'll help you warm up. I'll just lean against the rock."

"Well . . ." I hesitate. The idea of having a warm body to press against is powerfully tempting. In fact I am almost desperate for it all of a sudden. For the warmth, and maybe even for the contact. But Tavik is . . .

"Come on, I'm harmless," he says, like he's reading my thoughts.

"I call bullshit on that."

"What, because I'm a convicted felon?"

"Yes. And."

"And? What 'and'?"

"And . . ." I put my arm out in an all-encompassing gesture. "Oncoming train, and. Tough guy, and. Lots of and."

"Really." His eyes seem to go liquid, and darker, and they pull at me.

"See?" I say, and swallow. "Put that away."

"What?"

"That non-harmless look." I'm telling him to stop looking

at me like that, but . . . I don't hate the feeling it gives me. It's better than most of the other feelings I've been experiencing lately. I could fall into this feeling and stay there for quite some time, and it would be . . . distracting, at least.

"This is just the look of me appreciating how your mind works," he says, not stopping.

There's a long, fraught pause where we are totally still, until finally I look away, breaking the connection.

"So . . ." Tavik says, then swallows. "What ever happened to poor Isaac?"

"Oh. Well . . ." I don't want to talk about it, really, but my mind is racing with thoughts along the lines of *What the hell did I just almost do . . . ?* and this is therefore a welcome change of subject. "After the play, Isaac tried for the rest of the school year to make up with me, but I was too upset. Then last summer I realized maybe I should give him a chance. But when school started, he was with Autumn again, which sort of . . . crushed me . . . even though it was my own fault. It made me insane, having to see them together at school. Then . . . he broke up with her during the December break and sent me this long e-mail saying he was still thinking about me, and he knew his thing with her was a mistake. . . . But it was too late because I wasn't . . . in the right headspace. That's about it."

"Sad story," Tavik says.

"I guess. Yeah."

"You're still shivering. Come here."

"But . . ."

"Let's not be dumb. You're freezing. We've slept in the same tent all this time, and I can help you warm up. I *am* harmless, as in, I mean you no harm. Not even the fun kind."

"Fine."

"Good. Come." I turn and let him pull me back between his legs, my back against his chest. Then he wraps his arms around me, and I drop my head back against his shoulder because he is so amazingly warm, and the closeness of him is confusing enough to scramble my misery.

"See?" he says. "Helpful, and mostly harmless."

"Okay, sure," I say, pressing myself even closer.

"I'm too tired to cause any trouble tonight, anyway," he says, and yawns.

And then I yawn. A bone-deep warmth is kicking in, giving me a sleepy, stoner sensation.

"I should go," I whisper blearily, a few minutes later.

In answer, he tightens his arms around me, and says, "Shh. You're going to sleep with me."

That gives me a jolt, and I start to pull away.

"Sleep," he says. "If I meant something else, I'd say so. Haven't we covered this?"

"Is that what we were covering?"

"You're driving me nuts. Let's go to sleep."

"Won't we get in trouble?"

"What are they going to do? Anyway, I wake up early. We can sneak you back then. Come here . . ."

He pulls me close again, and then drags over the pile of stuff he uses for a pillow, clicks off the reading light, and eases us both down onto the ground, wrapping himself around me in spoon position.

I am so toasty, so weary, and so sore, I can't imagine leaving.

"Okay," I say.

"Wise choice," he says.

I wake early, the sky just lightening, with Tavik breathing into the back of my neck, arm still around me, and fast asleep. It's a strange feeling, waking up with someone. It feels intimate, vulnerable, warm.

But mornings are hard for me. Mornings are when I'm too sleepy to fend off images of Mom crumpled on the floor with the bottle of pills, and when I wake up sometimes, heart racing, looking for a window to kick in.

I carefully slide out from under Tavik's arm, stifling a groan as I start to feel how sore my muscles are from yesterday. I almost can't move at all, and it isn't just my arms, back, and shoulders, it's my abs, sides, hip flexors . . . even my fingers. Still, I collect my hat, and duck out of the lean-to, staying close to the ground until I get to mine in case anyone does happen to be looking. Then I push my sleeping bag into my rickety structure and carefully climb inside .

An hour later my eyes meet Tavik's over our respective bowls of fried granola.

"Morning, Ingrid," he says, completely casual.

"Morning," I say, the same way.

"Good sleep?"

"Awesome," I say.

We both smile, then look away, and the warm buzz that gives me, deep in my chest, is hard to ignore.

Chapter Twenty-Nine

PAPER DOROTHY
(Age Fifteen)

Mom was still unconscious when the ambulance arrived.

In the hospital they pumped her stomach, which would get rid of some of the alcohol, but wouldn't help with any medication that was already in her bloodstream.

All we could do was wait. The substances would work their way through, and she would be fine, or not. I had cuts on my legs and arms, and blood on my clothing, and one of the nurses was kind enough to bandage me up, but I hardly noticed it happening.

The waiting gutted me.

Those were some of the darkest, most frightening hours of my life to that point. I could not see there being life past her death. If she died, I would die too. I felt like I was dying already.

And I ran through, over and over, what I could have done differently, and tortured myself with the idea that this was my fault for doing the play, for letting myself get so distracted with

my own happiness that she'd walked to the edge and been standing there, and I hadn't noticed.

Finally, in the early hours of the morning, she woke.

She woke like nothing had happened—sharp and wasp-
ish and insistent on getting up and out of bed. She literally
pulled the IV out of her arm, and marched/hobbled out of her
room. Andreas had to pick her up and carry her back. But
they couldn't legally keep her in the hospital now that she
was lucid.

"But you overdosed," I said, almost shouting. "You almost
died!"

"Don't be absurd," she snapped. "You two are acting like
drama queens."

I opened my mouth, then shut it again, at a loss for words.

By ten in the morning we were back home, where she refused
to go to bed and instead zoomed around, quarterbacking the
cleanup of the mess in her room, even going so far as to scold me
for damaging the door and breaking the window. We stripped
the bed, and Andreas cleaned up the broken glass and put a
temporary cover on the window.

"Insurance is not going to cover that, you know," she said.

"Insurance wouldn't have helped me much if you had died,
either," I said sullenly.

"Enough with this subject," she said, but then she started to
tremble, and her face turned red, and a single tear made its way
down her cheek.

"Oh, Mom." I melted instantly, and rushed to put my arms
around her. "Mom, Mom . . . shhh . . . it's okay . . ."

She was shuddering, silently sobbing, clutching me close.

"Margot-Sophia Lalonde should never be so foolish, so weak," she said. "Promise me you will never tell."

"Sure, sure . . ."

"No!" She pulled back to look me in the face, holding my shoulders. "Not 'sure, sure.' Never. Tell. You must promise."

"Fine, I promise. According to you there's nothing to tell anyway."

It was late afternoon and we'd just ordered takeout when the landline rang. Only then, as it was ringing and I realized my phone had been dead for hours, did I see the time and realize . . .

Oh noooooooooooooooo . . .

I was supposed to be onstage in twenty minutes.

It was Isaac, of course, calling me in his official role as stage manager.

"I can't come," I told him.

"What?"

"Look, Autumn probably knows my part. You'll have to work it out."

"Ingrid, are you kidding me? We can't do this without you. And half the audience is already here. What's going on?"

"I can't do the show. Please . . ." Tears were streaming down my face now, but I swallowed, trying to sound normal. "Please apologize for me. . . ."

And then suddenly Margot-Sophia grabbed the phone.

"This is Ingrid's mother," she said. "Please forgive my daughter for frightening you. Of course she will be there . . . Yes.

No, this was simply a misunderstanding. Ingrid will be there. Thank you. Good-bye, young man."

She hit End and put down the phone.

"Mom, I can't leave you. And I can't go out there and . . . sing about rainbows right now."

"Are you such a coward?"

"What?"

"You have a bond of trust with your audience. No matter what pain you're in, no matter what is happening in your life, you must not break that trust, ever. The golden rule is that you show up. Always."

"Mom, you just—"

"I just nothing! When you are performing, you show up. Unless you are dead, you show up. You are not free to indulge in cowardly emotional weakness when you make a commitment like this. You must be strong. I certainly don't want you here, sniveling and watching my every move. I am fine. I will not be fine, though, if you don't go."

"Ingrid has had a very difficult time," Andreas said. "She may well be in shock . . . ."

Margot-Sophia waved him off, her gaze both fiery and empathetic, somehow. Because she could do both at once, even less than twenty-four hours after overdosing.

Then she pulled away, marched up to her bedroom, and came back in a fabulous electric-blue dress, flats, and lipstick.

"I for one have paid for a ticket, and I expect to get my money's worth," she announced, a slight quaver evident in her voice, but with her chin up. "And I want to see my talented daughter perform. Andreas, my love, get the car."

Somehow I did it. I couldn't tell if it was good or bad, and I don't know what I did differently, but people cried during "Over the Rainbow."

Not me, though. Inside me was an ocean and I had to funnel it through a straw. This took everything I had—it took even what I didn't have. Margot-Sophia was out there, and she expected me to do it, and so I got it done.

At the final curtain call, there were flowers, tears, congratulations all around. Backstage, after, was gleeful pandemonium. People wanted me to celebrate, but I was not who I'd been yesterday, or the day before that.

It felt like that girl had died. Like Dorothy before and after the tornado, but worse. So much worse, because I didn't feel plucky and brave and certain and strong. I couldn't go back to Kansas, either.

I was like a paper doll, or a bullet-riddled target practice figure, on my feet, standing at the closing-night party only because I didn't know what else to do.

Andreas and Mom were waiting for me—together at least—and so I didn't stay long.

Isaac intercepted me at the dressing room door, on my way out.

"You're going?"

"Yup." I had an armload of flowers.

"Not staying?"

"Going means not staying last I checked."

"Ingrid, please . . ."

"If I want a ride home, I have to go now."

"What happened to your hands?" (My hands were discreetly bandaged, and Isaac was the only person to mention it.) "And . . . what happened? Something happened."

I stared at him, then shook my head.

"Ingrid . . . we need to talk. I need to explain to you . . . about Autumn and—"

"I don't care about Autumn right now," I said, my self-control almost at an end. "And I don't want to talk to you. I can't."

I was about to start bawling right there in the dressing room, and everyone was going to think it was about him, but really I just didn't have one more iota of energy to give to Isaac at that moment, or to anything else. Maybe I'd overreacted about Autumn, though I didn't think so, and in normal circumstances we'd have been able to work it out. But not now. Even if I loved him, which maybe I had. In fact, in that moment, I knew I had. That only made everything worse, and more impossible.

I was Paper Dorothy. Flimsy, and full of holes, barely standing.

"Forget it, Isaac," I said, and pushed past him, jaws tight and lips pressed together to keep me from crying. "Good-bye."

Chapter Thirty

OPTIONS

(Peak Wilderness, Days Fifteen to Eighteen)

The canoeing days are long. Six or seven hours of paddling under the hot sun with aching shoulders, back, arms, and obliques. Lots of time to ponder how much longer this pain is going to last, hour by hour, day by day. It's agony. Long agony. We take turns at the bow and stern positions, and in our canoe one person has to be the "princess," which is the person who sits in the middle on their pack because there isn't a seat.

It turns out paddling and steering a canoe takes coordination not just of oneself, but with others. And we are a group of people at odds with ourselves *and* others. There are long periods of determined silence in our canoe, broken by bursts of grumbling and bickering when one of us gets out of sync, or our paddles whack each other, or the front person sends a big splash of water onto the people at the back, or the canoe is suddenly going the wrong direction. Ally does more apologizing than bitching, but Jin and I bitch.

In fact, Jin is noticeably out of sorts, and I soon realize she doesn't like being on the water, not that she'd admit it.

"Good thing we didn't try this before the hiking," I mutter at one point.

"We'd have drowned," Jin agrees grimly.

This is one of our more positive exchanges.

When everything goes smoothly, though, which happens more often as we get the hang of things, canoeing is almost soothing. Well, it's soothing in the sense that your body starts to be able to do its thing, and your mind can wander.

I'm not that keen on where my mind wanders, though.

Talking about Isaac and Oz to Tavik has had the effect of stirring up those memories for me, and I find my mind looping back through the horrific ups and downs, through the hours I spent not knowing if my mom would live, and over and over to her making me promise I would never tell anyone.

I am very close, with Tavik, to breaking that promise— close in the story itself, which I know he's not going to let go of, and close also because I'm angry she asked me to keep it secret. Keeping her secrets never did me any good, and didn't help her either, I don't think. And being out here in the wilderness, I've started to realize how tightly, how tensely, I have to hold myself all the time, how tightly *to* myself I have held everything about me for so long. I do it now by instinct. I do it because I don't know how not to, because I'm afraid not to, because it has become the way I am. I thought it was strength, this solitary absorption of all things, good and bad. But it has left me very alone, and maybe that is part of what freaks me out, here in the wild. I feel my aloneness, and my inability to easily cross the bridge to another person.

Other people, over the past few weeks, have opened up—some of them to all of us, some to just one or two others. Melissa, since Peace left, has talked about everything to everyone, and she is transformed.

Ally has been quieter about it, but she is changing too, spending hours with Seth, but also talking in circle, and there is a quiet competence growing in her. Almost everyone else, with the exceptions of Jin and me, has relaxed into a comfortable rapport with the rest of the group. Everyone else is friends by now, whereas we are only friend*ly*.

My body is stronger, and I have fantastic wilderness skills, compared to when this started fifteen days ago, and even some unexpected leadership skills. And I can speak my mind about something that pisses me off. All of that is good, I guess. But I am still trying to build up and reinforce the walls I use to keep myself strong.

Supposedly strong.

But definitely alone.

Maybe that's why talking to Tavik is so tempting.

Maybe that's why I spend so much of Day Fifteen thinking about whether I'll sneak over to his lean-to again tonight, and sleep with him curled up around me, and whether or not it's actually sleep I'm looking for.

Maybe that's why I don't go.

On Day Sixteen we pause for a breathless half hour to watch a moose near the side of the river. We've been seeing a lot more wildlife while canoeing than we did hiking, partly due to the higher speed of travel, but also Pat says hikers are so incredibly noisy that they scare the animals off, especially this far north, where there are so few humans. From the canoes, though, we've seen foxes, a couple of beavers, a few deer, and a ton of toads, in addition to the moose.

Because we're a little behind, Bonnie suggests we have what she calls a "floating lunch," which saves us the time it would take to get onshore, unpack the canoes, and so on. At the top of a long straight part of the river, we paddle close to one another and then hang our legs into each other's canoes, thereby creating a haphazard flotilla. Then Melissa, Henry, and Seth make us wraps from their food barrel, and we pass them along from canoe to canoe until everyone has one, and we drift down the river, happily eating.

We're just finishing this rather fantastic lunch when the river takes a turn, merges with another river, and widens out. Suddenly we're moving fast—really fast. We all scramble to disentangle the canoes, and quickly grab our paddles.

"Yo, Pat, is this a rapids?" Henry shouts.

"Nope, not a rapids," Pat calls back calmly. "Just a fast part of the river."

"*Rapid* is another word for *fast*," I point out.

"Don't panic."

Panic or not, Harvey and Tavik's canoe is soon stuck on a rock, and they're in trouble. Pat and Bonnie start to paddle back upriver to help, while we pass them, barely in control.

"Get to the shore," Bonnie says, jerking her head toward it. "And grab on to one of those branches. And be ready to catch their food barrel!"

I guess this is what they meant by "situation."

We somehow get to the side, and Jin and I half stand to grab on to the low-hanging branches, while Ally paddles to keep us steady.

Upriver, Bonnie and Pat send the food barrel our way.

"If I let go to catch it, can you hang on?" Jin asks.

I'm not sure I can, but I say, "Go for it," and brace myself to hold on once Jin lets go—hands tight, legs half wrapped around the seat below me.

She lets go, and my whole body jerks, but I manage to hang on, and keep the canoe under me too, as the barrel comes closer.

I tighten my grip again, trying to ignore my shaking arms. . . .

And that's when I see the freaking *bear*, standing not more than ten feet away from us, under the shade of the same tree I'm hanging on to. It's dark brown, and massive, and it's looking right at me. Ohmyfuckinggod.

Out of the corner of my eye I can see Jin leaning out as far as she can without tipping the canoe, and she almost has the barrel. We need that barrel—the food is planned meticulously, down to the last meal. Of course we might be about to *become* a meal. Facts race through my mind: Bears rarely attack humans. Bears mostly eat berries. Bears are not so hungry in summer compared to spring. Bears mostly attack only if you threaten their young and I don't see any young. Bears are as scared of us as we are of them.

Sure.

Please, Jin . . .

"Got it!" Jin cries, and then pulls the barrel close and heaves it into the canoe.

"Good job!" Ally shouts. "Great job!"

"Guys!" I say from my precarious position. "Not to freak you out, but we have to go. Now. I'm going to let go, and both of you start paddling away from the shore as soon as I'm down. Okay?"

Neither of them knows what the problem is, but by the way they move—quickly—they believe me. I let go of the tree and drop down in one as-smooth-as-possible motion, trying not to cause us to tip in the process, and they start paddling like crazy. I haul myself onto my seat, pick up my paddle, and do the same.

With the weight of the extra barrel in our canoe, we sit low in the water, the paddling is more difficult, and the result is slower. Too slow.

"Holy mother of shit," Jin says from behind me.

"What is it?" Ally says, her voice high with panic.

"Just paddle," I say.

"Bear," Jin says. "There on the shore."

Ally gives a squeak and paddles faster.

"It's not going to attack us," I say, trying to sound sure.

"But . . . they . . . can swim . . ." Ally gasps.

"Yep," Jin says.

"I think the response we're supposed to be having is how beautiful and majestic it is, and how lucky we are to have spotted it," I say, tight-voiced.

On the shore the bear is still watching us, and then it gets down on all fours and lopes along the rock and sand, almost keeping pace with our canoe.

"I'll be filled with wonder later on," Jin says. "Right now I might barf."

Finally we hit the center of the river where the water is moving faster. The bear seems to lose interest, and we leave it behind. Along with ten years of my life, I'm sure.

Dear Mom,

Canoeing has put me in a strange state. Almost like I'm having an out-of-body experience some of the time. Like I am floating along beside myself, or above myself, and thinking about things from a one-step-away position. Or I go wandering off in the forest, away from myself entirely. This, it occurs to me, could be "meditative"—i.e., a good thing—or it could be "dissociative"—i.e., I am going batshit crazy. I'm just spacey, maybe.

I might be depressed. . . .

Except I don't feel sluggish or heavy, and when I need to wake the hell up and respond to something, I can do it. It's like a switch is flipped, and I go back into my body and do what I need to do. And that feels good.

But when I am back outside myself, I feel a little bit sad for the me that I'm watching, and yet I am cheering her on.

I could have been eaten by a bear today.

But I guess I also could have drowned or choked or had a freak accident.

I built a decent lean-to tonight. I could stay in it and test my courage further. Or I could go sleep with a very warm ex-convict who always wants me to talk. A different kind of test. A different kind of courage.

If that's what it is.

Five more days of this . . .

Good night, diva mama,

Ingrid

Tavik's light is flashing.

Anyone could see me going over.

But Ally and Seth are still talking by the fire, and there's no rule about visiting each other, and anyway, Pat and Bonnie's tent is down near the water.

"Hey," Tavik says when I arrive with my sleeping bag, and then ushers me inside.

"Were you signaling me?"

"Sort of."

I am in my body enough to know how cold and tired I am. In fact, it's hard to connect to that detached feeling at all when I'm around Tavik. Something about him requires all hands on deck, mentally speaking.

"You want to continue with our interview?" he says, a smile quirking at the corner of his mouth.

All I really want is to curl up next to him again, battle my lust for him for a few minutes while I get warm, and then sleep. But maybe it would be rude to just say so. Still, I am supposed to be using my true voice.

"Actually, I came to sleep with you," I say, meeting his eyes straight on, daring him to take it the wrong way.

"Again?"

"Again. If you don't mind."

He gazes at me for a moment, then shakes his head. "No, I don't mind."

"We can talk if you want, first. If you're not tired enough from the portaging and the near-death experiences and . . ."

"No, get on the bed," he says, patting his sleeping bag, "and let's do it."

I have to admit, I giggle. But within a couple of minutes, we're huddled together just like the other night, and as I warm up, the pain and soreness of the day seem to seep out of me.

But Tavik is wide-awake, and despite my fatigue, I am too.

"Know any bedtime stories?" I ask.

"What, like 'Baa, Baa, Black Sheep'?"

"Uh, that's a song."

"You would know."

"Nobody sang 'Baa, Baa, Black Sheep' to me, trust me."

"But did she sing to you? Your mom?"

"Of course. But it was Verdi. Puccini. Mozart."

"Classical shit. I don't think you lost out."

"Well, I guess whatever you didn't have, something was there in its place."

"Yeah. Like a kick in the ass," he says.

"Literally?"

"Yeah, but that's not a bedtime story."

"Mine isn't either."

"Maybe not, but . . ." His squeezes me closer. "I saw it in jail; everybody needs to talk at some point. To get it out. They reach this point when it's, like, oozing from them. You're like that. Or we could fuck."

I sit up fast, this comment a good reminder that this isn't a guy who'd just want to share a few dreamy kisses, if I were foolish enough to start something.

"Kidding, kidding," he says, dissolving into rude laughter, and covering his mouth to muffle the sound. "You should see your face."

"Tavik . . ."

"I'm sorry. Lie down. I told you a bunch of times: you're safe with me. I'm just trying to make you laugh. And, you know, get you to talk to me."

I glare at him for a long moment, and then lie back down, this time facing him.

"You're an asshole," I say.

"Hey, gimme a break—I've been in jail."

"All the more reason for me to be worried."

"Ah, so you think I'm a sex-starved desperado."

I shrug.

"I could be a sex-starved desperado just as a result of this trip," he points out. "Depending on my needs. But I just meant that I'm a petty criminal—I'm supposed to be bad-mannered and occasionally shocking. But I'm also honest, and hospitable, and not a rapist, and don't forget, warm and in possession of a large mosquito net."

"There's that."

"Not that I wouldn't fuck you under different circumstances."

"Thanks. I think."

"Under almost *any* different circumstances."

"Oh, like what?" I can't stop myself from asking.

"Like you saying yes?"

This should appall me, but instead it makes me laugh. Hysterically, and into my sleeping bag because I need to muffle the sound.

"See? You just think it's funny."

"I can't believe you said that."

"Doesn't it break the tension, though? I say it out loud knowing it's not happening, you confirm it's not happening, we leave it behind."

"Oh, is that what you're doing?" It reminds me of Juno and her "deal with the penis" lecture. I think we just dealt with the penis.

"Sure," he says. "Now, are you sleepy yet? I'm a really good listener."

"Actually," I say with a yawn, "I really do want to go to sleep."

"All right," he says. "Sweet dreams, Ingrid."

"Thank you for making me feel . . ."

"What . . . ?" he says.

"Safe . . . ?"

In the morning we wake at the same time, and early.

"Just build a piece of shit for your lean-to tonight," he murmurs into my ear. "And stay with me."

I nod, and try to ignore the ache I'm starting to feel, lying crushed up against him.

Day Seventeen is bear-less, but we have more rocks to contend with, plus another portage—two kilometers—and this time

Seth, in the lead and walking just two people ahead of me with a canoe, almost steps on a rattlesnake . . . and screams bloody murder while backing up as fast as he can, which causes a backward avalanche on the path, and then a stampede.

For once, neither Bonnie nor Pat equivocates about what we need to do.

"We go around," Pat says.

"We bushwhack," Bonnie confirms.

And so we very carefully pick up the fallen and dropped canoes and gear, and do it.

Bushwhacking is exactly what it sounds like—whacking and being whacked by bushes and tree branches as you forge your own path through the forest. It's hard, time-consuming, and super awkward with a canoe. We're heading for the first trip back when Seth has a total meltdown.

"I can't lead," he says, his face covered in sweat.

"What's the problem, Seth?" Bonnie says.

"A rattlesnake is the problem!" he shouts.

As he says this, I remember how he also wigged out when we were in the mud pit. If he has a phobia of snakes, this all makes sense.

"If you face your fear, it will begin to diminish," Pat says in his wisest voice.

"I faced it already. I keep facing it every single day out here. I'm not going back there!"

It takes the entire group to convince Seth not only to come back with us to get the next two loads of stuff, but also to lead.

Remembering how I helped Isaac years ago, I offer to sing as we're starting out, and sing a couple of soothing arias.

Then Harvey takes over for comic relief, telling Seth a long, ridiculous story about a potato-gun contest he went to one time.

When we get to the beach of tonight's camp, which is on a very pretty little island, Seth turns to all of us and says, "Since I just survived the scariest day of my life, I may as well add to it and tell you all I'm gay. And if that didn't scare the gayness out of me, I don't think anything is going to."

I can tell he expects us to react like his über-religious parents, because he's amazed to see all of us smiling, and people coming to hug him, pat him on the back, and congratulate him.

"No one cares?" he says, looking around in amazement.

"No one is surprised," Jin clarifies. "But all of us care."

We stand around chatting, and I feel a wonderful sense of connection from having gone through this day, and then this revelation, with Seth. Then Bonnie and Pat take him for a walk and talk, leaving the rest of us to set up.

All at once I'm alone again.

And I'm so tired, I just want to fall on my face.

In my lean-to.

That I still have to build, just to keep up appearances, even though I'm not planning on sleeping in it.

Tonight's circle conversation is all about facing fears and about surrounding yourself with people who support you—finding your tribe.

Seth is still terrified. His family might kick him out, and he would then be homeless, or forced to live with other, equally disapproving relatives. Henry and Harvey tell him he can take the bus to the city and come to their house if that happens.

"Our mom likes to take in strays," Henry says. "Uh, not to call you a stray."

"My folks aren't fit to host anybody," Ally says. "But in a couple of years when I'm eighteen, me and you could get an apartment. If you can handle being around a baby—well, a toddler by then. And if I can find a job, and if I have her back."

"You could come to my house too," I say, and then turn to Jin. "And that goes for you as well, if things go badly with your aunt. Even if I'm in London, my parents . . . It would be fine. My room will be empty anyway. And Andreas, my dad, is great in a crisis."

"We can be your people," Melissa says to Seth.

I wait in my flimsy lean-to until the camp is quiet, then tiptoe over to Tavik's.

"I almost thought you weren't coming," he says, as I duck inside.

"After my second performance of *The Wizard of Oz*, my mom overdosed, and almost died," I blurt out. "Supposedly by accident."

"Whoa," he says.

"Sorry, I'm out of practice talking about these kinds of things. Well, I was never *in* practice. Should I have built up to it?"

"No . . . you do it how you want. I'll roll with it."

"Okay, so the thing is, I spend a lot of time thinking that it might have been my fault."

"For singing, and doing the play?" he says.

I nod.

"Bullshit," he says.

"Thinking that and believing it are two different things," I say.

He nods slowly.

"I promised her I would never tell anyone. She made me promise."

"So why did you just tell me?"

"Because sometimes I am so messed up, and I feel so . . . I feel like breaking things."

"Promises?"

"Yes. And actual things," I say, my hand going to my shin.

He's very still, and watching me with deep, steady eyes.

"Sometimes I feel too much," I continue, eyes locked on his, everything slow-motion, loaded. "Other times I can't feel anything."

"What are you feeling right now?"

I am feeling like I want to break down and tell him the whole sad story, and like the whole sad story is too much to tell. I am feeling like his eyes on my eyes are sustenance. I am feeling like if I could put my hand on his jawline and then trail it down his neck to his chest, then I would know if I was making his heart beat faster, and that would be better than all the talking in the world. I am feeling like I could sleep a thousand years, feeling like crying, like singing, like touching my lips to his, like crawling into a hole and hiding there for the rest of my life. I am feeling like lying on my back and looking up at the sky and letting the stars fall into my eyes and change me, drown me, light me up.

"Are you cold?" he asks finally when I don't answer.

"I should be able to move on," I say, ignoring his question.

"From?"

"All of it. The overdose. The boy I liked dating someone

else after I rejected him. Losing our first life, and Mom's voice, and . . . all of it. Sure, I was left to deal with lots of things on my own, but I managed. So many worse things happen to people. Here in this group, much worse things have happened to people. I just . . . Where is it all supposed to go when you move on from it?"

"I don't know," Tavik says.

"But it's also . . . I am afraid of what I'll become, going to London, studying music. Afraid to fail, afraid to succeed, afraid of being too much like my mom, afraid of not being enough like her. Afraid of my motivations, because . . . I want to surpass her. Why do I want that? Am I allowed to want that? What am I doing . . . if I succeed at that? What does that make me?"

"It makes you the person who succeeds, I think. It makes you your mother's daughter. And she's an adult. Can't she take care of her own reactions?"

I let out a pained gasp of breath and look away.

"This 'being responsible for her' business is dumb," Tavik continues. "But what do I know? I know zip about classical music, or any of this. I'm just a guy who's probably going to end up fixing people's toilets or cars, and that's if I think big."

"Oh, Tavik, I'm sorry, I—"

"I don't mean it like that. I don't have high aspirations. I'm just hoping for a normal life. I'm good with it. Just, Ingrid . . . don't be afraid. That's all I can say. Or be afraid, but do it anyway."

"I think . . . I feel like I'm looking for a sign. You know? Something that lets me know, or gives me the feeling of knowing . . . that I'm going in the right direction, that everything is going to be all right."

"No point worrying or looking for signs," he says. "It is or it isn't."

"Aren't you supposed to lie to me and tell me that it is?"

"You're already here to sleep with me," he says with a hilarious wink. "I don't need to tell you any lies."

I smile, while my mind gets busy peeling his clothing off one piece at a time, running my fingertips over his many beautiful muscles, but my body simply does what it has done every night I've spent with him, and curls up, humming, and eventually goes to sleep, exhaustion and caution winning over lust.

Day Eighteen. There are three more days until Day Twenty-One, when we all go home. The canoeing is better and worse now—we are better, but the terrain is worse. We're on a new river system, which widens and narrows with no warning. We don't have to paddle as hard, because there's a current. On the other hand, we have to steer like crazy. There are more rocks and multiple close calls and everybody gets stuck at least once. Melissa, Seth, and Henry bail when they take too sharp a turn, and the rescue and recovery is epic, but luckily sans bears. We stay in our canoe, but barely.

The eighteenth night is cold again, and I stay late beside the fire, shivering from my evening swim—aka stubborn exercise in self-torture—and wishing my hopelessly tangled mop of hair would dry before I go to bed.

The journal is on my lap, but though I planned to write, I find myself just holding it, still waiting for a sign.

Chapter Thirty-One

🍂 🍁 🍃

OZ, ET CETERA

(Ages Fifteen to Sixteen)

Oz became a category of memory—Oz, et cetera—the *et cetera* part encompassing all the ensuing pain, confusion, drama.

After Oz, et cetera, things got slowly better—in the sense that they weren't total crap, not in the sense of my overall happiness, which was at an all-time low.

I'd been brave, broken out, detached from the pattern of worrying about Margot-Sophia before worrying about myself, and I had been happy. But I couldn't help feeling the universe had decided to smite me for it. I had learned a lesson, and the lesson was that the price was too high, too painful, and always would be.

There would be no more singing or acting or music. Not when I was all the time carrying this hot, spiky ball of fear and fury inside me. Not when I woke bathed in sweat in the middle of most nights from vivid dreams in which Mom was lost, or dead, and I was running, always running, trying to find her or save her.

Andreas moved back in, and there was no more talk of breakups. He bought her a light-therapy lamp, and read up on depression, quietly passing along his findings and conclusions to me. It wasn't about finding a cure, Andreas said; it was a matter of management.

She was back on medication, and she used the lamp every morning while drinking her coffee, and she didn't consume any alcohol for six months. Andreas got her a gym membership, based on research that exercise is a natural antidepressant, but she didn't take to the gym. She did, on the other hand, sign up for weekly group therapy, and seemed to find it helpful.

I kept my head down, studied, finished tenth grade.

Isaac kept trying to talk to me until nearly the end of the school year, texting me, e-mailing, showing up at my locker with puppy-dog eyes, or angry, frustrated eyes. I missed him, and I nearly broke a hundred times, but I was too messed up, and hurting too much to risk it.

Fortunately by late spring Mom seemed her normal self, and in the summer, Andreas, Mom, and I flew to Vancouver, and then Andreas flew back home while Mom and I crossed the country by train, getting off to see a bit of each province. We read books aloud, pasted maps and postcards into a bound journal, and took photos and sent them to Andreas.

It felt like old times.

It felt like healing.

In the autumn of eleventh grade, Andreas's adoption of me was finalized, and we flew to New York for the weekend to celebrate.

I had a dad. It was the best.

One day at school I was walking by the theater and found the stage door open, with everything I missed wafting out, calling to me. I stepped cautiously inside. Seeing no one, I went up onto the stage. The lights were dim and there was nothing but the piano on it, and I ached, standing there. I ached for myself, for Mom, and I saw the years and heard the music and felt the performances, hers, mine, all that I'd seen, tumbling one over the other, and knew . . . that of course she was right: that life could not guarantee happiness of the steady variety.

And yet.

I went to the piano, sat down, placed my fingers over the keys. I'd done all that singing for the play, but I'd barely touched a piano since I was little. I didn't know if I could even play anymore.

I chose an old classic—Debussy's "Clair de Lune"—and played the opening notes. This was a piece I'd been able to play in my sleep, almost, at age ten. Now it was a mess, my fingers stumbling. Still I continued, trying again. It went better the second time, but more important, something finally clicked. It felt like falling into a warm bed, like home, like solace.

I was midway through my third attempt when I felt someone watching, and looked up to see Rhea.

"Don't stop," she said.

But I had.

"I . . . sorry. I just . . ." Damn, I was crying.

"I'll leave you alone. Go back to it," she said.

"No, I—shit, I'm a mess." Then I flushed. "And now I'm swearing in front of you! I'm so—"

"What sort of tears—good or bad?" she asked, coming to lean on the lid of the piano.

"I have no idea. I'm a teenager—aren't we supposed to be overly emotional?" I said, attempting a chuckle.

She leaned closer. "Two things, and then I'll leave you. One: I am going to give you a key to one of the practice rooms on the third floor."

"I don't—"

"As a hobby, as an outlet, as a space to yourself."

I swallowed hard. "Thank you."

"Two: I've been thinking about this, and now that I see you here, playing . . . I know the headmaster at a very special music school in London, England. It's called Ayerton. They take students in their final year of high school with the goal of helping each student zero in on their strengths. Most go on to be accepted either at their own college conservatory program, or at other top-notch music schools. They take only the best, auditions are by invitation only, and they accept three North American students per year. I can get you an audition," Rhea said.

"I . . ." London? Music school? It was like she'd uncovered my deepest and most secret longing—secret even to myself, until now. My throat was dry, and I was sure if I tried to stand up, my legs wouldn't work. London. Music.

"I can help you talk to your parents," she said.

My parents. Right.

"I can't," I said, swallowing hard. "Thank you so much. It sounds like . . . a dream come true, if it were to happen. But I can't audition, because even if I were to be accepted, I can't go. Besides . . ."

"Yes?"

"I was just thinking only five minutes ago, they don't lead to happiness, those careers. Usually not, I mean."

"So you are not a starry-eyed fool," Rhea said with a solemn shrug. "Nothing guarantees happiness. I'm not certain happiness should be the goal. Satisfaction, maybe. A sense of purpose. Contribution. Authenticity. Happiness? It's a lightweight goal. And meanwhile, I suspect that turning away from yourself will guarantee the opposite of happiness."

"I never thought of it that way."

"You could just audition . . . ." she said, looking into my eyes as if she could see how breathlessly, painfully, badly I wanted this. "Otherwise you'll never know."

"I'll have to live with never knowing."

I couldn't, though. Mom was so much better, and I wanted it. I wanted to at least try.

I got the key for the practice room and spent hours preparing.

I told no one.

I auditioned.

As usual, in these high-pressure performance situations, I nearly died of nerves, then afterward had no real idea how I'd done.

And so I put it out of my mind as much as possible, until the day in early December when Rhea called me to a meeting in her office, and I found Mom and Andreas there, and Rhea told all of us that I had been accepted.

"Ayerton is a top-notch school," Rhea said. "And unique."

"I know of it." Mom swiveled to look at me, eyes many fathoms deep. "I don't want this for you."

"I know," I said. "But, Mom . . . I do."

"Why don't you take the information home, and discuss it?" Rhea suggested smoothly, and before I knew it, we were all back on our feet, and she was handing me the acceptance letter and program description.

Mom rounded on me as soon as we were in the front door of the coach house.

"Why did you lie to me?" She always seemed taller when angry.

"I didn't lie; I just didn't tell you," I said with a calmness I didn't feel. "Because I didn't want to have to argue about it before we even knew if I'd get in. I didn't think I *would* get in. But I did, Mom. I got in! Please, please. You have to let me go."

"I don't *have* to do anything. How many times do I have to tell you that I want you to have an easier life? I don't want you to go through even the smallest bit of the pain I've been through."

"But I'm not you, Mom! What happened to you isn't going to happen to me."

"Why do you think I settled us here and worked so hard to give you stability, an education, a chance at a future doing something you can hold on to?" she said, earnest and sincere now, almost begging me. "Don't you see? You're good at more than one thing. You don't have to enslave yourself the way I did. Music isn't the only thing that could make you happy."

"How do you know? I'm sorry to disappoint you, but this life you're planning on my behalf? Sounds totally boring and unsatisfying to me."

"Ingrid, I understand you have . . . a strong feeling about music. But that feeling is fleeting. It's like an infatuation; eventually you come down from it and discover a world of nitpicking, backbreaking work that is mostly thankless. It's not just the loss of my voice; I gave up everything else to do what I did. I gave up everything except you. Perhaps you remember those years as romantic, but you were a child. You were shielded. You have no idea how hard it was. The rejection, the criticism, the people who want to rip you down . . . You have to be very strong."

"I am strong."

"The answer is no."

I felt like I was going to crack open and boiling lava was going to flow out.

"No?"

"That's correct. You are still a minor, and I am still the parent. When you turn eighteen and want to make your own way, you can do what you want. Until then, it's my way."

I glanced at Andreas, who'd been hovering in the background of all this—he was, after all, my other official parent now. But he had become wiser about jumping in too fast to try to fix things, and he gave a subtle shake of his head, a calming motion with his hand, and mouthed, Wait.

Wait? The entire course of my life was being decided here.

"Fine," I spat out. I'd reasoned, I'd laid my heart on the line, all for nothing. "But why don't you be honest? Why don't you just admit that you can't stand me having the thing you lost, the thing you're too much of a coward to try to recover? You want to spend your life playing out your little victim drama and taking no responsibility for your part—yes, *your* part—in losing your voice. And I have to suffer. I have to spend *my* entire life tiptoeing around you and trying to become something other than what

I actually am. I have to be the victim with you, and not hope for anything, and not want any of the things I actually want, for fear that my having them will hurt you. How is that fair?"

"How dare you—"

"What happened to the mother who used to tell me if I worked hard enough, I could have anything I wanted? Be anything I wanted? Where is she? She's the one I believe, not you. Let me just be really clear. I will never forgive you if you don't let me do this. Never."

And with that, of course, I stomped upstairs to my room, and slammed the door, and screamed into the pillows of my bed, and cried for five thousand million hours, before finally falling asleep.

We had a week to accept placement at the school.

We didn't speak for six days.

Andreas quietly told me he was working on her, and that he could make it happen, money-wise. Still, she looked pretty unrelenting to me.

On the seventh morning, she stalked into my room before I was even out of bed, and stood over me. In her hand she had a piece of paper and a pen.

"I will not always be here to help you," she said.

"Well, that's morbid," I said groggily, and rolled my eyes.

"I want you to have wide-ranging life skills."

"Yeah, I got that."

"You've never been away from home, been away from me."

"I know, but—"

"And I cannot come to London."

"They have dorms."

"My point is that you would be alone there, for the first time in your life."

"I know."

"But you may go—" She held a hand up to stop me from responding yet. "On one condition."

I sat up fast, heart leaping. "Anything. Yes. What?"

And here is the memory I've been replaying, trying to recall what was said, exactly. . . .

Mom held out a Peak Wilderness brochure—the one with sporty-looking kids standing in front of rustic timber-frame cabins.

"You will complete three weeks at this wilderness camp over the summer," she said.

I snatched the brochure from her, took a quick look.

"This is the one Ella did?"

Mom nodded. And it *might be* that she said something to the effect of, "Yes, or something similar."

"But . . . what does wilderness camp have to do with music school? What's the point?"

"You get something, I get something," she said.

"But why?"

"To toughen you up," she said, with an almost devilish grin. "What else?"

I didn't like it, I didn't get it, but whatever—it was just three weeks of my life. It wouldn't change anything.

"Fine," I said, too thrilled about Ayerton to bother with investigating further in that moment. "I'll do it. Where do I sign?"

Margot-Sophia might have sent me a link to the Peak Wilderness website sometime in the weeks after that. *Might have*.

I have a vague memory of it, but an equal feeling that I might have manufactured the memory. And if it's real . . . I *might not* have clicked on that link, because I was too busy Googling London, and dreaming about Ayerton. And so she might have purposely tricked me, or she might have been trying to warn me, or even to let me in on the process of choosing which program to sign up for.

I can spend my time wondering about "if" and "why" . . . but as the days pass, I wonder whether those are even the right questions to be asking. I can blame her forever, for everything, if I want to. But then it means that she is the person creating me, responsible for me, that I have no ability to make my own choices. If that's true, then what the hell have I been fighting for?

Chapter Thirty-Two

🍂 🍁 🍃

SPEED

(Peak Wilderness, Day Nineteen)

With only two days left before this trip is over, I should be feeling better.

I am feeling different, but not better.

In some ways I am feeling worse, because when I go home, the rest of my life starts. Peak Wilderness has created a transition, a before and after. And so the next thing is after. This makes me anxious.

But I don't have much time to dwell on my anxiety, or anything else, because on Day Nineteen we run our first "official" rapids.

We know they're official, because Bonnie makes us put on the helmets.

From a distance the rapids look pretty, and not particularly worrisome. But once we're in them, it becomes a crazy, rocket-speed, death-defying experience. We have only the smallest amount of control over our canoe, over our panic, and the wrong move, or the wrong rock jutting up in front of us, could be disastrous.

Ally is brave and strong and decisive. But Jin gets motion sickness and wigs out completely, curling into the bottom of the canoe, leaving Ally and me to do all the paddling and navigating.

"Remember this!" I shout to Ally as we go through it, her in the front, guiding us. "Remember when you get back, how you kicked ass at this!"

She raises her fist for a moment, between strokes, and pumps it.

Tavik and Harvey capsize, soaking everything that's not in a dry bag, and nearly losing one of the packs. Our canoe is the only one close enough to help them, and we somehow manage to do it—rallying Jin, then rescuing the sinking pack with a paddle, helping them to right their canoe.

We get wrapped around a rock immediately after, but luckily Ally is able to get purchase with one of her feet, and manages to push us off.

It's intense, fast, breathtaking, terrifying, full-on. And when it all goes right, and we make it through a tough patch and live to tell the tale, it's . . . a little bit amazing.

Terror mixed with amazing is, of course, followed by yet another portage. Jin and I have the gear, and Ally has the canoe.

I trudge along, my rapids-induced high fading, and hum of going-home anxiety ramping up. I'm wishing for the out-of-body feeling to come back, but it seems it can't be summoned at will.

Whatever. I just have to get through this day, and then the next, and the same for every day after that, once I'm home. I am settling into this train of thought when I realize everyone in front of me has slowed down, and then stopped.

We've only just set out, but the path has disappeared.

Ended.

And it has ended because the forest we were walking through is completely burned down from where we are, forward.

What's left is a charred field, littered with blackened stumps and root systems, leafless trees toppled onto one another in a gruesome tangle of death, and ghostly trunks—the few that are still upright—standing bare, blackened, and pointing toward the sky like needles. The ground is charcoal-colored mud with nothing growing out of it. The smell is foul and sharp—ash mixed with rot.

It's shocking, sickening, stark. It hurts to look at.

"Forest fire," Bonnie offers into our silence.

"Uh, yeah," Jin says, but she's not even trying to be sarcastic.

"Probably happened in the spring, or we'd already see vegetation coming through," Pat adds. "They just let them burn up here—nature taking its course."

"So no one even reports it? Puts it on the map to warn travelers?" Seth asks.

"This area's not traveled that often," Pat explains. "We'll report it when we get back."

"How . . . do we get across?" asks Ally, eyes wide.

"Very carefully and with difficulty," Pat says, but not in his fridge-magnet voice this time.

Together we study the map, trying to guess where the trail should be. Then Pat pulls a compass out of one of his many pockets, and he and Bonnie attempt to give us a general trajectory.

"Watch your step," Pat says, and then picks up his and Bonnie's canoe and takes the lead. I find this both alarming and reassuring, given his usual insistence on our figuring everything out on our own.

Ally's nervous, so I offer to take the canoe.

I hoist it up over my head and walk out into ankle-deep charred mud and discover quickly that there is no sure step to be found. Ally and Jin stay close, packs on their backs, one in front, one behind, and reach up to help balance the canoe multiple times.

Dark clouds blow in, making the already bleak scene even bleaker. My every muscle is tensed, and soon sweat is dripping from my face and down my back from the effort of balancing the canoe with such unsteady footing.

We climb over multiple stumps, huge trees. Jin's in the lead and therefore trips and ends up on her knees in the mud a few times, and on her face once too, but she does not complain. We're silent except to warn one another of obstacles ahead. It takes ten minutes to progress ten feet.

I am thinking of nothing except what my body has to do in the immediate future and whether I can keep doing it, which seems doubtful.

I said I was looking for a sign. . . .

If this is the sign I was looking for, it contains a dismal message—something about the necessity of going through hell, obviously. It's not even a sign with rays of hope—tiny shoots of new vegetation poking through, a single flower, or a pretty bird chirping in the middle of it. Nothing. Probably there'll be a pit of fire at the end.

And it gets worse.

As we approach the approximate halfway point, we see a pair of antlers rising up out of a pile of ash, and a little further along, what looks to have been a family of raccoons trapped under a fallen tree and burned into blackened statues.

Ally gasps.

Jin stumbles away and vomits.

I squeeze my eyes shut.

Jin rejoins us, and we march on. There are tears streaming down my face now, along with the sweat. They're from the physical pain. They're from *all* the pain. Sometime since we started across, every last shred of my inner fortification has burned away and I feel everything; all the memories, all of my pushed-down, blocked-out joys and sorrows and regrets lick up and down my insides, matching the searing of my muscles, the agony of a forest burned to the ground, the awfulness of the mother and baby raccoons. I weep and walk and climb and stumble, and my arms and shoulders and abs and back and legs and feet scream.

To the left of us, I see Tavik actually throw his canoe over a fallen tree, walk under the tree, and catch the canoe on the other side.

I have a moment to appreciate how cool that is before I take a bad step and my leg buckles. I go down, landing on hands and knees as the canoe falls on top of me, the front bench cracking over my mid-back and knocking the wind out of me.

My breath is returning as Ally and Jin lift the canoe off me, but instead of getting up, I pound both my fists into the mud and howl with frustration.

"I can take the canoe," Ally says.

"Or I can," Jin says.

I pound on the ground one more time, swearing, then push myself up to my feet.

"We're almost there," I say, swiping at the sweat and tears and only managing to smear mud across my face. "I'll carry it. I want to."

"But—"

"Let her," Jin says, cutting Ally off.

They don't ask me whether I'm okay, because whether or not I am is irrelevant. We have to get across. And then we have to go back two more times for the rest of the gear.

The three of us emerge from the final crossing with our arms around each other's waists to keep from face-planting, and then fall into a messy, muddy hug.

When everyone has had a short time to recover, we get everything together and head the short distance to the top of a nearby hill to find out where we are. Luckily, the river we're aiming for is on the other side, bubbling along below us. Unluckily, the way down is essentially a cliff.

"Of course," Jin mutters, and Ally and I laugh hysterically.

This time Pat *does* leave us to figure it out ourselves, and the final result is that we basically drop the canoes, and then the gear, onto the beach twenty feet below us, and cross our fingers.

The collective logic of a group of people this tired is obviously suspect, but it works, and everything plops down to the sand without breaking.

Jin says she is tempted to do the same thing with herself.

But instead, one at a time, and wearing our canoeing helmets and using rope as backup, we pick and scramble our way down the steep rock face, to the beach.

Dear Mom,

I get it now. Peak Wilderness is geared to breaking down your barriers—physical, psychological, mental. Bringing you face-to-face with the best and worst of yourself, teaching you things you didn't know about yourself, facing your demons.

My demon is you.

My best and worst is about you: how I need you and fear for you, how I fear for myself if I lose you, how I have let myself be defined by you.

The demon . . . is also what you lost, and the thing that took you down, over and over. Every time it happened, you stopped living, Mom. Stopped wanting to. I wish I could make you feel what that did to me, see how it changed the way I take every single breath.

I tried to live so lightly, so carefully. I tried to be someone you would love enough to stop letting yourself spiral down. I lost my voice, too, trying to keep you alive. But living like that is death, Mom.

And I want to live.

I felt it when Peace shoved me underwater. I felt it in the mud pit, on the trail, in the face of the bear, and in the devastated forest today.

I want to live. I want to sing, and tell stories and be connected with something larger than myself. I want to give everything I have, even if it hurts, even if it leaves me beaten down and hollowed out. I want it.

But I cannot make you want the same things for me, or for yourself. I cannot help you let go of your pain, or tether you to me, or keep you here.

If I continue to choose you over me, I don't live either, not truly.

So we both die, Mom.

How does that make sense?

I kept my promise to do this trip. I chose that. And now I choose to live.

Love,
Ingrid

Everyone jumps in the river, and I stay in until I am practically blue, somehow enjoying the ice-cold water on the heat of my sore muscles, and the many cuts and bruises I acquired today.

The nights are getting cold, the sun is setting earlier, and this is our second-to-last night. Hard to believe.

I put lots of layers on once I'm out, and sit cozily between Ally and Jin for dinner and circle.

Later, I watch Tavik saunter down to the narrow sandy area beside the river that's too narrow to be called a beach . . . and find myself following him.

He turns, dark eyes glittering in the bright moonlight.

"You look . . . better," he says.

"Ha! I've never been so beat-up and bedraggled in my life."

"It's your eyes. In your eyes you look better. Fast rivers and slow forests seem to agree with you."

"I heard you whooping and cheering like a maniac on the rapids."

He grins. "I like to go fast."

"That's obvious."

"Maybe you look better from talking to me every night. . . ."

"Maybe. I'm almost all talked out, I think."

"Too bad."

"There is one more thing you might find interesting. A couple of months ago I took an ax to my garage."

"What?" His shock is so extreme that I actually start laughing.

"Oh my God, it was worth telling you just to see your face!"

"Wait. What . . . an ax? Are you serious?"

"Dead serious," I say, and my laughter stops as abruptly as it started. "The garage was really old, built more like a shed. Big enough for a car, but barely. Anyway, I was upset. It was still light out—a little after dinner. I was . . . on a break from school at the time . . . but my best friend had convinced me I should go to the spring dance. Be social. Have fun. So. I had a dress and everything—I'd even put it on— but when it came to it, I couldn't make myself go. If I went, I was just going to stand there hating everybody and feeling like a freak. I was messed up."

"Because of your mom."

"That, and I heard Isaac was bringing some girl to the dance, and . . . somehow it all became too much. I just felt this . . . incredible force driving me to *do* something. Anything. So there I was in this fancy dress and fuzzy slippers, and I went and got the ax. It sounds crazy but it made perfect sense in my head. Chop down the garage. I just picked up the ax and started whaling on those old boards, and it felt incredible. Pretty soon I was covered in sweat and probably crying. I had a stepladder out there so I could hack at the roof, too. I wanted to take the whole thing down and I didn't care how much trouble I was going to get into."

"No one came to stop you?"

"Spring in the city," I say with a shrug. "People mow their lawns in the evening, and there's constant renovation—digging basements, building and fixing stuff over the weekends."

"So you just chopped away, no one saying boo to you."

"Yep. It was hard work, actually. Of course I'd never used an ax before, so I lost my balance mid-swing on the stepladder and chopped myself in the leg."

"Jesus."

"I know. In hindsight, it's almost funny."

"Not really," Tavik says.

"No, you're right. Not really. Anyway, I screamed, and my stepdad—my dad, that is—came running out of the house. It wasn't as bad an injury as we thought at first, but of course we left the garage—it was half down at that point—and went to the emergency room and I got stitches."

"Did your parents freak? About the garage?"

I swallow, shake my head. "Andreas bought a second ax the next morning and helped me finish the job. We did it together."

"Your mom must have thought you were both nuts."

"She's half the reason we're nuts."

"Sure, but—"

"We didn't give her any say in the matter," I say with a sudden harshness.

"Wow." Tavik backs up a step. "All right."

"So. Now you know—I'm a delinquent too."

"This was just a couple of months ago?"

I nod.

"How's your leg?" he asks.

"Wanna see?" Without waiting for his response, I sit on the sand and pull up the leg of my pants. Tavik kneels, peering at the scar in the moonlight.

"Still looks kinda angry," he says, and gently runs his fingertips over it.

My breath catches in my throat.

"Does it hurt?"

"Only when I'm upset. Which makes zero sense."

"Huh." He places his whole hand over the scar, and warmth seems to radiate from it, into my leg and up through the rest of me. "What about right now?"

"No, it feels . . . fine right now."

He takes his hand from my leg, and without thinking about it, I catch it in mine and put it back.

"It feels good there," I say, seeing a shift in his eyes and feeling a shift in myself as I move from the edge of one precipice to another.

"Careful," he says.

"Of what?" I say, eyes locked on his.

"You love that boy . . ." he says, his hand nevertheless slipping around to the back of my calf.

"He's not here. He might be with someone else. I might never see him again. Meanwhile, you . . ."

"I what . . . ?"

"You are something beautiful," I say, on my knees now, face-to-face with him.

He exhales a laugh.

"What?"

"No one's ever said *that* about me," he says.

"I'm saying it." I place my hands lightly on his shoulders, then drop them to his chest. His hands are at my waist, fingers on my skin.

"You want me to help you forget," he says, tugging me close, so close that I am up against him, hip to hip, chest to chest.

"I want you to help me feel something good," I say.

"Ah. I might be able to do that," he says, one hand traveling smoothly up my back and expertly unhooking my bra, at the same time as his lips lock onto mine.

He smells like soap and fire, and he tastes like chocolate, like firesmoke, like the river. My hands can't get enough of his bare skin, my body can't pull him close enough, and mother-of-god, he knows what to do with his mouth and hands.

Tavik is not sweet and warm and careful like Isaac.

He likes to go fast, knows where he's going and how to get there, and soon we are no-holds-barred, on each other, shirts up, zippers down, hands everywhere, hot gasps exploding into the night air.

We stop short of complete nudity and actual sex, but it goes way past "feeling something good" all the way to feeling something very deliciously bad, to feeling ridiculously, explosively, desperately good.

Eventually we tiptoe/stumble our way back into camp, and I sneak into his lean-to with him and fall into a deep and heavy sleep.

Chapter Thirty-Three

🍂 🍁 🍃

LIVE

(Peak Wilderness, Day Twenty)

I dream of London, of Tavik, of Isaac standing on a stage, waiting for me. I dream of Mom standing on a ridge of crystal-lined granite. She's in my hiking boots, but they're covered in red glitter, and she's wearing one of her draped velvet dresses, which is whipping in the wind. She has a walking stick raised toward the heavens like she's some kind of unhinged Gandalf telling me I shall not pass. I rage at her from below, but she can't hear me. I have to climb the damned rock and somehow get past her, and on the other side is a stage door, and in it is a theater and I'm due there any second. My cue is coming. But I don't even know, have somehow forgotten, what the play is.

Tavik is still sound asleep when I wake. I extricate myself carefully, pull my sleeping bag around my shoulders for warmth, and go to sit on a rock by the river.

The birds are awake, and the sky is a thick, glimmering, ever-lightening silver.

The river rushes forth, filling every space it needs, stopping for nothing.

Like life, like love, like despair, like time.

Not like fear, though. Fear, I realize, can be pressed smaller, pushed out of the way, lived with most of the time without it taking over everything. On the one hand, you can live with it. On the other, it's hard to banish. It lurks. But fear can be battled with love, with strength, with hope. Can be overcome, over-ruled, by truth sometimes, I tell myself.

One more day and I will be home.

On our final day of canoeing, Day Twenty, the sky opens up and it pours.

Of course it does.

By now, as a group, we are practically the definition of stoic, but still, it's a wretched day. It's cold and wet. Paddling is hell. We eat lunch with our canoes on our heads, and stay onshore like that for another frightening hour when there's lightning and thunder in the sky.

Getting back on the river just in time for another rapids, still in the rain, sucks and is scary as hell even without lightning. Past the rapids, the paddling is hard going, the water choppy as we head back out onto the lake in order to cross to our final campsite.

Jin throws up over the side. Ally, though she has developed into a kick-ass canoe girl, is sweating, and her arms are shak-ing, and I feel like garbage too. Alongside us, the other teams are struggling just as much. Even Tavik looks done in.

Without thinking about it, I start to sing. I start with some Gilbert and Sullivan from *The Pirates of Penzance* because it's rousing and has a good rhythm. Immediately the paddling feels easier, and people chime in with hoots and echoes. I follow up with some Mozart, then some Wagner. This is my music. Mom's music—well, not the G&S, so much, but the rest of it. I fill the lake and sky with it. I sing the "Anvil Chorus" from Verdi's *Trovatore*, then "Libiamo" from *Traviata*, then circle back to more Gilbert and Sullivan, this time from *The Gondoliers*. I sing first to help, and then for fun, and then because, there in the middle of the rainy lake, even freezing cold and tired and miserable, it gives me joy. I sing all the way into the campsite, and finish to cheers and claps on the shoulder, and hugs from Jin and Ally and Seth.

Miraculously it's not dark yet—in fact, as we're pulling the canoes up the beach, the sun comes bursting through, giving us a final two hours of light and much-needed warmth. We set about gathering firewood and lean-to materials as fast as we can, and before long we're sitting around the admittedly anemic fire, having our last dinner together.

"Not gonna miss the rice and beans," Jin says, and everyone nods and/or groans.

"What's the first thing you're going to eat when you get home?" Henry asks her.

"A cheeseburger," she says, grinning. "And then some brownies—the two-bite kind."

"I'm going for sushi!" Seth says. "And then cinnamon buns."

"Indian food," Ally says, her bright, un-made-up eyes alight and full of so much confidence. "And then a chocolate sundae.

Or maybe an all-day breakfast—sausages, eggs, pancakes . . ."

"Steak and eggs," Harvey says, and Henry nods vigorously. "What about you, Tavik?"

"Nachos, or maybe a giant burrito, some beer, apple pie with vanilla ice cream," Tavik responds without hesitation. "You know, we talked like this in jail. That was my meal then, too."

"Did you have it?" I ask.

"You bet your ass I did."

"There's an Italian restaurant down the street from my house," Melissa says. "They make everything fresh. I'd have their pumpkin agnolotti with cream sauce, the bruschetta, followed by tiramisu and tartuffo—the kind with the dark chocolate and raspberry at the center."

"Mmm," I say, bowled over with delirious anticipation.

"And you?" Melissa says.

"I'd come to your meal," I said. "But I'll take a pizza."

"With what on it?" Ally asks, almost lustfully.

"Sun-dried tomatoes, green olives, prosciutto . . . and then ice cream, something creamy with caramel . . . But before that, a shower followed by a long, hot bath. In fact, if I could have the food in the bath, that would be perfection. That's it—I'm going to spend, like, four days in the bath, gorging myself. I just need someone to keep bringing the food so I don't have to get out of the water."

"I volunteer for that job," Tavik says. "Especially if you sing in the bath."

We all go on like that—about food and showers and other things we've missed. And then the talk shifts to what we'll miss about Peak Wilderness, which turns out to be rather a lot, considering.

Pat and Bonnie join us, and as we have so many nights, we move naturally into circle time.

We go around to each person again, like we did the first night, and everyone gets a chance to reflect on where they're at with the goals they set, what their challenges were, what they're taking away from it all. Unlike on that first night, I'm not freaked out by these people, not under the impression that I'm separate from them, stuck here by accident. I'm here for just as good a reason as anyone else.

I've seen each and every person here hit their own walls. I've seen them fight, I've seen them give up, I've seen them persevere even after they said they were giving up. For some it's been dramatic, for others more subtle. But the rigors of the trip, the interpersonal as well as the physical challenges, and nature itself, have all helped heal us, change us, make us stronger. Even some of the Peak Wilderness psychological garbage might have helped a couple of people. *Might*.

After a long, soulful, hilarious, tearful talk and the exchanging of contact info, we add more wood to the fire and sing and talk late into the night.

Bonnie pulls me aside to ask whether I'm planning to have Peace charged with assault, and I sigh.

"I'd like to just forget about him altogether."

"I know," she says. "A lot of people make that same choice. And the truth is, it wouldn't be an easy process. You'd have to go through it all again, emotionally, and it would take time and energy, and the court system . . ."

"Isn't set up to be kind or even necessarily fair to girls and women who come forward about this kind of thing," I finish for her.

She nods. Waits.

"And yet, if I don't, he gets away with it. And does it again, or something worse, to someone else. Which means I have . . . a responsibility," I say, the weight of this settling on me.

"There's that," Bonnie says.

"So . . . no big deal, but I have to choose between my own personal happiness and, like, the good of humankind."

"You wouldn't be alone," she says. "You have witnesses, and Peak Wilderness would support you. Pat and I would support you."

I nod, she gives me some details about who to talk to at the Peak Wilderness head office if I decide to go ahead, and then we both head back to the fire.

Tavik makes his way to my side, then, and stays connected to me by hand or thigh or shoulder until the group finally breaks up and it's time for bed. He and I are the last people still sitting at the fire.

"Come sleep over," he says quietly.

I look at him, smiling, eyes narrowed.

"I'll be good," he says.

"No, you won't."

"No, I won't. But come on—it's the last chance. And I made my lean-to nice and big."

"Why do I suddenly feel like you're the big bad wolf?"

He grins, exactly like the big bad wolf.

"Anyway, it's not the last chance," I protest. "You have my number in the city."

"I don't live in the city."

"Yeah, but we could . . ."

He gazes at me, shakes his head. "Let's not be full of shit," he says, eyes a little sad, but honest.

I wasn't, but he's right. This is *something*, but it isn't love. Not that kind of love. It doesn't mean it's shallow or purely physical, but it's hard to imagine how it would ever work, outside this very specific time and place. It's a "stays in Vegas" situation.

"Okay," I say. "I need a few minutes to myself, but I'll see you in a bit."

He goes off to his lean-to. I extinguish the dying fire, then walk down to the shore, take off my shoes and socks, and stand with my feet in the icy water.

Dear Mom . . . I compose, in my head, and then stop.

I know why she sent me. She did it so I would see hardship and experience it. She sent me here to have my strength tested, knowing it would fail. She sent me to be knocked down and get back up again, so that I would know I could. She sent me to learn about survival and be forced to own my choices and be ready to fight for them. She sent me to grieve what's past, and for a special tough-love variety of healing. She sent me to help me get clear— clear of her. It makes a certain, bizarre sense.

Still, there's more I need to resolve before I go to London. There will always be more.

But there's time for that tomorrow.

Instead I stand under the giant sky, counting stars, feeling scared and raw, but at the same time full, fierce, open.

And then I go to Vegas.

Chapter Thirty-Four

HOME

(Peak Wilderness, Day Twenty-One)

In the early morning, we break camp and make the short trip across the bay to the Peak Wilderness outpost/office where Duncan stays, holding all the confiscated luggage hostage, and waiting to come harass/rescue/instruct while programs are running. We take showers—hot showers! with soap, shampoo, and conditioner!—then change into clean clothing, and head back to the original landing field where we board the same tiny airplane and fly back to civilization.

As arranged before the trip, there's money in my wallet, and I use it to take a taxi home from the airport.

Then I stand in front of the coach house, key in hand.

Despite my fresh clothing and glorious-smelling hair, I feel wild and grubby and surreal.

And I feel suddenly afraid again because nothing has changed here from when I left.

I have changed, I remind myself. If I can survive what I just survived, I can handle going inside my own house. Still,

I do so in a breathless, almost slow-motion way.

Key in the lock . . .

Turning . . .

Click.

Push.

Feet on terra-cotta tile of threshold. Smell of home all around me . . .

I close the door gently, set down the duffel bag.

Loud silence. God, there's that silence.

"Hello?" I call out, voice like an echo.

A voice calls back from upstairs, "Hello?"

There are footsteps above and then on the stairs, and someone appears. . . .

Not Mom.

Andreas.

He stops halfway down at the sight of me, beams.

"Ingrid!"

My heart sings to see him, and I want to run forward, leap up, and hug him. But instead we're both frozen in place, and though he's beaming, his love always steady, he looks at me with caution, with uncertainty, with concern.

"Yep, it's me," I say, and clear my throat. "You know anyone else who can just . . . let themselves in here with a key?"

I try to smile like this is one of those everyday jokes between people, funny ha-ha, but the joke doesn't exactly fly.

"Do *you*?" Andreas asks, watching me.

Truth.

"No," I whisper, and shake my head.

He waits.

"No, I don't," I say with more force, holding his gaze even though my voice is breaking and *I* am breaking from finally saying it out loud. "Not anymore."

"Ingrid . . . sweetheart . . ."

He comes slowly down two more steps, like he thinks I'll bolt if he moves too fast.

"It's just us," I say. "It's okay."

"No, it's not," he says. "And it doesn't have to be. It shouldn't be."

"Well, no, but . . . I . . . I will be. I'm not, but I will be. I'm sorry. I know I've made it so much harder. . . ."

"Shhh . . ."

"Thank you for not having me committed or whatever, because I know sometimes you must have thought I was completely bananas. . . ."

"Never," he says.

I press my lips together, but it doesn't stop my face from crumpling, my hands going to clutch my chest, the avalanche from coming. Doesn't stop Andreas from flying to me and wrapping his arms around me and holding me tight . . .

As I finally let the truth all the way in.

My mom . . . is gone.

Gone since New Year's Day.

And I will not be talking to her or showing her the letters I wrote, or ever seeing her again.

She must have realized she meant to overdose. She must have

found herself wishing she'd succeeded. She held on as long as she could, I suppose. Waited for the adoption papers, waited for us to have one last summer, one fall, one Christmas.

And then she made a very thorough and tidy job of dying via carbon monoxide in the garage. We found her together, Andreas and I.

Back inside the coach house, she'd left a letter on the sunroom chaise, along with the registration confirmations for both Peak Wilderness and London.

I did not read them or even really look at them.

There was also a pile of thirty sweaters and hoodies in various colors and fabrics, packets of socks and underwear, pajamas, a collection of classical literature in hardcover, including *War and Peace*, five books on how to choose a career, another three on time management and work habits, and the journals—one hundred of them. Some had silk-screen covers, some were leather-bound, one was an old-fashioned diary with a key, all were beautiful and interesting-looking. One hundred. Like she knew that after she did what she was going to do, I would have something to say about it, would need to write about it, possibly for a lifetime.

There were multiple homemade frozen dinners with dates and descriptions on them in the basement freezer, and for Andreas there were twenty pairs of indoor/outdoor slippers, a beautiful leather jacket, photo albums from trips they took together, and ten pairs of reading glasses—he's always losing or breaking them.

She also left many pages of instructions about what she wanted done, and how.

It is my wish for you to honor our deal, she had written under her signature on the Peak Wilderness registration. *You must be stronger than me, not to mention better.*

I couldn't even comprehend the gall of this, couldn't process it, or the pain, or the fact of what she'd done.

So . . .

I spent the next few months . . . not exactly pretending she was alive, but fiercely, determinedly ignoring the fact that she was dead. I thought of the garage door and put one in my mind, pulled it shut, the fact of her death firmly behind that door.

We didn't do a public obituary, and I refused to attend the cremation or the small service she had organized and paid for in advance. I ignored the existence of the beautiful cloisonné vase Andreas brought home and set inside the dining-room cabinet among the formal dishes.

In fact, I stopped going into the dining room at all.

I stopped going to school, too, and only managed to pass the rest of the year because Andreas let me homeschool. I don't know whether my classmates knew or whether they didn't, because the only person I saw was Juno, who came over a couple of times a week to tell me the latest gossip. Andreas had talked to her—I could tell because she didn't say a word to me about Mom, or about anything serious at all, but instead seemed to think it was her duty to entertain me.

At home we simply went forward, Andreas and I, one day to the next.

We tried to choke down one of the frozen dinners, a lasagna, but neither of us could do it.

Neither of us really wanted to eat at all.

Andreas gave the dinners to a women's shelter and then he made our meals, sat down to eat with me every night, had breakfast with me every morning, set aside time to try to help me with physics, or anything else I needed.

And, without exactly encouraging or engaging in it, he let me pretend.

And when I lost it completely and did what I did to the garage, he understood. And helped me finish the job, and didn't say a word.

"You don't have to go," Andreas said as he watched me pack for Peak Wilderness.

"Mom wants me to," I said, jaw tight. It was almost like I was going to spite her at that point. And to keep her alive, somehow. It didn't make logical sense, but it made emotional sense, at least to me. It gave me something to fight about, to fight for. "So, I'll go."

"Ingrid . . . it might be too much for you."

"No. It'll be fine."

"I'll be here," he said. "When you get back, and always."

Normal people probably don't need these kinds of assurances, but Andreas knew I did.

And here he is today, as promised, catching me as I fall, catching my delayed grief.

Looking at him, I notice for the first time how the pain has stained him, bruised him—dark circles under his eyes, a new shock of white from his temples, the tired set of his shoulders. . . .

"I haven't been here for you." My voice is raw, and the tears are threatening to return.

"Ingrid," he says, shaking his head, "I'm the parent. It's my job to be here for you, not the other way around."

"Who's there for you, then?"

He shrugs.

"That's not fair."

"I'm okay," he says. "I'm better now that you're better."

This strikes me as funny, and I let out a ragged chuckle. "I seem better to you?"

He chuckles too, then gives me a beautiful smile.

Chapter Thirty-Five

🍂 🍁 🍃

FOREVER

Dear Mom,

I'm going to keep writing to you for a while. Maybe forever. Maybe that was your plan. But I must say, for someone who wanted to die, you were awfully invested in controlling everything that happened after you left. You could have just stayed and made sure we kept doing what you wanted. Now we might not.

But I will write, because I'm not ready to be without you. I'm angry and wrecked and I'll never fully understand. But I really miss you. I'll miss you forever.

About Peak Wilderness: I know you did it to make me strong for the future, and also to keep me from falling down and dying of grief. To give me something to fight with, to rage against, to focus on. In some way, if not in exactly the way you intended, it worked.

Although that program . . . I don't think I deserved it. But you know that already from the other letters. Or you don't. I'm going to pretend you do.

So, it worked, sort of, but it could have scarred me for life. Scarred me more, that is.

And I wish, for karmic and practical purposes, that before you left me, you'd had to spend a few days collecting your dirty toilet paper in a Ziploc and sleeping on the wet ground with a smelly, snoring pervert. At the same time I wish you had seen one of the sunsets, swum in the freezing lake under the stars, sat around a campfire (roasting your undies), and grappled with your weaknesses and found your strengths and eaten bugs for dinner and learned to put up a tent, build a fire and a lean-to, tip a canoe, follow a path in the wilderness.

It just occurred to me: if purgatory is a real thing, it might be just like Peak Wilderness.

Where are you . . . ?

I hope you are somewhere. Somewhere better—with the happy little bluebirds, maybe.

Anyway.

I nearly lost my virginity to an ex-convict, which was really fun.

And when I got home, Andreas told me that a boy named Isaac had stopped by. My heart lurched, hearing this. I thought he'd moved on, was ready to give up for good.

"I invited him in," Andreas said.

"You what?"

"I wanted to take his measure. We had coffee."

"And . . . ?"

"I could tell he likes you, so I made very strong espresso," he said with a mischievous grin. "He drank it."

"This is your testing method for young men?" I said.

"One of them, yes. I'll develop more as needed."

I laughed.

"I believe he is . . . good. So if you like him . . ."

At this I gave another laugh, but a less comfortable one. "Like" is such a simple word.

"It's been so long since I've even spoken to him," I said. "What did you say?"

"Beyond pleasantries? Only that perhaps you would be ready to talk with him when you got back, and that I would . . . encourage you to. He left his number."

"I have his number."

"And his summer workplace information . . ."

I smiled. Tried to breathe.

"But I believe Juno is in Paris?" he said. "You could go there, and then I could meet you and take you to London to check out your school. Maybe this boy can wait . . . ?"

I laughed again. Cried again. Imagined myself at the Louvre, the Eiffel Tower, in the cafés and shops and hostels, laughing with Juno, using our terrible French to chat up dashing Parisian men.

But in the end I needed to be here with Andreas for the rest of the summer, helping him tend the garden he's planted where the garage used to be, here in our house with all my memories of you, with what's left of you, with what I have to build the rest of my life on.

Andreas has rented a flat in London, and he's going to base himself there so I won't have to be alone. I know I will be seeing you—remembering you there, feeling like you're around every corner, which I guess you are. You are around every corner of me.

You told me once I could be anything, and I believed you.

I'm choosing to continue believing it, even if you stopped.

Forever,
Ingrid

Epilogue

Isaac is working at a drama camp run out of an independent theater company.

I put on a jean skirt, my favorite ice-blue tank top, and my newly washed boots from Peak Wilderness because although they're ugly, by now they feel both earned and symbolic.

I don't think about it too much in advance, and I don't warn him I'm coming.

I am nervous, but I am not a scared little girl anymore.

And I am done with having regrets when it comes to Isaac.

I arrive just as the doors are opening, and wait off to the side at the bottom of the steps as Isaac emerges with a gaggle of children and checks off each name on a clipboard as they're picked up by parents and caregivers.

He has too much going on to notice me, which is good news because the sight of him, actually *looking* at him after months of looking past/around/over him, has momentarily paralyzed me.

He is taller and scruffier-looking, and the hair on his arms has lightened with the sun. He's wearing jean shorts, and a black T-shirt with Mickey Mouse on it, and sandals. He's cute as hell with the kids, totally dialed in. As he waves to the last one—a little brunette who gazes up at him with giant, adoring blue eyes—my insides lurch.

He is taking a final look around when I finally get my legs functioning again and start up the stairs. The movement catches his eye and for a second he freezes.

And then, zoom, he's in front of me.

"Ingrid! Hi."

"Hi," I manage, rather dorkishly. "Andreas said . . . you stopped by."

"Yes, I . . ." He flushes, clearly at a loss for where to begin.

"Let me just say . . . I am an idiot." I dive right in. "I completely, unequivocally forgive you for not officially breaking up with Autumn before we started making out backstage during the play, and in fact, it's not even something that needs to be forgiven by me, anyway. I'm over it, in other words. And we don't have to rehash it . . . unless you want to."

"Wow. Okay."

"Also, I want you to be in my life no matter what. We can be friends, or . . . whatever."

He lifts an eyebrow. " 'Whatever'?"

"I'm comfortable with 'whatever' . . . as a starting point," I say, trying to act calm despite the somersaults in my stomach. I want to be honest and brave, but hopefully I can do so without acting like a freak. "I still care about you. I never stopped. But you might have a girlfriend. And I'm moving to London. We have a lot of talking to do. I have a story to tell you. If, that is, you're willing to hear it," I say.

"I'm free right now."

"It might take the rest of the summer," I warn him. "It's a long one."

"That's fine," he says. "I have time."

"All right, then." I say this, but then nothing further comes out of my mouth because all I can do is look at him, and somehow I am seeing and hearing the city around us—cars and buses and cyclists, small children playing in a park across the way, birds chirping, the sun casting its late-afternoon gold over everything—and at the same time there is only Isaac, standing on the stairs in front of me with a gaze so loaded, and yet so pure.

"I missed you," he says, into the too-long pause.

I catch my breath, still fixed to the spot mere steps from him.

"No one has ever driven me as crazy as you drove me," he says.

"I'm sorry," I manage to say.

"It's all right. You frustrated me, but you also made me think. And feel. And change. It's not a bad thing."

"It's not an easy thing, either, Isaac."

"Maybe not," he says. "But it was good. We were good."

"Past tense?" I say, then put a hand up to stop him from replying. "No, don't answer that yet. You can't predict how you're going to react until we've talked. I want to do this properly."

"That sounds both rational and wise," he says, and his eyes are so deep, so intent, so warm, staring into mine.

"I know I wasn't so great at communicating sometimes. I'm not so scared anymore," I say, the sudden urge to stare down at my feet, or up at the theater, or anywhere but directly at him belying my words. "Or . . . I am, but I'm going to do it anyway."

Isaac smiles like he can sense my struggle and is gently amused by it.

"What?" I say, chin lifted.

"Just . . . maybe it would diminish your fear to know that

whatever you tell me, nothing will change three particular facts," he says.

"Which are . . . ?"

"One: I'm very fond of London."

"Okay . . ."

"Two: I do *not* have a girlfriend."

"Oh. Okay, good," I say, trying to remain cool even though I want to start cheering and jumping up and down. "What's the third?"

"Three: I really, really want to kiss you right now."

"Oh!" I say, with an embarrassing gasp. "Um. Here?"

"The students are gone and we have the steps to ourselves," he says with a wave of his arm. "Not sure if that fits in with your plan of doing things properly, though."

"The plan . . . is flexible."

"Well, as always, we can discuss it," he says with a hilarious glint in his eyes. "At length, if need be."

"No," I say, melting and laughing at the same time.

"No kiss?"

"No need to discuss at length."

"Excellent. Fantastic," he says, coming closer. "Do we need to count to three?"

I grin and answer him, but not with words this time.

ACKNOWLEDGMENTS

Writing a book is a mostly solitary job, but getting it right, and then out into the world, takes the belief, hard work, and creativity of many people. To those people, I owe enthusiastic thanks and deep gratitude.

To my agent, Emmanuelle Morgen, who has incredible determination and dedication, more patience than I ever will, and who always pushes me to do my best.

To Leila Sales and Lynne Missen, my dream team of editors, whose intuition, instincts, and total commitment to the book have made it so much better than it could ever have been without them, and who have been so incredibly approachable and attentive.

To copyeditor Laura Stiers, for her incredible attention to detail, and particularly for saving me from the typo that would have had Ingrid going to a "pubic school" instead of a "public school."

To Janet Pascal for being another set of eyes during copyediting, and for sharing her expertise on the subject of opera.

To Theresa Evangelista and Lisa Jager, for coming up with the stunning U.S. and Canadian covers.

To the publicity, sales, and marketing people at Viking, especially Katie Quinn, and to Vikki VanSickle (publicity) and Liza Morrison (head of sales) and their teams at Penguin Random House Canada. The work you do is absolutely vital, and I am lucky to have you.

To all the sales reps who will be going around to stores with ARCs and catalogues, I know you have other books to promote too, so thank you in advance for time you give to mine.

To my foreign rights agent, Whitney Lee, for doing such an excellent job selling rights.

To my wonderful publishers Scholastic UK, Carlsen Forlag in Denmark, Piemme in Italy, and Gallimard in France. I can't wait to see your editions of *Everything Beautiful Is Not Ruined*.

To Shaylyn Saville, for info on canoeing and camping, and Sue Saville, who sent me stunning photos from Shay's trips.

To Gillian Stecyk, who helped me with information about vocal training, specific pieces of music, opera singers, and the world of opera.

To Stephanie Saville, my go-to person for insights on at-risk teens and addiction therapy, and always a person of deep wisdom.

To Brian Younge and my cousin Richard Younge for specifics about small airplanes and unconventional landing circumstances.

To Amanda Almeida for info on how high school plays are run these days.

To Alexander Galant, who came up with the name of the fictional school, Ayerton.

To the trusted readers who gave me feedback, or just let me talk through plot points at various stages, Bev Rosenbaum, Maureen McGowan, Jon Clinch, Caroline Leavitt, Adrienne Kress, Caitlin Sweet, Elizabeth Letts, Michael Wacholtz, Elyne Quan, and Madelyn Burt.

To my larger community of writing buddies, including those mentioned above, who make this whole thing less lonely, and often give behind-the-scenes support: Karen Dionne, Sachin Waikar, Keith Kronin, Renee Rosen, Lauren Baratz-Logsted, Joanne Levy, Eileen Cook, Martha Warboy, and the members of the Torkidlit group, plus the many friends I've made at Backspace.org.

To Mike Kleinberg, for his help in 1990, and Christine Thompson and my other teachers and Holy Trinity School—when you read the book, you'll know why.

To the late Patricia Kern, whose stories about the opera world, told in bits and pieces over the years, seeped into my bones and took up residence, and whose passion, eloquence, and sense of humor, always inspired me.

To my parents, Cindy and Gary Ullman, for exposing me to so much opera and theater as a teenager, for helping me see so much of the world, for sending me on a certain camping trip, and for believing in me, even when they don't always quite understand what I'm up to.

To the many awesome members of the Ullman, Saville, Younge, and Wacholtz families, including my dad, Brian Younge, and Jim and Beatrice Wacholtz, who continue to be such enthusiastic readers and supporters.

To my husband, Michael, for being my most passionate and stalwart supporter, cheerleader, butt-kicker. And my two smart, adorable, hilarious girls, T and S, who, along with Michael, shower me with love, and pull together to keep things running when I'm on a deadline. You are the loves of my life.

Thank you.